A MALEVOLENT CONNECTION

A Regency Cozy

LYNN MESSINA

potatoworks press • greenwich village

Never miss a new release! Join Lynn's mailing list.

To Emmett and Luka,
the most marvelous connections of all

Chapter One

❦

Having insisted on the presence of pineapple at the breakfast table every morning, the Duchess of Kesgrave was extremely reluctant to admit that she did not, in fact, like the fruit.

She did not hate it either, for there were aspects about it she quite enjoyed—its juiciness, for example, or the unexpected way a biting tartness offset the sweet flavor. But it also had a peppery note, a faint hint of spiciness that lingered for several seconds after she swallowed, which she found unappealing. She had not noticed it at first because she had been too enamored of the novelty of sampling an indulgent morsel procured directly from the duke's own pinery at her request.

At Portman Square, it had been very difficult to secure even the most mundane provisions because Aunt Vera kept a miserly eye on the shopping list. Understandably, she refused to satisfy her daughter's plea for drinking chocolate, as nuts were expensive and required a specialized tool to process in addition to a good deal of the kitchen maid's time.

No such complaint could be lodged against apples, which

were commonplace and effortless, and yet Bea was allotted only two per week.

Alas, the uniqueness of the situation could distract her for only so long, and slowly she began to realize that the pineapple's subtle piquancy was disconcertingly strong.

By the end of the first week, it was all she could taste.

Her dislike had not posed a problem when the fruit was served only at breakfast because Bea could nibble daintily on a slice and then proclaim herself full. Mrs. Wallace, noting the meagerness of the new duchess's appetite in the morning, modified the size of the portion accordingly and provided fewer pieces.

But now pineapple was present at every meal.

It was, without question, an impressive feat, and the chef, André, was to be commended on his ingenuity in incorporating the delicacy in so many preparations. Few cooks would have the creativity to devise pineapple potage and duck à l'ananas.

Indeed, Bea was awed by the assortment of recipes he managed to produce on a daily basis, and if they sometimes strained the limits of what was enticing (turbot glazed with pineapple jelly!), they always paid homage to what was possible.

Naturally, she was gratified by the effort the servants made on her behalf, for she knew their desire to please her was an indication of their regard.

Previously, she had earned their esteem by figuring out who among the residents of a neighboring establishment had ruthlessly slain its celebrated chef. Their respect, though sincere, had been a tepid thing mixed with a vague sense of embarrassment at their employer's outré behavior. It was pleasing, yes, to have a mistress who was clever and daring, because her audacity reflected well on the duke, who had had his pick of the Marriage Mart and could have easily settled for an insipid milk-and-water miss like so many of his contemporaries.

The new duchess had pluck!

But impertinence had its consequences—namely, the gauche interest of shopkeepers, among others—and many of the servants found it increasingly difficult to conduct their daily business without being pressed for information. All one wanted was to purchase mackerel for that evening's meal, not evade a dozen questions about decapitated Frenchmen.

'Twas thoroughly vexing, for none of the other house-keepers in Berkeley Square were obliged to endure the vulgar curiosity of the fishmonger.

The staff's opinion of her, however, rose dramatically when Bea managed to repel a murderous attack by the Earl of Bentham. One moment she had been reading a book in the comfort of her own sitting room, the next she was gasping for air as his lordship's hand pressed against her mouth and nose. Trapped beneath his weight, she freed herself from his suffo-cating grip by driving a magnifying glass into his eye, then ramming her foot between his legs.

That was the moment the servants entered the room—when Bentham dropped to the floor with so much force, the magnifying glass flew out of his eye.

It was an appalling sight, blood dripping from the gaping wound onto the pristine rug and Bea's stunned gaze as she sought to comprehend fully what had just transpired. The onlookers, possessing even fewer facts than she herself, perceived at once what had happened, and the revelation of their deficiency horrified them.

Somehow the duchess had come within an inch of losing her life while tucked cozily in the supposedly safe confines of her own bedchamber.

Obviously, some catastrophic failure had occurred, and every member of the household, from the staunchest footman to the youngest kitchen maid, felt complicit in the attack, as if in failing to thwart Bentham, they had in some way aided him. That Bea's continued good health owed nothing to them was a challenging reality for them to accept, and they were all absurdly grateful to the duchess for successfully discharging their duty.

Marlow, in particular, felt the lack keenly. Having made a career of swatting the pernicious flies that swarmed the front steps, he could not comprehend how he had allowed a wasp to slip through the back door.

Thankfully, Bea suffered no ill effects from the assault, save for a small round bruise on the top of her lip where the earl's signet ring had pressed into her skin. Even the carpet, with its blush-colored flowers, had been scrubbed clean by Mrs. Wallace, who firmly told the fishmonger two days later that, no, she did not find her grace's competence demeaning.

"I am sure we all sleep better knowing she is equipped to defend herself if necessary," she added.

Bea, who had considered the cause lost from the moment she asked the housekeeper about her flirtation with the beheaded chef next door, had never expected to earn the respect of the other woman and was extremely reluctant to do anything that might jeopardize it. She realized, yes, that asserting a slight aversion to pineapple was a rather minor admission, but even that insignificant confession might undermine Mrs. Wallace's admiration.

Or possibly one of the other servants'.

Although the staff extolled her bravery, Bea knew herself to be something of a coward. The only reason she had insisted on the daily provision of pineapples in the first place was that she'd feared disappointing the housekeeper, who would expect a duchess to be exacting in her tastes. Overseeing the finest residence in London, Mrs. Wallace would be deeply troubled to learn that all her new mistress needed was a book, a comfortable chair and enough light by which to read.

Imagine if the fishmonger discovered that!

Compelled by rank and duty to make at least one unreasonable demand, Bea would hold fast to it, for it seemed egregious to admit she did not even want the only thing she had claimed to require. Even if she were not worried about their perception of her, she would never reveal the truth. To divulge an aversion to pineapple would be to indicate that there was something even minutely unappreciated about their kindness—and there was not.

Bea wholly appreciated it.

And yet the existing state of affairs could not continue, for now pineapple had invaded her beloved rout cake. It was a trifling addition, only a few dried pieces of the dreaded fruit dispersed in the doughy deliciousness, but recognizing it as an ominous harbinger of things to come, Bea knew measures had to be taken before the incursion became a full-fledged conquest.

At the moment, the particulars of those measures eluded her, for she had only just identified the unpleasant flavor, but she knew they would have to be indirect and subtle.

No hint of her true feelings must be detected.

Perhaps the problem could be physical, in which case it would be no fault of her own if she could no longer consume pineapple. Maybe she could develop a mysterious reaction, such as gastric distress or a rash. Flora had recently demonstrated how easy it was to simulate a stomach complaint. All one had to do was clutch one's belly in pain.

Oh, but a rash would be more convincing, she thought, although also more difficult to simulate. Obviously, she did not want to afflict herself with horrible itchy patches all over her skin. A few splotches on her forearm, however, would not go amiss. Maybe some bumps as well.

The question was, how to produce them?

It should not be very hard, she thought, recalling her childhood in Sussex, which was bedeviled by cuts and scrapes caused by various features on the house grounds. She had fallen out of a lot of trees, which was not the least bit helpful now, but once she had dropped into a bush of stinging nettles and suffered an unsightly rash on her calves that lasted for little more than a day. It had been uncomfortable as well, but applying a cool compress to the area deadened the itchiness.

Another factor in its favor: Stinging nettles were a relatively common woodland plant. If she could not locate a specimen in Hyde Park, then she was almost certain to find one on Hampstead Heath.

Would not that be a picture, Bea thought, the Duchess of Kesgrave trouncing about the woods examining leaves. She smiled as she contemplated Jenkins's baffled expression, for surely she would not be permitted to wander around by herself. In the week since the assault, she had barely been allowed to enter her office for rout cake enjoyment without a servant first performing a thorough inspection to make sure the room was empty of intruders.

Perhaps the more viable approach was to address the problem at its root—literally, she thought, contemplating the pinery itself. It was true that she knew nothing about growing pineapples, but she felt confident she could find at least one book on their care and cultivation in the house's vast library. Sabotaging a tropical species in an inhospitable climate could not be hugely complicated.

Even so, the plan presented a significant challenge. The Matlock family seat was situated hundreds of miles away. It was not as though Bea could effortlessly dash outside to incapacitate the pineapples and then just as quickly scamper back inside. First, she would have to travel to Cambridgeshire, which would, she realized, provide her with ample time to reflect on the immorality of destroying an entire crop simply to preserve the sanctity of a rout cake.

So, in fact, there were two insurmountable obstacles.

Well, three, she acknowledged, as she contemplated the complexity of the scheme. She would not flourish in her career as a duchess if everything she did entailed an elaborate plot.

It was better to simplify.

Kesgrave, she thought.

If he could just be prevailed upon to tell chef André that he was weary of so many pineapple dishes and desired more variety at mealtime, the whole problem would go away in an instant.

But the duke was too amused by her predicament to do anything to alleviate it. He found it very funny indeed that a woman who had jammed a magnifying glass into a killer's eye would cavil at providing the housekeeper with updated information about her culinary preferences.

He was a fine one to talk, Bea thought, with his own deep reluctance to do anything that might disturb the smooth running of the household. In the middle of a fevered hunt for the blackguard who unceremoniously chopped off the head of Mr. Réjane, he had insisted they cool their heels before searching Mrs. Wallace's office because the late-night intrusion might upset her.

As if one slightly disgruntled housekeeper was anything compared with a coldhearted murderer!

No, Kesgrave could not be relied upon to act as an ally.

Maybe there was some way to maneuver Aunt Vera into alleviating the situation. She was an easily excitable woman, and if she could be made to believe pineapples had a deleterious effect on one's health, she would demand that Bea stop eating them.

But how to convince her?

Flora, she thought, was a likely prospect, for her cousin's recent spate of food poisoning incidents made her appear unduly susceptible to provisions that were less than perfect. If she complained about terrible stomach pains caused by pineapple consumed at Kesgrave House and the physician who was summoned could be persuaded to warn her of the terrible damage the fruit could do to her digestion, then Aunt Vera would be turned staunchly against it.

She would march to Berkeley Square and demand that the cook cease serving it at once.

Well, actually, no, Aunt Vera would not, for she was awed by grandeur and would never presume to issue orders to a duke's chef. If anything, she would marvel in wonder at his expertise with the prickly fruit, praising every aspect of his deft handling, from the way he cut slices to his technique for inserting them into rout cakes.

And that was only if she managed to raise her eyes from the brass accents on the hob grate in the hearth.

Contemplating the machinations she would have to employ to lure Aunt Vera to the kitchens of Kesgrave House made Bea smile, and she allowed that this latest scheme was just as intricate as her previous ones.

Sighing deeply, Bea clutched the book in her lap and glanced at the clock to note that she had spent a full twenty minutes thinking about the matter.

That would never do.

In the past week, her reading time had become despondently scarce as Kesgrave implemented a demanding schedule of instruction to ensure she was able to defend herself should another depraved villain try to murder her in the comfort of her own sitting room. She had committed herself fully to the lessons, not only because she was deeply moved by his faith in her abilities, but also because she had no desire to be slain in the comfort of her own sitting room.

Or, indeed, anywhere else in Kesgrave House.

Although she had never done anything to deliberately provoke a killer into attacking her, she accepted that the fact of her investigation was often enough of an incitement. Given how many murderers were naturally inclined toward violence and how little they relished being identified, the only surprising thing was that more attempts on her life had not been made.

Truly, Bea was fortunate to have scraped by for so long without possessing the skills necessary to protect herself and was genuinely eager to acquire them.

Even so, she could not help but wish her rigorous training allowed for a little more time to read. To be sure, the activities at which Kesgrave insisted she become proficient, such as fencing and fisticuffs, required a great deal of physical exertion, and as such were incompatible with quiet study. But surely there was some element of defense to be gained from familiarizing herself with the battle tactics of successful generals.

Sun Tzu, for example, had much wisdom to impart from his triumphant career as a military strategist during the Zhou dynasty. His treatise on warfare detailed every aspect of a winning campaign, from how terrain affected the outcome of a skirmish to the importance of obtaining reliable information about your enemy.

There had to be other books of that ilk.

It would not be so terrible, the reduction in her reading time, if the lessons were her only obligation. Alas, she was also required to make social appearances, attending routs, plays and dinner parties. Just a few days ago, she had been dragooned into spending an evening at Almack's by her cousin, who was determined to appear utterly indifferent to her beau's defection. That Mr. Holcroft was not present in the assembly rooms to witness her gaiety had little bearing on

Flora's plan, for she was convinced that word of her enjoyment would reach him quickly enough.

Bea, who thought the scheme had almost no chance of prospering, could not help but admire the resolve her cousin brought to the project. The giddiness on display was persuasive, and while the point of the exercise had not been to attach new suitors, Flora had in fact gained the interest of several young men.

During her visit yesterday, Aunt Vera had revealed herself to be at once delighted and aghast at her daughter's sudden popularity, for never before had so many gentlemen left their cards at 19 Portman Square.

Mr. Locklin had even sent flowers!

It was thrilling, yes, contemplating the bright prospects that lay ahead for Flora, as there were so many possibilities. But it was disconcerting as well because Mr. Locklin's father had once numbered among Vera's own swains, and it would be very strange to establish a family connection at this late date.

She had no cause for concern, for Flora did not care two figs for anyone save Mr. Holcroft, a fact she made crystal clear with her mopey sighs and dejected manner. But Aunt Vera had never allowed the lack of a reasonable excuse to stop her from worrying about some minor detail in the past and she refused to permit it now, rattling off the various faults that had long ago prevented her from accepting Mr. Locklin's offer, which, to be clear, had never actually been extended.

"*He* did not possess a high phaeton, but his brother did and obviously I could not ignore the implication," Aunt Vera had said.

Before her aunt could launch into an extensive list detailing the many inferences she had drawn from the ownership of such a conveyance, Bea had interrupted to request her help in hiring a new footman.

"The fourth, to be precise," she added, which, though considerably fewer than the eight Aunt Vera supposed a great establishment such as Kesgrave House to employ, was still enough to disconcert her timid relative.

Consequently, her aunt jumped to her feet at once and announced that she had to be off. "Another engagement," she explained as she hurried to the door. "I am sure you understand. Do extend my apologies to Kesgrave for missing him."

It had been amusing to watch her aunt scurry out of the house, but Bea knew that the larger matter would not resolve itself so easily. Flora's efforts to obtain Mr. Holcroft's attention would only grow increasingly more drastic the longer he remained impervious to her efforts, and Bea wondered if it was time she decamped to the country. The plan had much to recommend it, for it would mean fewer social engagements and an opportunity to spend time with the duke away from the clamor of the city. Furthermore, she had yet to see the country estate.

And, she realized with a grin, it would carry her over the first insurmountable hurdle by placing her in close proximity to the source of her pineapple problem.

That left only the ethical question, which she felt certain she could work her way around to resolving soon enough, for she was deeply immersed in Voltaire.

Or, rather, she thought as the clock struck five, she was *trying* to immerse herself deeply in Voltaire. Alas, she was too distracted by the inane contemplation of pineapples to make significant progress.

Thoroughly disgusted, she tilted her head firmly down and focused on the essay she had begun more than an hour before. Given the little time that remained, she would be lucky if she managed to finish the chapter before dinner. Any minute now, Mrs. Wallace would return to collect the tray and ask Bea when she would retire to her dressing room to change.

Indeed, Bea had no sooner had the thought when a knock sounded on the door and she looked up, expecting to see the housekeeper.

Instead, it was Joseph.

"I apologize for the interruption, your grace, but you have a visitor," he said, his tone tentative as he stood in the doorway. "I explained that you were not at home to callers, but she asked me to convey her presence regardless, for she felt confident you would agree to see her. She says she is your aunt and long overdue for a visit."

Puzzled, Bea tilted her head, for the guest in question was obviously not the woman who had raised her. Aunt Vera would never be so bold as to press her case with a footman dressed in the fine livery of Kesgrave House. She would leave her card and then grumble endlessly to her husband about the new duchess being too high-flying to spend time with her family.

Furthermore, Mrs. Hyde-Clare was already known to Joseph. Just yesterday he had led her to the drawing room while she marveled over the extravagant floral arrangement in the entrance hall.

"My aunt?" Bea repeated.

Helpfully, he added, "A Mrs. Welpton."

Ah, yes, she thought. Aunt Susan.

Since Susan was Vera's older sister, she bore no direct kinship to Beatrice and had in fact shown very little interest in the young orphan during her childhood. Every year at Michaelmas the Hyde-Clares would visit the boisterous Welpton family at their home near Reading, Capstone Manor, where Aunt Susan bestowed gifts on the cousins. It was always the same: Flora would get a sleek rocking horse and Russell would receive a lavish toy theater and Bea would be handed a miniature piece of furniture such as a bed or a table meant for a dollhouse she did not have. The first time it happened, she had been beside herself with excitement, for she naturally assumed she would be getting one soon—for Christmas, which was only a few months away—and she waited and waited for the little home in which to install her slightly threadbare settee.

It never came, of course, for the gift was precisely what it appeared to be: a worn cast-off from her own daughter's collection.

Mrs. Partridge, the kindly housekeeper at Welldale House, noted her disappointment and took pity on her by giving her a fruit crate to house her motley collection of furnishings. Painted celestial blue, it served its purpose well and after several years, Bea assembled a cozy little scene of a country cottage of a gently bred woman who had come down in the world.

Most recently, she had seen Susan in March, when Aunt Vera, deeply distressed by her niece's increasingly erratic behavior, enlisted her sister and brother-in-law to help keep an eye on Bea during the Lelands' ball. It had been a communal effort, with every member of the family assigned fifteen-minute intervals during which it was their responsibility to make sure she did nothing to embarrass them.

And even with their coordinated effort to regulate her conduct, Bea still managed to mortify them. The expression on Aunt Vera's face when she found her on the terrace berating Lord Duncan for his hypocrisy! It was a horrifying mix of shame and fury. She could not conceive of anything more humiliating than Beatrice acting with such daring impertinence in front of a duke.

Aunt Vera firmly believed her niece was undergoing a mental disintegration sparked by the discovery of the corpse of a spice trader during a weeklong stay in the Lake District.

In fact, she was courting Kesgrave.

Recalling the exchange now, Bea smiled and wondered why Aunt Susan would pay a call while out of the company of her sister. In the twenty years Susan had known Bea, she had never spent a single moment alone with her.

A poor little orphan girl held no interest for her.

Ah, but she was none of those things now, and the residence she called home was so palatial, it made Capstone Manor look like a dollhouse.

Even Aunt Susan could not resist the lure of a duchy.

Fleetingly, Bea considered denying her entrée. She wanted to finish the chapter, it would be time to change for dinner soon, and she owed the woman nothing save a few weeks of misery and confusion when she realized the settee she had been given would not be followed by a setting.

Aunt Vera would not blame her for rebuffing her sister, for she would consider her persistence in the face of refusal to be an insupportable presumption and laud Bea for withholding her consent. Impudence must not be rewarded!

Well, not *laud,* Bea thought in amusement, for Aunt Vera could never quite bring herself to praise anything her niece did. But she would condone the decision as proper.

Although her relative's reluctant approval was yet another reason to turn the visitor away, Bea instructed Joseph to show Mrs. Welpton to the drawing room. "And ask Mrs. Wallace to send up a pot of tea."

She was tempted to request a plate of rout cakes without pineapple, citing her aunt's aversion, but decided calling attention to the fruit now might undermine efforts to remove it from the menu later.

Joseph left to admit her guest, and Bea leaned stubbornly back in her seat, determined to at least finish the page before attending to her obligations as hostess. But the oddity of Aunt Susan's solitary visit, the fact that her business was so pressing she could not wait for her sister to accompany her, proved more compelling than Voltaire. Clearly, her purpose in calling was not to wish the bride every happiness in her new marriage.

She wanted something.

Her youngest daughter, Julia, had made her presentation earlier in the year, and the family had hosted a modest party in their London home to launch her into society. Perhaps she sought the support of the Duchess of Kesgrave to more firmly establish the girl or thought she could be persuaded to throw a lavish affair in her honor.

Securing a ball at Kesgrave House would certainly be a coup.

Although Bea could very easily imagine Aunt Susan pursuing such an arrangement, for she possessed little of the humility or restraint that ruled her sister, she knew the woman was too clever to make the request so boldly. Rather, she would step lightly around the topic, utilizing her sister's relationship to reaffirm the connection first.

No, Aunt Susan was here on a weightier matter.

Money, Bea thought, was an excellent spur, and she pondered the possibility that Uncle Lawrence had amassed a debt so large he required financial assistance to settle it. He was a temperate man, and she could not believe he would lose a vast sum at the gambling table.

But an investment that went awry?

Yes, she could see that happening.

And Aunt Susan would not want her sister to know she had made the application.

Even so, it was a shocking audacity to ask the orphan girl whom you ignored for decades for a loan of several hundred pounds, and Bea could not conceive of any relation of Vera Hyde-Clare being so bold.

On a deep sigh, Bea acknowledged the futility of trying to

read while the mystery of her aunt's presence bobbed around in her head. Closing the book, she stood and left the amiable comfort of her office for the imposing grandeur of the drawing room, where she expected to find her relative examining its contents with curiosity if not awe. One did not have to be a Hyde-Clare to appreciate the mastery of the frescoes decorating the vaulted ceiling or the superiority of the plasterwork, which was intricate and precise. The sculptures adorning the niches were by Coysevox, the fireplace was made by Adams, and the large canvas on the far wall was by Brueghel.

In the room full of treasures both large and small, Aunt Susan had chosen to examine the edge of her glove. Sitting in a mahogany chair with scroll arms, her posture more rigid than usual, she fiddled with the trim, her fingers running over the border as if to detect some minor imperfection.

Without question, the edge of one's gloves was an engrossing subject, especially when trimmed in an elaborate thistle pattern in lavender and puce, and Bea had spent a good portion of her social career scrutinizing the seams of various articles of clothing. But surely the Murano chandelier, with its brightly colored glass molded into delicate flowers, was slightly more interesting?

Bea herself was fascinated by the glasswork and marveled at the skill of the craftsmen.

She made no comment to that effect, however, as she crossed the threshold, for one could not vaunt the quality of one's own possessions, especially when one did not actually feel as though one possessed them. Instead, she greeted Aunt Susan politely and announced that tea would be brought in shortly as her relative rose to her feet. Then she observed that the other woman looked well.

In truth, she looked too well.

The hair was correct, tinged with gray as befitted a lady

who had turned fifty only a few years before, and her cheeks had that overly pink cast of rouge applied to mimic the vigor of youth, which her aunt had sported the last time Bea had seen her.

But her neck was smooth, unmarred by wrinkles and displaying none of the gentle droop that had of late vexed her sister.

And the height, Bea thought as she approached her aunt, was off by two inches. The change itself was not remarkable, for a pair of tall heels would easily make up the difference, but the woman standing before her was wearing silk slippers.

Patently, her caller was not Mrs. Welpton, and as she raised her gaze to look the impostor in the eyes, she recognized her at once: Miss Brougham.

Chapter Two

❧

"Y ou must let me explain," Mrs. Norton said firmly.

Calmly, Bea regarded the heiress who had maliciously undermined her social career by cruelly mocking her dowdiness and then sought her ruin by maneuvering her into a compromising position with an actor. She could see her plainly now beneath the paint and the powder she had applied to alter her appearance: the even features, the appealing brown eyes, the pert mouth that was accustomed to getting what it wanted.

It had almost worked, her plan to feed Bea to the gossips, and had faltered only on a careless slip of the tongue. (Well, that, *and* the grisly murder of one of the scheme's participants. But Mrs. Norton could not know yet what horrible sight lay just beyond the door.)

If she had been a little more thoughtful in her determination to shuffle her victim down the corridor, Bea's reputation would be in tatters now and her marriage to the duke over before it began.

Kesgrave would have resisted her decision, she knew, arguing fiercely that he could not care less if his wife had

18

been caught cavorting with an unclothed man in the back room of a wretched little stable in Milford Lane. But she had her own sense of honor with which to contend and could never have allowed their betrothal to stand, not with muck dripping from the hem of her dress.

The faint splatters of blood had been intolerable enough.

In her impatience, however, Mrs. Norton *had* spoken injudiciously, which provided Bea with the warning she needed to avert disaster. Realizing she had been lured into a trap, she had spun sharply on her heels and marched away from the tawdry room toward the courtyard.

But the calamity that Mrs. Norton orchestrated was not the one that transpired, and Bea's progress was halted first by the spiteful heiress's screams and then by the dead man who lay on the bed in the dark little room, a gaping hole in his stomach.

That was the moment Mrs. Ralston arrived—of course it was, for no tale of licentiousness and immorality was complete without a zealous scandalmonger to spread it far and wide.

It would have been fitting if Mrs. Norton's plan to destroy Bea's reputation had wound up damaging her own as well, which was exactly what would have happened if Mrs. Ralston found them in the presence of the bloodied corpse. Fortunately for both of them, Bea managed to fend off the notorious prattle-box, and dragging Mrs. Norton to Kesgrave House, she obtained the full details of the plot against her.

Despite her enthusiastic participation, Mrs. Norton was not actually its author. That honor belonged to Lord Tavistock, Kesgrave's neighbor to the north who desired to align his family with the duke's through his daughter. An affianced bride presented an impediment to his ambition, so he arranged to remove her from the situation.

It was not personal, of course, just a matter of business.

Tavistock was sure Kesgrave would not mind at all.

Alas, he did.

Infuriated by these machinations, the duke had Mrs. Norton's vouchers for Almack's summarily revoked, which was a fitting punishment for a London hostess whose worth depended on the number and quality of gatherings to which she was admitted. It was virtually unheard of for someone of her stature to lose entrée to the famous assembly rooms, and her change in fortune caused quite a bit of chatter as the beau monde speculated as to what she could have possibly done to earn such a punishment.

Her status had suffered accordingly.

Bea saw no reason to devote any time to following the travails of a woman who had sought her destruction, but Flora relished keeping abreast of the affair and had insisted on providing her with regular updates during the intervening six weeks. Most recently, Mrs. Norton had been disinvited to Mrs. Godbee's garden party, which had been a particularly crushing blow, for the hostess was her godmother and as such had resolved to stand by her. And yet, as the date of the affair grew closer, Mrs. Godbee found herself unable to bear the shame of associating too closely with the child she had sponsored. She suggested Mrs. Norton attend a separate gathering, a more selective one limited to just their intimates.

Her cousin had found that tale to be especially diverting because Mrs. Norton had been seen just the day before at the Western Exchange purchasing a new hair ribbon in anticipation of the event.

Examining her now, Bea saw nothing in her affect that indicated an alteration in her position in society. If anything, the firmness with which she spoke signified an increase in importance, for now she was telling the Duchess of Kesgrave what she should do.

Coolly, then, almost dispassionately, Bea replied, "Must I?"

Although she managed to imbue the words with genuine disdain, as if what the other woman had to say was of no importance to her, she was in fact extremely curious to discover what scheme was afoot now. It had to be something very elaborate, for nothing short of Byzantine could account for her archnemesis appearing on her doorstep in the guise of a distant relative.

Bea's sense of the ridiculous, well honed and without caution, reveled in the utter strangeness of the situation.

Swayed by the apathetic note in Bea's voice, Mrs. Norton pressed her lips together tightly and her nostrils flared. Her tone, however, revealed none of her distress, and evenly she reiterated her plea. "Yes, you must, your grace, for I have news that pertains to you and the duke, and I am confident you will want to hear it. As well, you will want an explanation for why I am dressed as Mrs. Welpton. I will tell you that, too. I promise it will all make sense if you would just allow me to explain."

Bea very much doubted it would *all* make sense, just as she could not quite believe her ruse was anything more than an elaborate bid for clemency. It seemed highly unlikely the other woman had information that would interest her, but she nevertheless indicated to the chair.

Mrs. Norton acknowledged the gesture with a dip of her head and retook her seat, murmuring gratefully as she folded her hands primly in her lap.

Joseph entered the room with the tray, which he placed on the low table next to the settee, and Bea, leaning forward to pour the brew, tried to imagine Kesgrave's reaction if he returned home to find her calmly serving tea to the woman who had tried to ruin her.

Angry, she thought.

But surely intrigued as well by Mrs. Norton's decidedly odd costume.

Even if he did not credit her with possessing pertinent information, he would want to know what nefarious deception she was weaving now by pretending to be in possession of pertinent information.

Mrs. Norton accepted the teacup and thanked Bea again for generously agreeing to allow her to explain, adding that she was undeserving of such graciousness. "But I am not surprised, for you have proved yourself to be an elegant and kind duchess. You are a credit to the Matlock name."

Oh, dear, Bea thought wryly, the situation must be very hopeless indeed if her archnemesis was resorting to flattery.

"Am I?" she asked softly as she filled a second cup of tea.

Mrs. Norton nodded. "Obviously, I am in awe of your handling of the Pudsey affair, rescuing Fawcett from certain death *and* extricating yourself from Bentham's clutches. It is astonishing that anyone could accomplish such feats, but for a gentlewoman like yourself it is truly extraordinary. Paying tribute to your many achievements, however, is not why I am here," she said, then blinked several times as she contemplated Bea thoughtfully over the rim of her teacup. "Unless you want it to be. You are so very impressive, I could spend the entire afternoon heaping praise on your head, and since my goal is to endear myself to you as much as possible, I am eager to defer to your preference if you would but let it be known."

Amused by the overture, Bea was tempted to allow the other woman to make the effort, for she felt certain she would run out of encomiums after only a few minutes. But as much as she would enjoy watching her nemesis grapple for compliments, she valued her reading time too highly to waste any of it teasing Mrs. Norton.

Smoothly, Bea thanked her for the offer and assured her it was not necessary. "You may proceed to the next item on your agenda."

But Mrs. Norton could not.

No, first she had to praise the duchess's pragmatic approach and inspiring efficiency, and Bea, enduring several minutes of breathless admiration, was forced to reconsider her previous conclusion and concede that her guest could in fact pass several hours in glorification of her.

Only when she was satisfied that her host's sensibleness had been fully appreciated would Mrs. Norton consent to move on to the purpose of her visit, which was to make amends.

"But not easy amends," she hastily added. "Never that, for my sins are many and require much atoning. It is a process, your grace, one that is long and painstaking, and I have spared myself no quarter. Yes, I have taken a harsh light to my soul and discovered many unpleasant truths about myself. I have been cruel and unthinking. Falling in with Tavistock's plan was a terrible mistake, not because it failed to succeed in its precious goal but because it represented the worst of humanity. Blinded by my own prejudices, I could not conceive how the duke's regard for you could be deep or sincere. It simply seemed impossible to me that he would enter into a union with you willingly and must be a prisoner of some horrible trick from which he was much too gallant to extricate himself. But I perceive the error of my ways and can only marvel at my earlier incomprehension, for it is no wonder that he cherishes you. You are remarkable in every way."

Fearing that this description of Bea's positive qualities was not fulsome enough, Mrs. Norton supplemented it with a list of adjectives—brave, kind, clever, shrewd, thoughtful, courageous, resourceful, compassionate, creative—that threatened to extend the interview well past the last drop of tea.

"Thank you, yes," Bea said, interrupting the catalogue. "I perceive now what you mean."

"Of course you do," Mrs. Norton said with a knowing smile. "For you are too astute not to understand precisely what I mean. Your ability to grasp the entirety of a situation is one of the things I admire most about you. If you were not so quick and agile in your thinking, Tavistock's plot would have harmed both our reputations, for I would never have had the presence of mind to turn Mrs. Ralston away. I could not marshal a single clear thought after seeing Mr. Hobson, for my mind was consumed by the ghastliness of the scene. But you remained calm and conversed with her as if nothing were amiss. At this astounding display, I should have realized then that Kesgrave's attachment to you was genuine, for why would he not seek out originality in his bride? A man who is so feted and admired by the *ton* must naturally crave something out of the ordinary. All those Incomparables with their pretty eyes and plush lips are so alike as to be almost indistinguishable from one another. But your style is unique."

Here again, Mrs. Norton's conversation devolved into an inventory of attributes to better explicate what she meant by the word *unique*.

'Twas a peculiar sensation, listening to the woman who had consigned her to drabness describe her now as effervescent, lovely, emotive and vibrant. But Bea did not doubt the other woman's sincerity, for nothing had improved her appearance as much as the assumption of a duchy. The gleaming curls skillfully wrought by her new maid had nothing on the luster of the Matlock name.

But even Mrs. Norton's ingenuity had its limitations, and after applying the few descriptions that had occurred readily to her, she foundered for additional terms that could be perceived as laudatory.

Keenly aware that *refreshing* and *fairish* fell well short of her own high standards for fawning, Mrs. Norton ceased her catalogue and apologized for embarrassing Bea with her effusiveness. "It is simply that I wish for you to understand the depth of my contrition. Kesgrave was right to have my vouchers revoked and thus deal a fatal blow to my social status, for the humbling experience has been wholly transformative. I sit before you an entirely different woman."

Yes, Bea thought in amusement, and that woman was her Aunt Susan.

"But you must not assume that reevaluating my actions and feeling ashamed of my past behavior are the extent of my atoning," Mrs. Norton continued. "To fully make amends, I need to take active steps to counter the harm I have done and to be made to feel uncomfortable in the world. I hope you can understand how extremely uncomfortable I am right now, your grace, sitting in this drawing room talking to you about my past misdeeds."

In fact, Bea could comprehend it, for she knew how strongly the other woman resented her and having to debase herself so thoroughly in the hopes of reclaiming her vouchers had to be above all things demoralizing. The words themselves must burn in her throat.

"This wig is abhorrently itchy," Mrs. Norton said plaintively as she reached up to scratch lightly behind the ear. "The powder is so strangely heavy, I feel almost as though I am wearing a cloth on my face. The padding I added to make my waist appear thicker is awkwardly situated. It is a constant battle not to endlessly adjust my position in hopes of finding a satisfying one. But I am not complaining. Each new discomfort is an opportunity to demonstrate my worthiness of your mercy, and I have suffered many to bring this information to you. The bench outside Danby's coffee shop comes to mind as being particularly awful, for it was hard *and* cold, as well as the smell inside the establishment, which was redolent of sour coffee and the perspiration of men who do not bathe at regular intervals. And then there was the wart, which I used to further disguise my appearance. The first time I applied it, I foolishly placed it directly below my eye so that I felt perpetually teased by a fly in constant need of swatting. It was an intolerable sensation."

Bea, who had not thought the situation could grow any more bizarre, listened to this catalogue of complaints and wondered if Mrs. Norton's expulsion from Almack's had done grave damage to her ability to think. Clearly, she was desperate to get back into Kesgrave's good graces, but setting for herself a series of arbitrary and outlandish challenges was not the most auspicious way to go about it. If determined in that course, she should have at least consulted with the duke in advance to ascertain which sorts of physical discomforts he wished her to endure.

She was about to clarify this point when Mrs. Norton added, "I do not list these experiences in an attempt to gain your sympathy, although I am sure you would instantly grant it in your munificence, but to demonstrate the sincerity of my repentance. I have done the work, your grace."

"The work?" Bea asked, placing her teacup on the table with a slight rattle.

"Yes, the work," Mrs. Norton affirmed. "I would never dare present myself to Berkeley Square if all I had to offer were remorseful mea culpas. You are a woman of action, your grace. You are brave, courageous, daring, valiant—"

"No," Bea said, raising her hand to halt another barrage of flattery. "You are much more likely to achieve whatever it is you are here to achieve if you cease with the endless blandishments. I shall take it as assumed that accompanying each sentence you utter are five accolades that remain unsaid. Here, let us establish them in advance."

"In advance?" Mrs. Norton asked uncertainly.

"Yes, the five unsaid accolades," Bea replied. "Let us say them now so they do not have to be repeated. What is your preference? I would advise you not to select adjectives directly related to my duchesshood because they have a way of feeling unearned, but you are of course free to choose whatever words you like."

Although she blinked her eyes several times in confusion, Mrs. Norton straightened her shoulders and gamely complied with her host's instructions. "*Bold, dashing, intelligent, benevolent,* and *cunning,*" she said, then immediately shook her head in disagreement with herself. "No, no, *cunning* will never do, for it has a slightly sinister connotation that does your ingenuity a disservice. Let us replace it with *witty.* I have heretofore made no observations in reference to your humor, which is widely known to be sly and diverting. You are marvelously droll, your grace, and I have found—"

"Uh-uh, Mrs. Norton," Bea tsked with a disapproving shake of her head, "we settled on five. I must insist that you abide by our agreement."

Briefly, the beautiful heiress pursed her lips as if annoyed by this comment, but she allowed no other indication of her peevishness to slip through and swiftly smoothed her features. "You are right, and if I may deviate from our compact momentarily, I would add that your ability to be fair-minded is humbling. I have done little but torment you since our first season together, and yet you are willing to allow me to sit here and present my case. I am fully cognizant of the honor you do me. You are genuinely kind, and I do not say that lightly. I expected to be forcibly ejected from the drawing room the moment you recognized me, and yet here I remain," she said, a hint of bewilderment in her voice, as if she was not quite sure how that had happened. "Regardless, I made you a promise so I shall return at once to the matter of my penance."

"Yes, please do," Bea said with a glance at the ornate clock on the opposite wall. She could not be sure when Kesgrave would return, and she wanted to know the whole of Mrs. Norton's scheme before he did in fact have the woman unceremoniously tossed out of the house.

"As you may recall, my understanding of the duke's situation was dreadfully incomplete, and for that reason, I did not consider or anticipate the consequences if Tavistock's plan went awry," Mrs. Norton said, her fingers once again fiddling with the embroidered border of her glove. "I'm sure having my vouchers for Almack's revoked was nothing less than what I deserved, and I have had a terrible time of it ever since. The snubs and speculation have been wretched, but what I truly cannot bear is my husband's response. Norton is so very angry and disappointed in me. I tried to hide the truth from him with a bagatelle about a harmless mix-up, but he would not be assuaged and eventually I had to tell him everything. He was appalled by my behavior and stunned to discover that I would put any woman in danger, let alone one who had done me no harm. I tried to explain what harm had been done, but that only angered him more, for he had no recollection of the exchange that affected me so deeply. You cannot know, your grace, how humiliating it is to realize the event that had a profound impact on your life was but a passing moment to everyone else. More than a month has passed, and Norton is still furious with me. It is intolerable. I spent five years being the ideal London hostess and society wife, carefully weighing every decision to ensure that it reflected well on myself and my family. I never made a single misstep, and with one error in judgment I lost everything."

Despite the wrinkled edge of her gloves, which revealed her agitation, Mrs. Norton's tone remained matter-of-fact. "Obviously, amends had to be made, and I knew the best way to do that was to perform a service for you and the duke. Painfully aware that there was nothing I could offer socially or materially, especially from my position of disgrace, I cast about for another way to provide assistance. I decided that if Tavistock objected so strongly to your diverting Kesgrave's wealth from his accounts and he is only a neighbor, then perhaps a family member would also take issue. I began my search with his presumptive heir, Mr. Mortimer Matlock, and spent several days observing his activities and noted nothing suspicious. To interview his associates, I assumed the guise of Mr. Twaddle-Thum, the *London Morning Gazette*'s scurrilous gossip, whose identity is entirely unknown. I spoke to several of his closest confidants, and they all assured me that Mortimer did not covet the dukedom or resent his cousin's marriage. I turned next to Mortimer's father, Lord Myles Matlock. He was a different kettle of fish."

To say that Beatrice was taken aback by this communication was to grossly understate the matter. She was astonished by the actions undertaken by the former Miss Brougham.

No, completely dumbfounded.

Nothing in the spiteful heiress's history indicated a capacity for diligence or cunning or even creativity. Lodging an accusation of dowdiness against Bea, for all the damage it had wrought, was little more than childish name calling. 'Twas also an act of a lazy and unimaginative mind, for Bea was in fact quite drab. Her participation in Tavistock's plot was likewise without industry, for she had, by her own account, merely gone along with his scheme. Conceiving none of the particulars herself, she had followed the steps with which she had been provided and the moment the situation diverged from the prescribed outcome, she collapsed.

Within minutes of discovering Hobson's corpse, she had admitted to everything, the entire conspiracy. She did not even make an attempt to improvise a plausible explanation to salvage some element of Tavistock's plan.

And yet now she had devised an entire identity for herself.

That Mrs. Norton would embark on such an enterprise did not surprise Bea, for the woman was unequivocally desperate to have her social standing restored.

No, what was shocking was that she had the ingenuity and adaptability to make it succeed.

Social ostracism, by all appearances, had had an improving effect on her intellect.

Revealing none of her thoughts, Bea raised her teacup to her lips and said mildly, "Lord Myles Matlock?"

Mrs. Norton folded her hands in her lap as she nodded in confirmation. "Yes, his grace's uncle. His father's younger brother. As I am sure you know, the fifth duke's first wife died in childbirth. She managed to push out a pair of sickly sons before promptly expiring, and the boys did little better, surviving barely a week. In his grief, the duke, who was very young at the time—barely more than twenty—vowed never to wed again, and Myles, taking him at his word, eagerly stepped into the void, courting a woman, wedding her and producing a presumptive heir in rapid succession. Mortimer securely inhabited that position for eight years before the duke had the poor taste to impregnate his mistress and the even poorer taste to marry the girl. Five months later Kesgrave was born, cutting his cousin out of the line of succession and enraging Myles, who had grown quite possessive of the title and the estates in the interim. It is said that his uncle tried to kill him several times in his youth."

Although Bea kept her features smooth as Mrs. Norton shared Kesgrave's history, her mind reeled at the account and she felt a strange compulsion to press her hands to her ears. She did not want to hear more of it, any of it, not another single solitary word.

It was utterly irrational, Bea knew, her overwhelming desire to shut out the ugliness of Kesgrave's past, and yet she could not claim to be unfamiliar with the sensation. For several weeks now she had been avoiding the issue of his parents, and although she had resolved on several occasions to broach the subject, the moment never seemed suited to the weightiness of the topic. Despite Bentham's attack on her life, which came disconcertingly close to succeeding, she was still a woman in the first blush of marriage and strongly disinclined to do anything that might dim the rosy glow of contentment. Eventually, however, she would have girded her nerve.

But now, like most matters one was loath to discuss, it had sat down in her drawing room and presented itself as an inevitability.

Obviously, Bea could not explain to Mrs. Norton the source of her anxiety, not only because she would never reveal such highly personal information to her archnemesis but also because she did not entirely understand it herself. She worried, yes, about causing the duke pain by raising what was probably an upsetting subject for him—as the subject of her parents was deeply troubling to her—but that was just the tip of her apprehension, the narrow end that pricked her skin like a needle.

Forced to examine her deep reluctance now, for she could not scurry out of her own drawing room like a frightened animal, she supposed it most likely stemmed from fear.

Most likely? Bea thought wryly.

Quite clearly, her inability to raise the topic with Kesgrave was the product of terror.

Yes, but what aspect in particular frightened her?

That was the more puzzling question, and she sought to answer it by pondering what it meant to consider the duke in relation to his father.

But it was not just his father, she thought. It was the whole line of Matlocks stretching all the way back to the Peasants' Revolt—twenty generations of untold wealth and privilege.

It was daunting to situate Kesgrave within that historical context.

He had been placed there previously by the dowager herself, who had lulled Bea into a sort of waking sleep with her seemingly endless recital of illustrious forebears. There were so many lord presidents of the council and chancellors of the exchequer occupying various branches of the family tree it was shocking the trunk did not collapse under the sheer weight of their importance.

But there was a quaintness to those ancestors. Picturing them, Bea saw knights in effigy, beloved hounds at their feet, heraldic shields in their grasp.

There was nothing charmingly antiquated, however, about the man who had sired her husband. No, the fifth Duke of Kesgrave was a man so assured of his supremacy and so cruel in its implementation that he delighted in wringing his own tenants dry like cloths. Coolly, without any concern for morality, he would have made his son's unworthy betrothed disappear.

Damien wielded the same power and was forged in its potency. Swaddled in influence and bathed in wealth, he had known naught but the heady elixir of self-determination from the moment he drew his very first breath.

Bea knew this to be true, and yet all she could see when she looked at him was a wondrous anomaly existing outside of time and space.

It was an incongruous perception, she knew, for at the

very same time she credited much of his character to his upbringing. His genuine indifference to the opinion of others, for example, must be attributed to his position in society. Only someone who knew he was unaccountable could behave with such flagrant disregard for accountability.

Without that disdain, he would never have allowed himself to love her.

The contradiction should have been impossible to sustain, and yet somehow it only strengthened her sense of Kesgrave's inexplicable singularity. Discovering the truth about his parents, however, would deal the illusion a fatal blow, for she would no longer be able to imagine he had sprung fully formed from his father's head like Athena.

Rather, she would know fully the terrible forces that formed him.

Naturally, that was a terrifying prospect because those forces continued to exist and bear down on them—as evidenced by Mrs. Norton's presence in her drawing room. Calmly drinking tea while implausibly dressed as Bea's rarely seen Aunt Susan, she was the embodiment of the past's determination to encroach on the present.

Alas, there was nothing Bea could do save refill the teacups and she duly lifted the pot while glancing curiously at her guest. "Would you like a little more?"

Slightly taken aback by the query, for it was not the response she had anticipated to the revelation that her grace's husband's life had been repeatedly imperiled by his uncle, Mrs. Norton fluttered her lashes several times before agreeing. "Yes, that would be lovely, thank you."

As Bea refilled her cup, she urged the other woman to continue. "You were explaining your concerns regarding Lord Myles Matlock."

"There is much to be concerned about regarding Lord Myles," Mrs. Norton replied, "but first I was reminding you of his unsavory reputation, for I do not know how familiar you are with the history. Much of it is gossip, which is notoriously unreliable, and can easily be dismissed or ignored. I tend to think it is on the mark because I do not believe any boy could be quite that accident-prone. You may recall, I have a young son of my own and while he has got himself into quite a few scrapes, he has never fallen down a well or been bitten by a poisonous frog. I also believe there is some truth in the reports detailing the bitterness between the two brothers. Lord Myles contended publicly that the duke only married his mistress to spite him, to which his brother replied that Myles did not warrant even that much consideration in his decision-making. I imagine their enmity was quite painful for the dowager."

Mrs. Norton paused to sip daintily at her tea, noting the exquisite perfection of the blend, and Bea waited impatiently for her to continue. Identifying the source of her reluctance had the gratifying effect of ridding her of it, and she was now eager to know everything.

Her agitation, however, remained.

Indeed, it had increased many times over, rising to such an intolerable pitch she could barely keep her hands still. It required every ounce of her self-control not to rise from the cushion and seek out Kesgrave immediately. Roiled by horror at all that he had suffered, she longed to provide comfort, to tend to his wounds, to press kisses against the tender skin where injuries had once marred his body. He bore no scars from his calamities—she knew that intimately—but then neither did she, which only underscored how poorly the physical marks of childhood served as a map of an adult's pain.

And yet just as ardently as Bea ached to soothe the duke, she desired a moment alone with his grandmother, for she was overcome with a sudden, intense compulsion to be in the presence of the one person who loved him as much as she.

She did not doubt that Mrs. Norton's speculation was correct and the dowager found the rift between the brothers to be excruciating, but as an innately decent human being her ultimate sympathy would lie with the helpless babe. Bea was sure the old duchess protected her grandson as well as she could, and she wanted to know all of it—every action she had taken to keep him safe, every reprisal she offered when she failed.

Oh, yes, Beatrice was very anxious indeed, and contemplating the unbearable tautness of her nerves, she was amused to realize her ability to hide her disquiet was the most appropriately ducal thing she had done since assuming the title. How astonished Mrs. Norton would be if she knew the true state of her hostess's emotions.

Smiling blandly, Bea murmured, "I'm sure the dowager was most upset."

"Knowing the history as you do, you cannot be startled to learn that Lord Myles is most displeased by the duke's marriage," Mrs. Norton continued. "To be clear, he is displeased with the duke marrying at all and, unlike the beau monde, takes no particular objection to you. In fact, he is happy that Kesgrave wed a plain spinster for that should make it easier."

"It?" Bea asked.

"For history to repeat itself," Mrs. Norton clarified.

Finding the oblique answer of little help, Bea struggled to comprehend the implication. "You mean for me to die in childbirth?"

"Gracious me, no," Mrs. Norton replied with an emphatic shake of her head. "He does not want to let the situation progress that far because there is always the chance that the child will live and then where will he be? He will have to start all over again with the wells and the frogs! No, the history he wants to repeat is for the duke to be so devastated by his wife's untimely demise that he resolves never to remarry. He is thrilled that his nephew chose an old maid because it means he is deeply in love. He is convinced your death would utterly destroy the duke, who would waste away to nothing and obligingly slide into an early grave. That is why he is determined to kill you."

Chapter Three

Bea's first impulse was to laugh.

Her nerves already frayed from constraining her anxiety while struggling to appear calm, she found the idea of Lord Myles Matlock conspiring to kill her to be wildly implausible and highly risible. The brooding uncle waiting in secret for decades to visit the sins of the villainous father on the innocent son whom he had failed to murder in his infanthood was simply too closely related to the plot of a gothic novel for her to take seriously.

A giggle almost escaped her.

But Bea restrained it.

Of course she did.

Having narrowly escaped death only the week before, she harbored no illusions about her own safety. In a blink of an eye, a young woman could go from reading quietly in her sitting room to desperately staving off an assailant, and Bea had no reason to assume Lord Myles's resentments were not as lethal and longstanding as Mrs. Norton described.

Swiftly, Bea looked toward the bank of windows at the front of the room as if expecting to see Kesgrave's uncle heaving himself over the sill with a cutlass clutched between his teeth.

Needless to say, nothing so alarming met her gaze and she watched a row of trees sway gently in the breeze for several seconds before returning her attention to her guest.

Revealing none of the distress she felt, Bea said with bland interest, "And you discovered his intentions during the course of your investigation?"

"Atonement," Mrs. Norton corrected. "I discovered the truth about Lord Myles's intentions while *atoning* for my sins against you. And it was not easy, I assure you, for I had to assume a dozen different disguises to keep him in my sights for several weeks. I followed him to his club, to his lawyer, to his mistress, to assorted gaming hells—all at considerable danger to myself. Naturally, that is not worthy of consideration right now, for we have more pressing issues to deal with, but I have kept a detailed list of the perilous situations in which I placed myself for your perusal at a later date. I know you will want a full account of my actions before making your decision, as you are a fair-minded woman who would insist on considering every aspect of my penance. For the moment, it is more vital that we discuss the threat against you. Currently, I occupy two positions in Lord Myles's life."

Flabbergasted by this communication, Bea made no attempt to hide her astonishment. "*Two* positions?"

Her response pleased Mrs. Norton, who smiled and explained that Lord Myles knew her as Mr. Twaddle-Thum and as a barmaid at an establishment called the Rosy Compass, on Clarice Street in Holborn, which he visited every Sunday afternoon. "It is attached to a brothel, and there is a certain lightskirt of whom he is fond. Mr. Twaddle-Thum arranged permission to install a spy in his establishment to observe Lord Myles. Although I pay the tavern owner handsomely for his compliance, you must not fear that

I will present you with a bill for my expenditures at the conclusion of my atonement. I have no desire for reimbursement. Nevertheless, all monies paid on your behalf will be included in my final accounting as proof of my commitment to the project. I trust it goes without saying that your goodwill is priceless to me."

Incapable of imagining the fashionable London hostess serving tankards of ale at a public house, Bea said, "I am quite taken aback by what you have managed to accomplish."

Dipping her head modestly, Mrs. Norton insisted she could not have achieved any of it without guidance from her grace's theater company. "Miss Calcott was so very helpful in explaining how to perform a convincing character. It is not just in the tone and texture of your voice, although that does play a significant part, but also in your posture. Miss Calcott was emphatic on the importance of holding oneself appropriately to convey status and mood."

Mrs. Norton continued in the same vein for several minutes, detailing the lessons she had learned from the actors at the Particular and identifying the institution as belonging to the duchess. At first Bea thought she was using the term as an affirmation of the connection—that was, as the place where Bea had conducted one of her investigations—but the longer she talked, the more it became clear that she meant it in the literal sense.

Her visitor was under the impression that Bea owned the Particular.

Convinced now that Mrs. Norton was making a May game of her, Bea considered rising to her feet and briskly showing her the door.

Owning the Particular!

Every other aspect of her story, though improbable, contained some fragment of possibility, but the assertion of ducal proprietorship of a theater on the Strand was simply one absurdity too far.

Whatever wicked scheme Mrs. Norton was brewing, she had badly overplayed her hand.

And yet Bea remained firmly in her seat because she simply could not believe the disgraced society matron was so hen-witted as to return to the well that had ill served her before. Having failed so catastrophically to ruin Bea previously with an elaborate ruse about a consuming mystery, she would at least have the sense to attempt something markedly different.

Placing herself in the center of another rackety plot would be to invite disaster.

After all, Kesgrave had expelled her only from Almack's. He had left every other establishment in London available to her, a kindness that could easily be revoked. Mrs. Norton, who had already suffered the excruciating mortification of being disinvited to her own godmother's garden party, had to understand the danger she was in if she tried to gammon Bea again.

Why would she seek more indignities to bear?

Hoping to clarify what could only be a genuine misapprehension, Bea interrupted to say that she did not own the Particular.

Mrs. Norton nodded understandingly and said, "Of course, yes, Miss Drake and her father continue to own the larger portion, but given your investment, it is not an inaccurate statement. You must not be shy in taking possession of the many assets of the Matlock estates. The reluctance is understandable, especially in an orphan of your unique history, but they are rightfully yours now as well."

Although Bea was indeed timid in this respect, she did not doubt Mrs. Norton spoke the truth and concluded that Kesgrave had followed through on his pledge to invest in the

Particular. Bea thought it had merely been a ruse to gain access to the theater company during their investigation into Mr. Hobson's murder, but she recalled how zealously he had conducted the negotiation. At the time she had marveled at his inability to consent to any agreement that was less than ideal even in pretense.

Bea realized now that was because he had always intended to hold true to the pact.

Why, then, had he failed to mention it to her?

Misunderstanding the look of confusion on Bea's face, Mrs. Norton rushed to explain that she was familiar with the ownership arrangement at the Particular only because she had paid a call on Miss Drake in the wake of Hobson's death. "I assure you the information is not widely known. After everything that happened, I felt so awful about my part in it and wished to know more about the victim, whose murder was directly linked to Tavistock's wretched plan. I considered it part of my penance. That was why I consulted with the company when I needed help disguising myself as Mr. Twaddle-Thum. It was Miss Calcott who taught me tricks for blending into the background and not calling attention to myself. It comes to you naturally, of course, but for someone of my appearance, it is quite a difficult feat to accomplish. The secret is to keep your eyes down. People do not notice people who do not notice them. She is inordinately clever for an actress. Or perhaps she is the standard amount of clever. I am not acquainted with enough actresses to make general assumptions."

Although Bea's experience was almost as limited, she agreed with this assessment of Miss Calcott, for the actress had struck her as unusually knowing and sly. That fact that she was able to successfully tutor Mrs. Norton attested to those traits.

"Everything she taught me was so helpful," Mrs. Norton

continued, "for she assured me that Lord Myles would not look too closely at the woman who brought his ale. And it was true, for he never once raised his glance above my bosom, and I was able to linger near his table without his noticing. That is how I was able to discover his plan to kill you. He was looking for someone to perform the service and talked openly about it with several prospects."

Accustomed to holding many notions in her head at once —conversing with a suspect, for example, while evaluating the evidence she had already collected—Bea was disconcerted to discover she could not quite form a coherent thought. So many different ideas whirled about in her mind, from disclosures about Kesgrave's parentage to revelations about his investment in the Particular to images of her archnemesis donning the rough frock of a barmaid to eavesdrop on Lord Myles. She did not know on which to concentrate first.

Her murder, of course.

Yes, she should ascertain the details of her impending death before focusing on anything else.

Consequently, Bea asked what precisely Lord Myles was planning.

Mrs. Norton grimaced before taking another sip of tea and admitting she knew none of the particulars of the planned murder. "And it is the most vexatious thing! I barely slept a wink last night picturing all the terrible ways you could die before restoring my vouchers: a robbery gone awry, a carriage careening out of control, a fall out of a high window. I do not know whom he chose for the assignment in the end, for the decision was made either away from the Rosy Compass or at a time when I was not there. But yesterday he was in an unusually jovial mood, smiling at everyone in the tavern and making ribald jokes about my décolletage. He even threw a couple of coins at me and told me to buy myself a dress with a lower neckline. And his grin! It was chilling, so predatory and voracious as he told the man at the table next to his that all of his problems were about to be solved. That was when I knew I had to come and warn you despite not knowing the precise details of what he planned."

"A prudent decision," Bea remarked with a mildness she did not feel, "what with your vouchers at stake."

Aware of the misstep, Mrs. Norton winced at the comment and said that naturally she feared for her grace's life more than her own social career—even if failure to redeem herself carried dire consequences for her daughter's future. "I chose my words poorly only because I have worn myself to a nub over worry for you. Showing up on your doorstep with vague warnings was the last thing I wanted to do, your grace. I had hoped to be able to tell you the specific nature of the threat so that concrete steps could be taken to ensure your safety. But the time for subtle machinations has passed, and now brute force must be applied. I am convinced his lawyer knows something, for Lord Myles spends a frightful amount of time bracketed in his office, no doubt working out the details of his nefarious schemes. The duke must visit Mr. Jordan and demand answers. He is a slippery man, with a droopy left eye that makes it look as if he is perpetually winking. Unfortunately, he has resisted all my efforts to gather information from him. He was decidedly rude to Mr. Twaddle-Thum. But he will submit at once to the force of Kesgrave's personality and position, I am certain of it."

"Mr. Jordan," Bea repeated, as if committing the solicitor's name to memory.

"Douglas Jordan, yes," Mrs. Norton affirmed. "His offices are in Tucks Court. The duke must call on him at once, for there is not a moment to lose. And until he does, I would advise you to remain within these walls. It is the only place you are safe."

Indeed, it was not, as recent events attested, and recalling the attack the disgraced visitor blanched and quickly added that she did not expect Kesgrave to take her at her word. "My husband is apprised of the situation, for I could not subject myself to danger without first gaining his consent, and he stands ready to confirm everything I have said. I trust you or the duke will not hesitate to contact him for corroboration."

It was another deft move, Bea thought, offering Mr. Norton's imprimatur. He was, as far as she knew, an honorable gentleman with all the right opinions. He would never have a hand in harming the reputation of a young woman, let alone the wife of a powerful peer. "Thank you, yes, I suspect Kesgrave will require some confirmation. He will most likely desire a word with you as well."

Mrs. Norton flinched at the prospect, recalling, no doubt, her last interview with the irate lord, but smiled gamely and said, "Yes, of course."

Then, as if afraid the duke might magically appear in the drawing room, she rose to her feet and announced that she had taken up enough of the duchess's time. "You must desire the opportunity to digest this information in peace. It is overwhelming, I know, but do not lose heart. The die is not cast. You can extricate yourself from the grip of death as handily now as you have in the past, and everything will be as it once was."

In truth, it sounded as though the fallen society matron was trying to rally her own spirits, and Bea could not smother the smile that rose to her lips. "I will keep that in mind, thank you."

Satisfied with the response, Mrs. Norton nodded and took several steps forward, toward the door, then halted and said with some hesitancy, "And when this is over and your life is secure again, we can discuss my repentance? If you do not consider my saving your life enough of a service, I am happy to perform another. I will perform as many as necessary to earn your forgiveness."

Her sincerity could not be in doubt, and Bea, who considered her life to be of significant value, agreed to the proposal.

Mrs. Norton's relief was palpable. "Thank you, your grace. Thank you very much for being so kindhearted and fairminded. Yes, I know those are not among the five compliments upon which we agreed, but you must let me say them. Well, no, you *must* not do anything you do not want to do," she added quickly, "but I hope you will allow me to say them, for, truly, I know I do not deserve forgiveness for what I have done."

Before Bea could reply to this earnest statement, Flora swept into the room.

"He is gone, Bea," she said with an anxious frown as she strode toward her cousin. "Up and left London with naught but a polite note expressing his regret that he will not be able to join me for tea with the duchess. I cannot imagine what he is about, writing such a—"

Abruptly she broke off when she realized there was another person in the room. Flora's expression turned to confusion as she beheld her relative. Startled, she gasped, "Aunt Susan! But how are you here? Mama was in a tumult this morning over the message you sent announcing your terrible cold. You said you could not raise your head from the pillow, let alone pay social calls. When I left her, she was fretting dreadfully about your health and ordering Mrs. Emerson to make a poultice of dandelion and garlic."

As Mrs. Norton's disguise was convincing with only the most cursory inspection, Bea knew better than to try to brazen it out. Furthermore, allowing Flora to believe her aunt had recovered enough to visit Berkeley Square would inevitably end in farce, with Aunt Vera angry at her sister for fobbing her off with the flimsy excuse of illness and Aunt Susan taking a pet at the unfounded accusation.

"I understand your confusion, but this is not our aunt," Bea said, threading her arm through Flora's as she led her to the settee. She did not truly believe her cousin would assault the other woman when she learned of her identity, but she also saw no reason to take the risk. "It is Mrs. Norton. You remember Mrs. Norton, I am sure. She made her presentation the same year as I. We just had a very cordial visit and now she is about to depart."

Although Flora stiffened at the mention of her cousin's archnemesis, for if the former Miss Brougham was the sworn enemy of Bea's, then she was the sworn enemy of Flora's as well, she displayed none of the enmity she felt, smiling amicably and asking if her family were well.

Mrs. Norton, disinclined to linger now that her objective had been achieved, provided a polite but succinct answer to this query. Then she thanked the duchess for her consideration and time. "I look forward to hearing from you. It was lovely to see you, Miss Hyde-Clare, however fleetingly. Please give Mrs. Welpton my best. It is so disagreeable to be under the weather."

Flora, replying easily, pledged to convey her regards to Aunt Susan and thanked her for being so thoughtful. Then as soon as the other woman left the room, she leaped up from the sofa and ran to the threshold to watch Mrs. Norton depart. When she was satisfied that the other woman was indeed out of earshot, she turned to her cousin with a solemn expression and assured her she did not have to say a word.

She knew precisely what was going on.

Chapter Four

❧❦❧

Fear pierced through Bea as she imagined Flora frequenting waterfront taverns in her brother, Russell's clothes and asking indelicate questions about Lord Myles Matlock. She knew, yes, that her cousin could take care of herself, for she had efficiently disarmed a murderer, thereby saving herself and Mr. Holcroft with the swing of a wood plank, but could not help believing that luck had played a significant role in her success.

If the house had not been so dilapidated...

If the floorboard not been loose...

It was too much to hope that fortune would strike again, and a man who would kill a child was utterly without conscience.

Flora must cease all activities in regards to Kesgrave's uncle.

Before Bea could launch into her protest, Flora's demeanor underwent a radical change and she squealed with excitement. "You must let me help!" she demanded.

"Help?" Bea asked, confounded by the transformation.

"Do not try to gammon me by insisting nothing is afoot,"

Flora said. "You are planning something to repay Mrs. Norton for her crimes, and whatever it is, I want to help. I am sure it is very clever and convoluted and a little vicious. Is Kesgrave involved? Oh, yes, of course he is. Please tell me what is happening so that I may play a part. Her strange costume has something to do with it, does it not? She looks so disconcertingly similar to our aunt. Ooh! Is that your ruse? To have her apprehended by the authorities for pretending to be someone else? But is that even a punishable offense? And is it wise to draw our family into the intrigue? If something goes astray, Mama will be quite vexed. You know how fervently she seeks to please her sister," she said, her eagerness dipping just a tiny bit as she contemplated her mother's displeasure. Then her tone brightened again. "No matter! I am confident you have thought of everything."

Bea shook her head and insisted she was planning no scheme against Mrs. Norton. "Rather, she is determined to get back into my good graces and as such has discovered troubling information about Kesgrave's uncle. It is nothing for you to worry about."

But of course Flora found this development to be even more concerning, for she could not believe Mrs. Norton was genuine in her efforts to help and proposed that they pay an immediate call on Tavistock to discover what terrible disaster he had planned for her now. "Obviously, he is behind this new ploy, for she is not clever enough to come up with her own scheme. But why would he have her dress as our aunt?" she asked thoughtfully. "To lull your suspicions, perhaps, by calling forth feelings of familial fondness?"

Amused by her cousin's charmingly naïve assumption that Bea felt the same affection for the woman as Flora, Bea laughed and said there was no cause for worry on that score.

As lightly as the comment was stated, it nevertheless struck Flora forcefully and she said with anxious recognition,

"There is none, is there, for Aunt Susan and Uncle Lawrence have been as beastly as the rest of us. I am sorry, Bea, truly I am. I had hoped finding Mr. Davies's killer for you would go a long way to make up for my own complicity in our family's cruelty, but since he did not exist, all I did was make a muck of everything and almost get Mr. Holcroft killed."

As her cousin had described her pursuit of Theodore Davies in only the most larkish of terms, as a daring escapade embarked on in the spirit of adventure, it had never occurred to Bea that her pursuit could have been spurred by anything else.

And why would she?

Flora had appeared so proud of herself for wresting a mystery from her cousin's tight grasp.

That was true, Bea thought, but she also knew that Flora was not quite the giddy puff of air she had styled herself as, in hopes of making a good match on the Marriage Mart. It should come as no surprise to her that her cousin's motivation ran deeper than an eagerness to be perceived as a heroine, and the fact that it did shamed her a little.

Perhaps Flora's wish to make amends also accounted for why she had lately begun to refer to the new duchess as her sister.

Naturally, Bea had attributed the modification to a desire to align herself more closely with a coronet.

Heartened by these revelations, Bea sought to cajole Flora out of her bout of self-pity by pointing out how very much she accomplished in her pursuit of the fictitious man's killer, a list that included the apprehension of an actual murderer, the downfall of an immoral judge and the ruination of a corrupt system designed to prey on people when they were at their most vulnerable.

But of course Bea overspoke, for she was only trying to improve her cousin's mood, not accurately represent the state of the Chancery, and Flora rushed to correct her, explaining at length the many ways the court still perverted justice. It was a wondrous little speech—informed, insightful, coherent —and Bea listened with delight as her cousin discussed land law, sinecures and equitable distribution.

Alas, the notion of equity returned the topic to Aunt Susan and Flora ended her brief lecture with a tirade against Mrs. Norton's evil intentions. "I do not care what she says about Kesgrave's uncle. She is conspiring against you and will try to lead you again to your doom. I will not allow it!"

Given that her cousin seemed on the verge of marching out of the room and physically accosting the former Miss Brougham, Bea sought to distract her by reminding her of the original reason she had called. "You were out of sorts with Mr. Holcroft. Please do sit down and tell me what is the matter."

As her grievance with Holcroft had momentarily slipped her mind, Flora stared at her cousin with a bemused expression, as if truly uncertain which topic to pursue: Mrs. Norton's deceitful scheme or Holcroft's intolerable defection.

Plan or pain?

In the end, anguish prevailed and Flora tossed herself woefully onto the settee much in the way Lady Abercrombie had once advised Bea to do when nursing a broken heart.

"I am wretched," she said sadly, "utterly, *utterly* wretched. It is over. He has left town without a word."

As the gentleman in question had seemed quite besotted with her cousin, Bea was surprised to learn that he was so peeved by a minor disagreement as to decamp. "But did you not say he sent you a note?"

Flora sighed heavily and amended her statement slightly. "No kind word. He just dashed off a stilted missive. Here," she said, holding out a slip of paper.

Bea accepted it from her cousin's languid hand and read a

polite explanation as to why he would be unable to join her for tea at Kesgrave House. It was brief, without question, but he did express sincere regret, which she pointed out.

"Fine, then, no *very* kind word," Flora said petulantly. "I do not see why you are taking his side in this. You are *my* cousin."

Before Bea could respond to this particularly absurd bit of nonsense, Flora lifted her head from the cushion and nodded excitedly. "That is right, you are my cousin, not his. *His* cousin is hiding in disgrace in his rooms at Lyon's Inn. Yes, of course, Mr. Caruthers. I wonder how I did not think of it sooner, for it is so very obvious. We must go at once," she said, leaping to her feet.

Bea, however, remained firmly seated.

Flora waved her hand impatiently. "Why are you dawdling? We must go at once to Wych Street and coax Mr. Caruthers into an outing. It is the very thing! I am astonished I did not think of it sooner."

"It is too late in the day to pay a house call on a gentleman I've never met," Bea said reasonably, although that was not the true source of her objection. Having just learned several distressing facts about Kesgrave's past and her own future, she had no intention of leaving the house until she had spoken to him. She was not only agitated by the thought of somehow missing him before he went out for the evening; she was also too distracted to hold a rational conversation.

And yet the alternative was scarcely more appealing, for she knew she would be incapable of doing naught but pace the room apprehensively.

It was far better to at least make an attempt to engage herself in Flora's problem.

"And if it were not too late, I am disinclined to go haring off to Lyon's Inn without fully understanding the reason," she added. "Now do retake your seat and tell me why we must visit Holcroft's disgraced cousin."

Despite the churlishness on her face, Flora complied with this request and explained that Holcroft despaired of Mr. Caruthers ever emerging from his crypt. "That is what he calls his rooms because he fears his cousin has buried himself alive. But when I visited him a few weeks ago to gather information on Mr. Brooks, he responded to what Holcroft described as my matter-of-fact yet sympathetic manner. He seemed to come out of his self-pity for a little while, which pleased Holcroft so much, he insisted on helping me find Davies's murderer. Obviously, if making his cousin laugh delighted him, then convincing his cousin to go for a drive in Hyde Park will send him into paroxysms of joy. You must let me do that, Bea. Then Holcroft will forget his sullenness over my spending so much time with Nuneaton—which was only to ensure your social success!—and return to London immediately to lavish gratitude on my head for rescuing his cousin from misery. Do say you will help! I know you are too kind-hearted to consign a man to a life of sadness and solitude simply because the hour is imperfect."

"It is not the hour that is imperfect," Bea muttered, "but your plan. As charming as you are, Flora, I think you are over-estimating your appeal if you believe all this poor man needs to emerge from his crypt is a little encouragement from you."

"Not just me," Flora pointed out quickly. "You as well. He was appropriately impressed with my relationship with Kesgrave, for naturally I assured him that the duke would take an interest in rooting out the corruption that is so pervasive to the institution. By bringing you along, I would be demonstrating his commitment to that cause. That is, of course, unless you think Kesgrave could be persuaded to come. In that case, your presence would not be required at all."

Her cousin sounded so hopeful at the prospect, Bea could not help but laugh. Confidently, she replied that Kesgrave most assuredly did not want to visit a disgraced lawyer in his shabby rooms in Lyon's Inn. "And you are not to ask him," she added sternly.

Flora blinked her lashes several times in innocent wonder and swore she would never dare to dream of such a presumption. "I was merely ascertaining your opinion on the matter. And it is neither here nor there because you are a duchess, which is very impressive too. But you must come. You know I cannot do it alone, for Mama would never allow me to take the carriage and I could not possibly go for a drive in Hyde Park in a hack. It would create a terrible scandal."

The scandal the conveyance would create was minor compared with the one that would be incited by the sight of an unmarried young woman alone in a confined space with a known reprobate. Bea was necessary not just to provide a vehicle but also an air of respectability.

That problem only presented itself, however, if Caruthers consented to the plan, which, by her cousin's own account, he was unlikely to do.

As if hoping to forestall the refusal she feared was about to be issued with a pitiful display, Flora lowered her head sadly. "Of course you are reluctant to get involved. It is so very sordid, is it not? The only reason I am embroiled in this drama is I visited the rundown inn to find Mr. Brooks. Do you recall Mr. Brooks? He was the erstwhile employer of Mr. Davies, who also did not exist," she said softly, her eyes peering slyly at her cousin to observe how she was responding to this lugubrious display. "Had I but known he was a figment of your imagination, I would never have jeopardized my life to bring his killer to justice."

Since Bea knew exactly what Flora was trying to accomplish with her observations, she did not believe that yielding to her request counted as giving way to her manipulations. It was, rather, an acknowledgment of a hand very well played: Bea's lies had imperiled her cousin. If escorting her to Mr. Caruthers's rooms in Lyon's Inn helped discharge the debt, then she was genuinely happy to do it.

It would make no difference in the end, she was convinced, because she could not believe the lawyer would fall in with the plan. Nevertheless, the unlikeliness of the machination greatly improved Bea's mood and she consented to calling on Holcroft's benighted cousin.

"Perhaps tomorrow," she added, although she cautioned that it might have to be the following day or the next. "I must first consult with Kesgrave regarding the matter raised by Mrs. Norton."

"Thank you, darling. You are the best of good sisters," Flora said, cheerfully clapping her hands.

"But you must promise to abide by Mr. Caruthers's decision," Bea said, well aware of how relentless her cousin could be. "If he does not want to take a drive with us, then you do not get to browbeat him into agreement."

Flora shrieked happily as she clapped her hands and agreed to Bea's conditions, swearing that she would not know how to browbeat a gentleman even if she wished to. "I was raised to be submissive and compliant," she said, before adding with a wide grin, "just like you."

As Bea knew this to be true, she said nothing in response.

But she thought about it a few hours later as she tried to muster the pluck to ask Kesgrave about his parents and wondered if her reluctance was a product of her upbringing. How to avoid upsetting topics was the first thing she had learned as a newly orphaned child placed in an unfamiliar home.

Silently acquiescing to her relatives' every wish was the second.

She felt disconcertingly mute now as she watched the duke settle comfortably in a chair in the intimate library alcove, his golden hair gleaming in the candlelight as he apologized for being detained. Then he glanced at the assortment of dishes for dinner and laughed.

"Is that crimp cod with pineapple sauce?" he asked.

Startled by the question, for she had been too consumed by her dwindling courage to notice the plates, she looked now and noted the fish shimmered with a familiar yellow cast.

It was a measure of her anxiety that she was grateful for the wretched fruit's presence because it provided a benign (relatively, of course!) subject about which to comment. "It appears to be, yes, although I suppose it is more like a glaze."

"And the soup?" he said, leaning forward to examine it more closely.

"A classic potage printanier," she replied after a moment's examination.

But of course it was not, for the chef had added a fine dice of pineapple to the velvety puree of peas.

Delighted, Kesgrave chuckled again and advised her to inform the staff of her aversion to pineapple before even the wine was augmented with the ubiquitous fruit. "It will penetrate every aspect for your life, however minor. You may depend on it, for André is just clever enough to work it into a recipe for tooth powder."

As she could not imagine any incursion more appalling than her rout cakes, Bea received this warning with equanimity. "If you are worried about your dental hygiene, you must discuss it with him. I am sure he will be happy to defer to your preference."

Kesgrave assured her he had no concerns. "But if you do, I would urge you to do the same," he added somberly, as if conferring on a subject of great seriousness.

But he grinned!

Oh, did he grin, his eyes sparkling with utter mischief, and Bea, who had thought herself accustomed to his beauty after six weeks of marriage, felt her breath hitch in her throat at the sight. Somehow she was continually startled by the warmth of his gaze, for she could never quite forget the bored indifference with which he had originally scrutinized her, as if she were an especially uninteresting member of a colony of ants.

"I may have to," she admitted as the duke filled her glass with a deep burgundy-colored wine, "as the situation continues to grow more dire. This afternoon I detected flecks of pineapple in my rout cakes, and I am sure you are aware of what comes next."

"Chunks," he said, "then slabs."

"Pineapple cakes with a hint of rout," she explained.

"Oh, dear," he said with convincing alarm.

It was curious, Bea thought, how she frequently determined not to mention a particularly mortifying experience to him and then almost immediately blurted it out. Cowering behind the door in the butler's pantry, for example—she had sworn to take that absurd humiliation to the grave and yet she had told him about it at a bizarrely inopportune time: when they were searching the terrace for evidence of a young lady's guilt at Lady Abercrombie's murder mystery dinner party play.

Everything felt horrifyingly shameful until suddenly it was just funny.

Because the meal had begun so enjoyably—gleaming curls, gentle teasing—Bea considered keeping the conversation light. There were more than a dozen topics she could broach that would engross them for hours. Mr. Stephens and his recent fixation on cows readily came to mind, for the steward was determined to figure out which breed made the most milk so that he could optimize production. To date, he had filled three dozen ledger pages detailing type and yield as well as the specifics of the growing environment. It was a study not only of bovine productivity but also of pasture composition.

Bea found almost every aspect of his research fascinating, from the information he had gathered about the level of moisture in the soil to his compulsion to gather information about the level of moisture in the soil.

It would not be so awful, she thought, to delay the unpleasant conversation until after they had eaten. The meal would be difficult enough to digest with all that pineapple. Why make it worse by raising a thorny subject?

Reasonably, she could justify postponing it now, and she did not doubt that she could just as validly push it off again later. There was never an ideal time to talk about one's cruel dead father and murderous uncle.

It might as well be now.

But still she could not bring herself to jump headlong into the serious topic and decided to approach it cautiously from the side. As such, she asked why he had not mentioned his investment in the Particular.

Kesgrave, seemingly confused by the question, furrowed his brow and wondered why he would explicitly state something that had already been made plain. "You were present when we arrived at terms. Inevitably, my solicitor required a few amendments to better protect my funds, but they were only minor changes and not worth reviewing with you. All the significant concerns were resolved with Miss Drake, who represented her father's interests."

How logical he made it sound—as if every ruse to gather information was in fact a binding contract.

"I believed it was only a ploy to gain us access to the theater so that we could interrogate the company," Bea said.

"I thought you were negotiating an investment to which you had no intention of holding."

Now he stared at her as if incapable of comprehending her words. "Negotiate an investment to which I had no intention of holding? I would never condone wasting my own time nor anyone else's so flagrantly."

It was impressive, she thought, how he managed to imbue his tone with both ardent disapproval and earnest bewilderment. "It is not a flagrant waste of your time if it accomplishes a desirable result, such as granting us the opportunity to interview the acting company."

His expression remained baffled as he replied, "If I were inclined to behave in such a callous fashion, I would have agreed to whatever conditions Miss Drake put forth. Surely, the fact that I countered with my own terms was an indication that I was not engaging in a merely pro forma exchange."

Well, yes, Bea had thought he *was* that callous, though of course callousness had nothing to do with it. She had simply assumed he could not bring himself to make a half-hearted gesture. It seemed naturally of a piece with his pedantry.

Ably following her thoughts even though she said nothing, Kesgrave laughed and assured her that he was fully capable of reining in his penchant for detail when it was necessary. "I know you think my pedantry is a cudgel that I wield indiscriminately, but in fact it is more like a chisel that is deployed strategically."

Although this observation was not entirely correct, it was close enough to the truth for Bea to feel a warm flush suffuse her cheeks and she lowered her gaze to avoid the amusement in his.

Her embarrassment, however, did not stem solely from the discovery that she had misjudged him, something she had done before, most notably when she convinced herself he could never love a drab spinster. It also derived from a disconcerting sense of naivete. The truth was, she had grossly misjudged his wealth because it was beyond her conception to imagine having so much money on hand to invest hundreds of pounds at a moment's notice.

Kesgrave could endow a theater company as easily as she could purchase a book at Hatchards.

It was mortifying to realize that she could somehow still underestimate his position even after inhabiting it for more than a month.

"I am only teasing, Bea," Kesgrave said as he moved the soup tureen to the side so that he could grasp her hand across the table.

His touch was comforting, but the hint of genuine distress in his voice increased her dismay, for she loathed the prospect of appearing so fragile that she could not withstand a minor deflating of her vanity. Kesgrave endured such treatment on a far more frequent basis with good humor and grace.

Annoyed at herself for how poorly she was handling the situation, Bea stood and tugged the duke to his feet. Wrapping her arms tightly around him, she laid her head on his shoulder and sighed. "It has been a strange afternoon."

Soothingly, he ran hands along her back. "Has it?"

This was where she should have started, she thought. After an entire day away from him, she should have begun here, with the warmth of his body. Pressed against it, she felt some of her anxiety dissolve.

"We must talk," she announced, loosening her embrace with some regret as she took a step back and turned toward the settee.

If the duke thought this statement ominous, he gave no indication as he led her to the red silk sofa situated only a few feet away. As they lowered to the cushion, Bea resisted the urge to curl up on his lap and instead shifted to look at him directly.

"Mrs. Norton called today," she said.

The duke tightened his jaw at this communication but kept his tone even as he replied, "I trust she is enjoying her season."

Bea smiled faintly at the irony. "She is just as miserable as you would hope, your grace. Ensuring that her vouchers for Almack's were revoked was an excellent use of your influence. You are to be commended."

He accepted the tribute with a brief nod, then sneered lightly. "Let me hazard a guess. She deeply regrets her behavior and is very sorry for the danger to which she subjected you, and if you could just see your way toward forgiving her, she will become an eager acolyte and do everything in her efforts to promote your cause."

"Yes," Bea said, then paused a moment before adding, "and no. She did come here seeking absolution but not in the way you think. She is determined to earn it."

"Is she?" he asked with almost careless disinterest. "Unless she can journey to the past and undo time and space, I am reasonably sure that is impossible."

Although Bea's heart skipped painfully at the use of the word *past,* she kept her expression bland as she said, "She came dressed as my Aunt Susan."

He drew his brows together, as if trying to remember such a person. "Your Aunt Susan?"

"Aunt Vera's sister, Mrs. Welpton," she explained, "and somehow more awful. You've never met her. I rarely have cause to interact with her, so you can imagine my confusion when Joseph informed me she had come to visit. But it was not she. It was Mrs. Norton demonstrating her expertise in disguising herself so I would more readily believe the information she had to impart."

"Although I trust your judgment implicitly, my love, I must confess this sounds suspiciously like another scheme," Kesgrave said, winding his fingers through hers. "I would not be shocked to find Tavistock lurking in the shadows."

As Flora had assumed the same thing, Bea could not cavil at his observation and allowed that they would have to do a thorough investigation of their own before deciding whether to act on Mrs. Norton's information. "Nevertheless, she claims to have uncovered an alarming plot to make you a widower."

Chapter Five

Kesgrave's hand clenched.

Briefly and painfully, it clutched her own so tightly Bea almost cried out.

And then it loosened and he rubbed his thumb gently against her palm.

Murmuring softly, his tone perhaps slightly amused, he said, "Has she?"

Bea, whose fingers still tingled from the pressure he had applied, was not fooled by this composed display and inhaled deeply to settle her own nerves. Alas, it did not quite work. Her heart racing with apprehension, she said, "Yes, and she has identified the man behind the plot as Lord Myles Matlock."

Silence greeted this revelation.

Indeed, he gave no indication at all that he had heard her. His thumb, stroking her skin, did not hitch or pause.

'Twas unnerving, the lack of response, and she added uneasily, "Your uncle."

"Yes," he said evenly, "I know who my uncle is."

But it was too smooth, like a worn cord pulled taut to flatten its frayed strands. Sooner or later, it would snap.

As if aware of this vaguely menacing quality, he smiled warmly and raised Bea's hand to his lips. "Alarming indeed. But no doubt a tempest in a teapot. I shall look into it further and report back what I discover. Speaking of things that require further investigating, I understand from Stephens that you have begun to sort through the papers left to you by your parents. He reports that it is an intriguing assortment, some of which is quite valuable. He cites the shares in a Yorkshire mining concern in particular. He is less sanguine about Phillips & Company, as its prospects have dimmed in the years since its patents expired. I am, of course, happy to look through them with you. I do not pretend to have Stephens's head for arithmetic, but I am reasonably conversant in financial matters."

"Yes, thank you," she said calmly.

But obviously, no.

The conversation was not going to veer sharply toward benign topics like her parents' investments. She was not going to sit next to him and chatter inconsequentially about the contents of the chest lately removed from her relatives' attic in Portman Square or debate the value of holding on to her father's stake in the Phillips steam engine.

Did he truly think she would unresistingly submit to this blatant attempt to change the subject?

Or was it worse still, and he actually believed she could be so easily distracted?

Both prospects were remarkably insulting, and yet Bea held her temper in check, for taking a pet would do little to improve the situation. Additionally, it occurred to her that his intention might be to provoke her into starting an argument, which would serve as the true distraction.

If that was the case, she would not oblige.

In fact, she would not oblige him in any of the tactics he might employ to evade a conversation about his childhood.

Bea knew the exigencies of pain well enough to comprehend the compulsion to avoid examining it. Sadness lived inside her like a flower garden, an overgrown bed of roses deprived of sunshine and yet thriving in the darkness, prodding her constantly with their thorns. Always, it seemed better to give them a wide berth and hope they withered in the stale air of isolation.

If such an approach produced the desired result—if sequestering one's pain was sufficient to ending it—then she would have happily engaged in a conversation about the feasibility of steam power.

Alas, it did not.

The opposite, however, had a salutary effect, for light allowed you to see the thorns. You could not smother the roses, no, but you could at least give them a prune.

Mitigation, Bea thought, not elimination.

Having arrived at these insights only a few months before, she longed to share them with Kesgrave—to spare him pain, but also to somehow redeem her own by making it useful.

And yet it was not this project of redemption that consumed her thoughts as she contemplated the duke in his ruthlessly tailored coat, his square jaw as sternly set as ever as he adopted a pose of indifference.

Rather, it was a vague sense that something hugely significant was at stake if she could not persuade him to reveal his thoughts about his parents, his childhood, or his potentially homicidal uncle.

She had never expected to find herself in a place like this —not, to be sure, in an absurdly lavish palatial concern in Berkeley Square, although that was certainly beyond her ability to imagine, but in an extraordinarily satisfying relationship with a man who considered her to be his equal.

Too levelheaded for the starry-eyed illusions of other hopeful young ladies, she had never dreamed of a marriage of true minds.

Why would she have?

The notion was so outside her understanding of the world, she could not even have conceived what it meant.

Instead, she had pined for a union marked by comfort and kindness—a marriage of companionable silences enlivened by sincere affection and a cheerful fire in the hearth.

At best, she expected to have what her aunt and uncle had: a fondness interspersed with impatience, a blending of quirks and opinions, a slight disgust of each other that might sting at times but never smart. Eventually, her husband would get annoyed at her persistent studiousness and she would become irked by his lack of seriousness.

And that was it, the sum total of her grand romantic notions on the eve of her come-out, and if Miss Brougham had not altered the course of her first season, she would even now be content with its inadequacies.

But the spiteful heiress had changed everything with her snide observations, somehow, inexplicably, aligning Bea's trajectory with the duke's, and now she was here, in this place of utter happiness, but also at a marker clearly delineating a line that she was not supposed to cross.

If she heeded it, Bea knew, something irretrievable would be lost. Maybe that thing would be only her misapprehension about the nature of their bond. Perhaps Kesgrave had never actually considered her an equal and she had merely created that condition based on a few admiring remarks and a baffling desire for her body.

Although it seemed inconceivable to her that she could have misunderstood the entirety of their relationship, she allowed it was possible and thought it would be funny, in a desperately not funny sort of way, to discover her romantical schoolgirl illusions had been fantastically grandiose after all.

She could not be that deluded, could she?

No, it was not possible.

And yet what did it say about their communion if he was incapable of accepting comfort from her? If he could only give it, then what balance could be achieved between them?

More troubling still, she thought, were the limits he sought to impose on her knowledge of him. In creating a rigid boundary that she was not allowed to cross, he was denying her access to a part of himself. He was, in effect, asserting that this particular aspect was none of her business.

That would never do.

No, it would not, especially not when she had revealed everything about herself. If she had failed to properly convey the depth of her insecurity, it was only because the bottom of the cavern bore such a close resemblance to the top as to make one indistinguishable from the other. Had the walls varied in color or texture at any point, she would have duly articulated each facet of the distinction.

Having decided not to abide by his preference, however, Bea was at a loss as to how to alter it. She could not compel him to speak, and although the fact that he thought she could be fobbed off with an abrupt change in conversational subject indicated a diminished ability to reason, he was still too clever to trick.

Honesty, then, was her only recourse.

Consequently, she said, "The secret to the successful application of a wart to disguise your appearance is to place it somewhere on your face where it is unlikely to distract you. The chin, for example."

Kesgrave, his brow furrowed again, said, "Excuse me?"

Deliberately misunderstanding the source of his confusion, she explained that the chin was out of the line of sight, so the wart could not be perceived. "It is unnerving to see the appliqué on the edge of your vision, or at least that is what Mrs. Norton has found. Your experience may be different."

"Very practical advice," he said approvingly, "and I will be certain to keep it in mind should I need to disguise myself again. As you may recall, I had less than stellar success employing the mustache my valet secured for me. That said, I am confused as to what this has to do with the topic under discussion, unless one of the stocks your father held is in a company that produces warts."

It was a deft reply, Bea noted with admiration, implying that the conversation had always been about her parents' investments and the reference to Mrs. Norton was the digression rather than the other way around.

"I am not familiar enough with my inheritance to know whether a costume manufacturer is among the companies in which my father invested," Bea answered, "but it would surprise me if he thought a firm with such a narrow market was a good money-making proposition. Nevertheless, I will be sure to ask Mr. Stephens about it. But in mentioning it, I was only following your lead."

Mildly entertained by the comment, which was faintly disapproving, his lips twitched and he said, "My lead?"

He had no idea, she thought, struck by the trace of patronizing amusement in his response, how much was at stake, how incredibly important the next few minutes were to the future of their relationship. He thought she was being intentionally provoking or purposefully lighthearted.

"You changed the conversation from your uncle's plot to murder me to something trivial, and I was merely doing the same," she pointed out. "I can only attribute this abrupt switch to a desire to give yourself some time to process the extremely disagreeable information because any other explanation—that you do not consider me worthy of your confidences, you do not trust me with your pain, you do not value my input, you believe confiding in a woman is beneath you—would require me to question my position in your life and that I cannot do. So when I tell you that it's wise to make sure the padding you use to augment your stomach is as comfortable sitting as it is standing and when you tell me Mr. Stephens is on good terms with the minister who oversees the patent office, you will find the inconsequential prattle has calmed your nerves enough that you are able to tell me about your parents and uncle."

Bea spoke calmly, smoothly, as if expounding on a topic that bore no more interest to her than the weather, but inside her chest her heart was racing wildly and she discovered she could not hold his gaze.

She had tried.

Determinedly, she had lifted her head and regarded him directly, her eyes steadily trained on his, and yet her resolve crumbled at the first sign of irritation. Displeased with her calling attention to his digressionary tactic, the duke tightened his lips, and fearing what she would see next—disgust or anger or worse, the blank countenance a man committed to revealing nothing—she looked away, compelled suddenly to examine the line of books on the shelf along the wall.

Kesgrave said her name quietly, his tone sympathetic and sad, she thought, but also a little reproachful, as if rebuking a small child for fearing a monster might lurk beneath her bed.

Bea, having no idea what it meant, marveled at the strange intimacy of love, for while it felt to her as though she had known the duke for the whole of her life, it had in fact been only a handful of months. In truth, she knew her Aunt Susan better than her husband.

Terrified, therefore, that he would seek to appease her with a meaningless platitude—and succeed in breaking her heart in ways she could not yet begin to understand—Bea continued as if he had not spoken. "You see, that is the arrangement I always expected to enter. Before Mrs. Norton effectively ruined my chances by undermining my confidence, I assumed I would marry a man who treated me with kind condescension, patting me amiably on the head while dismissing my opinions and being highly amused by my intellectual pretensions. And I would have been content with that arrangement because life with my aunt and uncle had taught me that being worthy of condescension was vastly superior to being deserving of contempt. But then you came along, your grace, and set a rigorous schedule for acquiring the various skills necessary to defend myself when any other man in the world would have told me in uncertain terms that I would not be investigating any more murders. By treating me with more respect and dignity than I could have ever imagined, you set an expectation of equality, and if you are now going to revert to form, which, I concede, you have every right to do as the male of the species, then I must insist you allow me to leave this marriage so that I can wed a man who does not make me yearn for something more."

Silence met this speech—a silence that was inexplicably complete, as somehow the gilded clock on the pedestal table stopped ticking even as the fire in the hearth ceased to crackle.

Bea, who felt as though there was a literal gaping hole in her chest, as if she had actually cut herself open and laid her heart at his feet, stared with a frenzied intensity at the books: *The Faerie Queene, Orlando Furioso, Paradise Lost.*

Over and over, she repeated the titles (*The Faerie Queene, Orlando Furioso, Paradise Lost*) while battling a terrible, creeping fear that she had done irreparable harm by saying the thing out loud. Perhaps he had not known. With his arrogant conviction about his place in the world, it was possible he simply had not realized his treatment of her was extraordinary in any way (*The Faerie Queene, Orlando Furioso, Paradise Lost*) and now that it had been presented to him in stark, undeniable terms, he would be vaguely horrified by his open-mindedness.

Sometimes examining a rare and precious jewel too closely revealed it to be paste.

Her heart hammering painfully—unassailable proof, she thought, that it remained in her body and was not convulsing wildly on the floor—Bea wondered what she should do now (*The Faerie Queene, Orlando Furioso, Paradise Lost*). Ardently, she wanted to run away.

Race to the door.

Dash up the stairs.

Hide in her room.

She craved the safe isolation of her bedchamber more than her next breath.

Ah, but deserting the field in the middle of a skirmish?

'Twas the height of cowardice.

True, yes, but she would live to fight another day.

That was the goal of all military men, was it not?

In fact, it was not, for the man who had famously made that assertion after leaving the Battle of Chaeronea, where three thousand of his fellow Athenians died, was roundly censured for his despicable behavior.

Recalling the details of Demosthenes's life soothed the worst of her nerves, for it meant that her brain was still functioning, and she decided she could preserve some of her dignity by making a graceful exit.

Strolling to the door.

Walking up the stairs.

Retiring to her room.

If her steps were measured, revealing none of her terror, then she would be able to calmly evaluate the new state of affairs. She just needed a quiet space to think clearly.

How very funny, your grace, she thought as the irony struck her, desiring a quiet place to think when you are sitting in a room as silent as a tomb.

"Stephens would do well to have a friend in the patent office, for it is in fact a remarkably complicated and costly process, involving thirty-five steps and almost two dozen signatures, stamps, warrants and seals. It begins with the prince regent and ends with the deputy chafe-wax," he said coolly.

Bea's relief at his words was so acute her head actually buzzed with it, a humming whir that was as comforting as it was dizzying.

Belatedly, she realized it was the hiss of the fire.

Taking her first easy breath in what felt like hours but was surely only seconds, she swept her eyes from the books to the duke, who regarded her with a curiously placid expression.

She did not know how he did it, appearing so thoroughly unconcerned when she had nearly torn herself in half.

Nevertheless, she was determined to match his affect and arranged her own features into a look of sublime indifference. "I believe one of your great-uncles held the position of chafe-wax."

"Lord Privy Seal," he corrected.

"Ah, yes, of course," she said, her tone mild despite an almost overwhelming impulse to giggle. "I do extend my apologies to you and your ancestors for failing to discern the vast dissimilarity between the two."

But this reply was not contrite enough to appease him and he launched into a detailed description of the various differences between the positions—either as retribution or edification, she could not be sure which.

Bea nodded gravely, as if awed by the very great importance of the Lord Keeper of the Seal (fifth among the great officers of state!) and promised to keep the distinction in mind should an investigation require her to assume the identity. "Although what I think you are saying is that given the option I should always impersonate the chafe-wax because it is a minor sinecure."

"Well, no, that is not what I am saying because there is no circumstance in which pretending to be the chafe-wax would satisfy the requirements of the Lord Keeper of the Seal. As I have just explained, the two positions are not interchangeable," he replied patiently. "More to the point, however, is the fact that you should have no cause to assume either identity."

But Bea, who had recently acquired useful information on the adoption of disguises, explained that she was determined to find one. "I am quite eager to experiment with warts in particular, and nothing in your description of either position precluded the presence of a wart."

"Eager?" Kesgrave echoed with slight apprehension.

It was a thing of beauty, oh, yes, it was, the hint of alarm that colored his voice, the familiarity it implied, the awareness it connoted. He knew every detail of the contract into which he had entered.

"Well, really, your grace," she replied chidingly, "you cannot expect me to learn about the usefulness of warts in altering one's appearance and not want to test the efficacy myself. That would be like Newton, having discovered the concept of gravity, not applying it to the moon. It is the inevitable next step."

Gratified by the conceit, Kesgrave laughed and suggested that she might be overestimating the importance of facial disguises to the order of the universe. "I am not saying it is not on par with an apple, just perhaps not a celestial body."

At the sound of his laughter, Bea froze as love swept through her, swamping her with its intensity, subsuming her with its force.

She had thought she could do it, mimic his insouciance,

because tragedy had been averted and, more significant, events had made it clear that there had never been a tragedy to avert.

The alternate future she had envisioned never existed.

That other reality had barely a chance to take hold.

And yet Bea still felt as though some terrible collision had been narrowly avoided, as if the driver of her carriage had come within an inch of crashing into an oncoming coach.

But for a last-second swerve.

But for Miss Brougham's spite.

The capriciousness of fate, as wispy as smoke, made her breathless, and lightheaded with happiness, she hurled herself at the duke, knocking him sideways on the settee so that one arm had to reach out to the cushion to steady himself while the other encircled her waist.

Was he surprised by the gesture?

Bea could not tell, for any astonishment he felt was masked by his deft handling of the situation, effortlessly taking possession of her lips as if being accosted by giddy females was a regular feature of his existence.

Effortlessly, he shifted their positions so that she was lying beneath him on the sofa and softly saying, "I love you," over and over, like an incantation, as he placed searing kisses on her neck.

She could stay like this forever, she thought, her back pressed against the silk brocade, her skin thrilling to the heat of his touch, and because it all still seemed so fragile despite the reassuring weight of his body, she murmured, "I was so afraid it would go the other way."

His lips traveled upward, toward her ear, and he gently bit her lobe as he said with a gentle growl, as if offended by the idea, "Never. You already hold such a low opinion of me that I could not bear to sink further."

He was teasing—Bea knew it, of course she did—and yet

her emotions were just precarious enough to require affirmation. Dropping back slightly, she sought to look at his face as she protested the characterization.

But Kesgrave, seemingly aware of her thoughts, shook his head and said, "No, my love, no. 'Twas only a jest. Having never doubted your esteem, I am only humbled now to discover how deep it runs. The feeling is mutual, in every way. I could not love you so much if I respected you less, which is, I assure you, a constant surprise to me. As you noted on one memorable occasion, I had few expectations for a wife other than she be presentable, amenable and elegant. When I think of how easily *that* could have gone the other way, I feel something akin to terror."

Ah, so he felt it too, Bea thought, the mercurial suppleness of life, and giggling with delight, she scoffed at his dazzling understatement. "Presentable is for vicars and second sons. The Duke of Kesgrave would never accept anything less than a diamond of the first water. Why, think of the children. What kind of cherubs would you produce with a *presentable* wife?"

"No, he would not," he said with pointed emphasis, clearly besotted beyond reason if he was going to insist that the drab Miss Clare-Hyde rose to anything more than passable. "And I apologize for making you feel uncherished for even a moment. That was not my intention."

"You deflected," she said reprovingly.

"I did, yes," he replied, brushing a strand of loose hair behind her ear.

"You diverted," Bea said.

"Naturally. It works remarkably well with my grandmother," he explained. "As soon as she gets a bee in her bonnet about something, I ask about a particular ailment and the subject is permanently changed to the daft opinions of the numbskull doctor with whom I saddled her."

"You gave me your uninteresting-ant-colony look," she added.

Kesgrave, who had been prepared to submit to any and all charges laid against him, paused midway through a nod and said, "My uninteresting-ant-colony what?"

"Oh, no, your grace, you do not get to pretend you are ignorant of the way you look at people who do not rise to the level of your contempt," Bea said accusingly, "as if they are too minor a pest for you to notice. A glare, in contrast, would be a compliment, for it meant you had made the effort to be annoyed. It is quite devastating, and I speak from personal experience because you gave me the look several times at Lakeview Hall. It was infuriating, for I did so want to be worthy of your contempt."

"Then you may rest easy on that point, for I was quite contemptuous of your efforts to poke your nose into Otley's death when I had the matter well in hand," Kesgrave said.

Bea grinned. "How dare an upstart spinster presume to challenge your utterly ridiculous fiction about suicide!"

"That's right, brat," Kesgrave said amiably. "How dare your awe of me be so insignificant that you would question anything I say. You'll recall how politely all the other guests fell in line."

In fact, she did and remembered as well her own disdain for them. "Of course. Once the Duke of Kesgrave starts wrongly categorizing obvious murders as suicides, everyone in the *ton* will begin to wrongly categorize obvious murders as suicides."

"Precisely," he said, with just enough humor to reveal he was aware of the absurdity and just enough smugness to make it clear he expected it.

Bea considered pricking his vanity further, for she knew how delightfully he would respond if she pointed out the expansiveness of his ego, but they had weightier matters to discuss. "Now *I* am diverting."

"You are always diverting," he said fondly, his breath gentle on her cheek as he drew closer to kiss her. Although the embrace began sweetly enough, merely an affirmation of affection, it swiftly spiraled into passion, and Kesgrave, pulling away with purpose, insisted they change positions before his control slipped away. Primly, he indicated that he would sit on one end of the settee and Bea on the other. "Or are you composed enough now to have this conversation at the table over crimp cod with pineapple sauce?"

"I am never composed enough for crimp cod with pineapple sauce," she muttered peevishly.

"It will not work," Kesgrave said with forceful determination, as if eluding some masterful trap she had set. "You will not send me down a tangent regarding the importance of being able to hold a candid conversation with your staff. I will tell you about my sordid history whether you want to hear it or not."

Although Bea understood the duke's need to distance himself from her, Bea could not stand the complete lack of contact and slid just near enough that she was able to take his hand. "Sordid, your grace? Must I remind you that my own parents were murdered by their dearest friend and that for years my aunt and uncle believed my father had killed himself after slaying his promiscuous wife, who was about to bear an illegitimate child? And let's not forget, my mother wrote a treatise advocating for free love. Can you say the same for your own?"

Kesgrave allowed that he could not. "My mother was a courtesan and believed love should come at a premium. She charged well for her affection, which my father was happy to pay. He was suspicious of anything that came without conditions. In that way, they were very well suited."

"And in others?" she asked, squeezing his hand.

"Horribly mismatched," he said. "My father was a cruel man. He liked to say he was easily bored and required amusement, but the truth was he just enjoyed watching other people suffer. My grandmother believes it was the death of his first wife that caused the cruelty. She thinks losing her and their sons was so painful for him he was compelled to make everyone else feel it, too."

"Misery loves company," Bea said.

"Perhaps it does," he allowed, "but my father relished his isolation. He loved belittling people and making them feel every ounce of their insignificance. It was the reason he married my mother when she told him she was pregnant. He thought my uncle was growing too comfortable with the prospect of his son inheriting the title. Myles had begun to assure his creditors that my cousin would settle his debts as soon as he inherited the title, which of course got back to my father. It was a particularly stupid promise to circulate, but I do not think my uncle is especially clever. Devious, yes. Clever, no."

"But how old was your cousin at this time?" Bea asked. "Years away from attaining his majority, I would think. And your father was young as well."

"Yes, so I trust the implication is clear," he replied.

"The duke was going to suffer an accident in the near future," Bea said, "likely a fatal one. Your birth put a hitch in that plan."

"Only a slight one, for he soon turned his homicidal gaze onto me," he said. "Uncle Myles was not particular about whom he had to kill as long as murdering someone ensured his comfort."

Kesgrave spoke dispassionately, without a trace of bitterness, but Bea could not believe he felt no resentment. Rather, he had grown adept at containing it.

She wondered at what cost.

"Obviously, he did not succeed," Bea said.

The duke smiled faintly. "Obviously not. But it was not for want of trying, and my father found it amusing to allow him to make the effort. My earliest memory is of falling off a pony when my saddle broke. My father knew Myles had cut the strap, so he would not allow me to trot and held onto the reins so that I would not be trampled. But he allowed me to fall. I was four at the time."

"Damien, that is horrible," she said.

"Sordid," he replied.

Bea shook her head violently. "No, I know sordid and I am telling you this is horrible. I cannot believe it continued until you were four."

"It continued until my grandmother hired a strapping bare-knuckle boxer whose sole responsibility was ensuring my welfare," he said.

He did not have to say anything more, for all at once she knew. "Marlow."

Raising her hands to his lips, he pressed a kiss against her palm and said, "Marlow."

"And your mother?" she asked. "Did she have an opinion about the various attempts on your life?"

"Had she paid enough attention to notice, I imagine she would have objected on the grounds that it did not reflect well on her," he said. "She was only interested in me in so far as it furthered her career socially. When playing the doting mother worked to her advantage, she played the doting mother, fondly displaying her cherubic—I believe that's the term you like to use—child. I was very cherubic."

Now the bitterness seeped through, and unable to bear the thought of the lonely little boy, Bea slid across the cushion until her shoulder touched his. "And when it did not?"

Kesgrave shrugged. "She had no desire to be a mother, and I think she was genuinely appalled when my father insisted on making me legitimate, thereby forcing her to interact with me well after my birth. Presumably, whatever other children she bore were left on the doorstep of a workhouse. I do not think she even desired to move among the *ton*. She was a successful Cyprian and was content to remain in her place, but she could not refuse a duke and my father thought it was vastly amusing to foist his mistress onto the beau monde. Although she did not possess the skills to succeed in society, he immersed her in it as if it were water too deep for her to stand and then stepped back to watch her flail. She refused to accommodate him and did everything possible to earn the ton's acceptance. Sex, of course, was the only currency she truly understood, so she naturally defaulted to using her body to achieve her ends. At the same time, she denied my father access to her bed, which is why I am an only child. The situation between them might have devolved into the one wrongfully attributed to your parents, with my father killing her in a fit of rage, but scarlet fever accomplished the job first and less sordidly when I was seventeen. They died within just months of each other."

Bea, resting her head on his shoulder, was not entirely sure it *was* less sordid in the end.

"And that," he said with a heavy sigh, "is my family in broad strokes. There is plenty more to share and I am happy to tell you it all in the interest of proving how very worthy of my confidences I consider you, but I think that's enough for the moment."

Indeed, yes, she thought, it was more than enough for the moment, especially when neither the present nor the future had yet to be addressed. Cautiously, she raised it now, asking what he wanted to do with Mrs. Norton's information. "As I mentioned, she swears her husband can substantiate everything she told me. Do you want to consult with him before deciding how to handle your uncle?"

"It does not strike me as necessary to seek confirmation because killing my wife to protect his interest is precisely what my uncle would do," Kesgrave replied calmly. "Having failed to eliminate me at a young age, he decided to bide his time and wait for an easier target to appear. I am mortified to admit that it did not occur to me to consider how he would respond to my marriage. It has been more than a decade since I've seen him, and he knows to stay out of my way or suffer the consequences. The fact that he can barely afford his clubs let alone a tailor all but ensures he remains on the fringes of society and out of my sight."

"Consequences?" Bea asked.

"A good thrashing," he said plainly. "I have never laid hands on him out of respect for my grandmother, but I told him at my mother's funeral that if I ever saw him again, he would be beaten to within an inch of his life. He gave the eulogy, you see, because my father was already dead, and although he never said it explicitly, he implied in a dozen different ways that their relationship was more intimate than it should have been. It was quite a lachrymose performance. The *ton* was scandalized."

"And the dowager?" Bea asked.

"I do not know," he replied. "Scandalized as well, I suppose, although she could have few illusions about her sons by then. Once you send Dan Mendoza's sparring partner to ensure the welfare of your grandchild, I rather think the jig is up. I have never broached the issue with her because I do not want to make her sad, and she herself never discusses it. When she spoke of the de Lamerie teapot in relation to my mother a few weeks ago, it was the first time I had heard her mention her in years."

Thoughtfully, she nodded and agreed that it was best to

avoid raising the subject with his grandmother. "We do not wish to cause her further pain. It will be easy enough to gather information about him. As you said, he is deeply in debt. I suggest we start with the moneylenders."

Kesgrave's hand, which had been absently caressing her hair, stilled briefly before resuming its motion, and Bea waited for him to object to her participation. She knew he would and was prepared to counter with a logical argument. The situation was already too intense for emotional pleas. Rather, she would adhere closely to the facts, citing her qualifications like a governess listing the languages she spoke in an interview for a position.

Surely, the duke, with his gorgeous pedantic heart, would appreciate that.

But Bea did not get an opportunity to provide an orderly catalogue of her credentials because Kesgrave himself resorted to an emotional plea, making it a matter of trust, not skill. "You are my wife and I am asking you to trust me to keep you safe, not because I believe you cannot keep yourself safe—you demonstrated that unequivocally when you rammed Bentham in the eye with the magnifying glass—but because it is both a personal obligation, since he is my uncle, and a pleasure. You spoke of how my treatment of you raised your expectation of what a marriage should be. I feel exactly the same way, and as the man whom you consider to be your equal, I am asking you to let me handle this on my own. I assure you I am quite capable."

It was a very neat trick, boxing her in with her own words, and Bea looked at him with admiration mingled with aggravation. "I cannot argue with that, your grace. Nicely done."

"I know from experience that you *can* argue with it," he replied with humor, "and the fact that you choose not to means a great deal to me. Thank you."

Having promised not to interfere with his handling of the

situation, Bea debated whether asking how he intended to proceed counted as interference. Curiosity was an academic enterprise, separate and apart from meddling. She could be curious about Marlow's history without it having an effect on his ability to carry out his duties. It would be a different thing if she insisted on interrogating him while he was striding to the door to—

"I will call on him tomorrow," Kesgrave announced.

"Oh?" she said with an almost absent air, as if barely interested in the information.

Kesgrave laughed, not at all fooled by her attempt. "Yes, I will visit him at his rooms in Elder Street tomorrow to make certain he understands the precariousness of his situation. If anything happens to you, anything at all, I will repay him tenfold. At heart, my uncle is a coward. He was happy to terrorize a small child, but as soon as a bruiser with an iron fist entered the scene, he scurried away. I am confident that once he realizes his plan is known and there are grievous consequences to be suffered, he will decide that harming you is not worth the trouble. His circumstances are already not ideal with his gambling debts, which continue to mount, but I am happy to make them intolerable if necessary. I have thus far refrained from interfering in his life because I did not want to cause my grandmother more pain or provide fodder to the gossips."

"You might also point out the limited utility of his plan," Bea said, "for even if he succeeds in killing me, he will have done nothing but delay the inevitable, for you would be sure to marry again."

Horrified by the future she proposed, Kesgrave objected at once, insisting that upon her untimely death he would fall into a decline and rapidly wither away to nothing.

She shook her head, appalled that he would condone such selfish behavior. "By all means, do set up a shrine to me and make sure your second wife understands that she could never fill that empty hole in your heart. But you must consider the succession, your grace. It cannot be allowed to languish while you selfishly indulge your grief. You must think of the future chafes-wax you would be denying the kingdom."

Oh, but obviously he must not, for no Matlock would ever deign to undertake such a menial assignment, which, Kesgrave insisted, she knew very well. Her impudence, however, could not pass without penalty, and he launched into a comprehensive catalogue of the officer's responsibilities, which ran the dizzying gamut from melting the wax and applying the wax.

Delighted, Bea dutifully listened for several minutes before realizing it was futile to resist him and cut off the list at its source.

A full hour passed before they returned to the table, and Bea was distraught to discover that crimp cod with pineapple sauce was no more palatable for being cold.

Chapter Six

Although Mr. Caruthers treated Flora's invasion of his home with far more equanimity than Bea had anticipated when the gaunt gentleman opened the door to them, he remained resolute in his refusal to comply with her request.

Having rarely seen a scowl more intense than the one he had leveled at them, Bea was surprised he had actually admitted them and she entered the rooms reluctantly. Feeling none of her cousin's hesitance, Flora had marched confidently across the floor to the window, whose curtain she promptly pushed aside to raise the sash. Fresh air wafted past the worn blue curtains, which fluttered gently in the breeze.

Satisfied with the improvement, Flora strode to the fireplace, retrieved a kettle from among the items stacked haphazardly in a basket on the floor, filled it with water from a pitcher on a nearby table and skillfully placed it on the fire. Then, without pausing a moment to admire her own handiwork, Flora turned to Mr. Caruthers, apologized for not being able to compliment him on how well he looked and briskly explained that he had to accompany her on a drive through Hyde Park so that she could win back the affection of Mr. Holcroft.

It was an astounding sequence of events, and having witnessed it, Bea found herself suddenly much more intrigued by the outing than she had previously. Uncertain of the safety of going abroad after Mrs. Norton's warning, she had resolved to stay home and wait for Kesgrave's return. After an hour of anxiously pacing the drawing room floor, however, she could no longer stand her own company and sent a note to Flora consenting to visit Mr. Caruthers. Although she had embarked on the errand only as a way to take her mind off the duke, she realized now it was worthwhile on its own merits. Watching her cousin move with such confidence and competence was revelatory.

Mr. Caruthers, alas, was not nearly so impressed and replied with a firm "No."

"Oh, but you simply must," Flora said fiercely, "for your cousin has taken a pet over something I said, that I absolutely did not mean and he has left the city. I have to do something to impress him, and we both know how pleased he would be if you showed yourself in society."

Having set the kettle on the fire, Flora immediately forgot about it, and Bea, noting that the water was boiling, walked to the hearth to remove it. Thoughtfully, she looked around for a cloth to protect her hand from the heat of the handle and settled on a tattered towel.

Dashing across the room, Mr. Caruthers took the rag from her fingers before she could employ it and said, "No, please allow me."

"Ah, there, you see," Flora said triumphantly, "your gentlemanly instincts are as finely honed as ever so I know you will not be able to resist a plea from a desperate female in need of help. I am throwing myself on your mercy, Mr. Caruthers."

Although Bea was amused by her cousin's theatrics, she

could readily see that their host was not. His frown staunchly in place, he removed the kettle from the heat and placed it on the table. Then, as if indeed compelled by an irresistible force, he offered the ladies tea.

Flora opened her mouth, intending to refuse, for she had realized belatedly that partaking of refreshments in Mr. Caruthers's own quarters would hardly earn her Holcroft's esteem. It was better if they left the rooms immediately rather than linger over the tea she herself had started to prepare. But Bea darted her a quelling look and thanked him for his gracious offer.

"And we have yet to even be introduced," she added, "thanks to my scapegrace cousin, who immediately launched into her request without pausing for the proprieties."

"Why, yes, of course," Flora said, her expression brightening as she realized her oversight. "Mr. Caruthers, I am eager to present to you Beatrice, Duchess of Kesgrave. Presumably, you have heard of her, for she wields considerable clout. You have no cause to worry about anyone giving you the cut direct while you are in her company because the whole of the *ton* are tripping over themselves to garner her approval. Most recently, she defended herself against a deadly attack from the Earl of Bentham."

Mr. Caruthers poured the hot water into a teapot, covered it with a lid and allowed the brew to steep. "Word of that horrifying episode did reach me, and I must say, your grace, that you are looking remarkably well for a woman who narrowly escaped death."

"She repelled him using her magnifying glass," Flora said, "by driving it into his eye. There was blood everywhere."

"My cousin exaggerates," Bea insisted.

Flora, conceding this was likely true, amended her statement to say there was blood *almost* everywhere. Then she rushed to explain that the only reason she brought it up was to underscore Bea's importance. "She is hugely influential, to be sure, and one could not look higher than she, for one's first outing following one's ignominious fall from grace."

Noting Mr. Caruthers's discomfort with this description of his situation, Bea tried to smooth over the awkwardness by apologizing for her cousin. "She sometimes allows her enthusiasm to overcome her good sense. But I assure you there is no harm in her."

Flora, cheerfully pooh-poohing this notion, insisted that the opposite was in fact true. "My concern for Mr. Caruthers's welfare is a product of my good sense, for what is nonsensical is that he should cling to his shame when there is far worse villainy out in the world. The Master of the Rolls, the man charged with ensuring the integrity of the system, made corrupt bargains and sanctioned murder. I trust it goes without saying that I do not want to diminish Mr. Caruthers's crime, but accepting a few bribes does rather pale in significance in comparison, and it behooves us as his friends to make sure he comprehends this. It would never do to allow him to grow too precious about it."

The first hint of amusement lightened Mr. Caruthers's features as he said, "My friends?"

"Your friends, yes," Flora said emphatically, "for we are allies working toward a mutually beneficial goal. You wish to see Holcroft less often, and I wish to see him more. A drive through Hyde Park would accomplish both those objectives beautifully. Am I a *little* more committed to serving my own interests than yours? Well, yes, for I know how utterly devastated I am by his defection, but my concern for you is not insignificant. I think it is grossly unfair that you molder away in your dark crypt of a room when you were instrumental in bringing one of the most corrupt men the court system has ever seen to justice. Without your help, Grimston would still be lining his pockets at the expense of his poor litigants and that would be intolerable. Now do let's go commemorate your heroism with an excursion in the park. Bea, please be a dear and shut the window in the unlikely event of rain."

Mr. Caruthers, declining politely, poured the tea into a trio of mismatched cups and invited his guests to sit down. Flora resisted the offer, preferring to stand as if they were about to depart at any moment, and she glared at her cousin for making herself comfortable in one of the chairs.

Their host opened a small tin containing biscuits, which he arranged in a line on a plate with a narrow chip in the side and placed it in front of Beatrice. "A magnifying glass, was it? Although I did not have the pleasure of drawing blood, I once pricked Bentham with a tiepin. It was during my final year at Oxford. He had organized a mail coach race from London for the Henley and since I was friendly with his nephew, I joined them at the tavern to toast the victor. He gave a long-winded speech, ostensibly praising the winner but really lauding himself for being so clever as to organize the event. There was some talk, if I remember correctly, about the ethics of using the post horn to avoid stopping at toll-gates. At any rate, he was such a puffed-up ptarmigan, the only kind thing to do was try to deflate him. Alas, it did not work."

Bea selected a biscuit, which, though slightly stale, was delightfully free of pineapple flecks, slabs or chunks, and opened her mouth to respond. But Flora forestalled her by insisting that she save her reply for the carriage ride.

"There is no point in wasting your best conversation in the confines of this dreary room," she added. "Come, Mr. Caruthers, I promise you that you will find the duchess to be excellent company, for she is appallingly well read and capable of conversing intelligently on any number of subjects. And she is passionate about court reform, are you not, Bea?"

"No," Bea said succinctly. "But I am fond of my cousin

and know that she is sincere in her efforts to court Mr. Holcroft's good opinion. Is her scheme to coerce you into accompanying her on a drive through Hyde Park the best way to accomplish that? I cannot say. Frankly, it does not strike me as auspicious as a missive straightforwardly apologizing for the unintended harm she has done him. But I do think she is correct in her understanding of your situation. Your crime is not so egregious as to preclude your accompanying us on a brief outing. It will be harmless and it is such a lovely day."

Flora applauded her cousin's cogency in regard to their host's situation but sneered dismissively at the notion of sending a letter, insisting she was a woman of action. "I believe in deeds, not words."

Although Mr. Caruthers's demeanor was more relaxed than when they had first arrived, he remained inured to persuasion. Even so, he found Bea's line of reasoning compelling and promised to think deeply on it.

Pleased with what struck her as a sensible compromise, Bea took a sip of her tea and pledged to provide her support at a later date should he change his mind. "My cousin is correct in that I do have clout, and I am happy to employ it in your favor."

"Thank you," said Mr. Caruthers, who then had the presumption to ask how Flora had given inadvertent offense to his cousin.

Bea, darting an amused glance at her relative, leaned forward in her chair and said, "Ostensibly, it is Flora's fault for not carefully considering her words, but it actually speaks to the fundamental challenge of communicating, for she genuinely believed she was paying him a compliment."

Thoroughly intrigued, Mr. Caruthers forgot himself so much as to take a seat while a lady remained standing. "I am agog to know what she said, for Holcroft the Holy is usually indifferent to insults. I have hurled scores of varying vulgarities at him for months and he has never even flinched."

"No, no, this will never do," Flora said disapprovingly. "An intimate coze over a pot of tea does nothing to further my goal. We must leave these rooms. If a pleasant drive through the park does not convince you to emerge from your crypt, perhaps an errand to save a lady's life will serve as a better inducement? You are a solicitor and know other solicitors. Are you by chance familiar with a Mr. Jordan, Douglas Jordan?"

"What?" Bea asked sharply.

"If Mr. Caruthers knows him well enough to vouch for his integrity, then he could arrange an introduction and we could discover the extent of the plot against you," Flora said reasonably.

Appalled that her cousin would dare to use something so personally upsetting to satisfy her own ends, Bea swung her head around to glare at her. "A letter, Flora, is all that is required. Here, I will compose it for you: Dear Mr. Holcroft, I deeply regret calling you *staid*. Please accept my most heart-felt apology. Warmest regards, Miss Hyde-Clare."

Mr. Caruthers, whose confusion at the strange turn was writ plainly on his face, also looked at Flora. "My cousin took a pet at being called staid? But he *is* staid."

"I know," Flora said with frustration.

"He does as well," Mr. Caruthers added. "He frequently cites it as proof that his arguments are correct because he is too cautious and sober-minded to make any great leaps in logic."

As Flora replied that Mr. Holcroft's feet rarely left the ground, Bea shook her head as her agitation continued to grow. She had told her cousin about the threat to her life only because Flora kept insisting that Mrs. Norton meant her ill, and Bea feared the trouble the girl would get herself into if she acted on her wrongful assumption.

It was extremely unlikely, yes, that anything Flora did would bring her to the attention of Lord Myles, but the probability that she could stumble across a massive corruption scheme within the Chancery was also low and she had effortlessly accomplished that.

Her anxiety was caused not only by the careless way her cousin bandied about the private information, as if the iniquity of Kesgrave's uncle was no more weighty a topic than the weather, but also by the fact that Bea had promised the duke she would allow him to handle the matter as he saw fit. She had explicitly pledged not to interfere.

Asking about Jordan was in direct violation, and even though she had not been the one to raise the issue, Bea felt horribly complicit.

Discomfited by the sensation, she chastised her cousin for daring to exploit her situation to manipulate Mr. Caruthers. "It is grossly immoral."

Profoundly unsettled by the severity of the words, Flora paled and stammered an apology. "I'm sorry...I did not mean... I...I just thought...usually you *want* to gather information. I assumed that would be the case here as well or I never would have mentioned it even if I did believe it would be just the thing to encourage Mr. Caruthers to leave his rooms with us," she said, dropping into a crouch before Bea's chair so that she could look her cousin directly in the eyes. "It was horrendously presumptuous of me, I see that now, and actually very silly, for only a peagoose would think that all solicitors know each other."

Taking a deep breath, Bea acknowledged that what Flora said was true. Ordinarily, her response to an uncertain situation was to discover as much about it as possible, not wring her hands in helplessness, and the only reason she made no move to do so now was her promise to the duke, which Flora could know nothing about.

Consequently, she apologized for overreacting and allowed that her cousin's assumption was indeed a little peagoose-ish. "I am sure our host has never heard of a lawyer called Douglas Jordan."

"Actually, I know him well," Mr. Caruthers said.

Astonished, both women turned to stare at him.

"His office was down the hall from mine in Tucks Court," he explained. "Each of us had his own cases to work on, but there was a collegial atmosphere among the practices in the building, an informality, if you will. We frequently consulted with one another and did not stand on ceremony. I was often in Jordan's office and he in mine. I found him to be amiable and full of useful knowledge. I cannot believe, your grace, that your life actually hangs in the balance, for then paying a call on such a disreputable residence at Lyon's Inn would be the height of folly, but if Jordan has disturbed your peace in any way, I am eager and willing to escort you to his office so that you may settle the matter. Knowing him as I do, I cannot believe he meant to upset you intentionally."

Flora received this news soberly and held her tongue as she waited for her cousin to react. Bea, appreciating the display of forbearance, truly had no idea how to respond to the offer.

Obviously, she must decline it, for she had agreed to allow Kesgrave to deal with his uncle and interviewing Lord Myles's lawyer was not sticking fast to the compact. Previously, she had broken her word to him, and it seemed as though now that they were married she should be more steadfast in her commitments.

And yet that was not precisely true, for in each instance she had held to the particulars of the promise she had made. Having pledged not to investigate any more of the horrible murders that crossed her path, she had in fact ceased investigating the horrible murders that crossed her path.

In the months since she had given her promise, she had not pursued a single investigation that met that precise description.

Had she investigated the horrible murders whose path *she* had crossed?

Well, yes, because that was a different category altogether.

It was not her fault Kesgrave had failed to fully consider the possibilities when coercing his pledge.

Bea acknowledged that her reasoning was somewhat disingenuous—to argue that Pudsey's corpse had crossed *their* paths, not hers, was to insist on an extremely narrow taxonomical distinction—but she also believed there was a genuine line to be drawn between the spirit of the law and the letter. At heart, she was a formalist and reveled in finding the space in which to maneuver.

Sometimes it was no more than a hairsbreadth.

In this case, the gap was slightly wider, for she had agreed to allow Kesgrave to deal with his uncle.

Douglas Jordan was not Lord Myles Matlock.

Unquestionably, they were two different people.

If they were revealed to be one and the same, she would of course turn on her heels and immediately walk away.

Considering it, Bea wondered how she would know if Jordan was in fact Lord Myles.

Presumably, there would be a family resemblance.

Mildly amused by the patent absurdity of the digression, Bea knew she was putting off making her decision.

No, she realized, she was putting off acknowledging it.

The decision had been made before the question had been fully posed.

Bea was always going to accept Mr. Caruthers's offer

because what Flora had said was true: She met adversity with information.

"Thank you, yes," she said to her host as her cousin clenched her hand comfortingly before rising again to her full height. "I would like to pay a call on Mr. Jordan and appreciate your escort."

Displaying none of her earlier frivolity, Flora also thanked Mr. Caruthers for his willingness to assist her cousin and suggested that they return her to Portman Square before continuing to the solicitor's office. "To provide you with an opportunity to have a private discussion. Having overstepped my place already today, I do not want to do it again."

Bea appreciated her scruples but assured her it would not be necessary, and Mr. Caruthers, dampening the fire, lauded her good sense.

"The office is only a few blocks from here," he explained, "so driving to Mayfair first would be a significant detour."

Flora, seizing a biscuit from the table, slid her arms through her cousin's and assured her in the avuncular style she had recently adopted that all would be well. "Mr. Caruthers and I are here to ensure that nothing awful happens to you."

Verily, Mr. Caruthers was happy to provide these reassurances, but a look of worry flitted across his face as he wondered why they were necessary. "As I said previously, he is everything amiable and knowledgeable. I am sure he will be able to assist you without incident."

So saying, he extinguished the lamps that burned on the wall and closed the window. Then he escorted them to the door and through the hallway to the courtyard between the buildings, with its dappled sunlight.

Flora prattled affably about the clement weather, asking Mr. Caruthers if he had ever experienced such a beautiful spring day. "It is going to be a wonderful summer, I am certain of it. I know we have evolved past my persuading you to take a drive with us through the park as a way to endear myself to Mr. Holcroft, for now we are on a mission that could mean the difference between life and death itself, but if you are inclined in the future to go for that drive—for your own reasons, of course!—please know I would be happy to accompany you."

Passing through the wrought-iron gate that stood at the inn's entrance, Mr. Caruthers begged Flora to cease describing their excursion in such stark terms. "I find your references to a dire outcome unsettling in light of what happened the last time I helped you on a matter. On that occasion you were only looking for an old family friend, and one person wound up dead, you and my cousin were almost killed, and the Master of the Rolls was carted off in handcuffs by the magistrate. If something should happen to you, I would never be able to forgive myself, but more to the point, Holcroft would thrash me to within an inch of my life."

Although the point of this statement was to underscore his increasing anxiety about their errand, Flora took it as an affirmation of her beau's affection and asked with besotted fervor, "Oh, do you really think so? Within an *inch* of your life? Or merely just a hard knock to your jaw? Do think carefully before you answer, Mr. Caruthers, because I will put much stock in your answer."

"Please do not answer her at all," Bea said as she spotted Jenkins walking the horses in the street, "for she must not be encouraged in her ridiculousness."

Mr. Caruthers, displaying more good sense than Bea had believed him capable, replied that he did not think Miss Hyde-Clare needed any encouragement.

"You are hoping I will take offense and abandon my interest in a fit of pique," Flora said with a wide grin as she climbed into the lavish carriage that now belonged to her cousin. "But it is just the opposite. You are teasing me, so I know we are friends."

Bea listened inattentively to their exchange, her mind consumed by the imminent meeting with Lord Myles's solicitor, both with what he might say about the villain's scheme and how she would explain it to Kesgrave. The difference between poking her nose into a random stranger's business and inserting it into her husband's struck her forcefully as the carriage drew closer to Tucks Court.

She *could* justify her decision, yes, but that did not mean that she *should.* Previously, Kesgrave had met her rationalizations with varying degrees of frustration, most recently all but shrugging his shoulders when she barged into their neighbors' home to question its residents on the decapitation of their celebrated French chef. Indeed, he had owned himself heartened by her audacity, which she would need to succeed in her career as a duchess.

The two circumstances, however, were not comparable, and to pretend that conducting an interview with Mr. Jordan was just another act of impudence that Kesgrave would ultimately find charming was to do them both a disservice.

What trust could there be between them if she did not defer to him when expressly asked?

With that thought swirling in her head, Bea watched as the carriage drew to a stop in front of a light-colored building with an elegant facade and gracious portico.

It was not too late to turn around.

But actually it was, she thought, opening the door, for at heart she was not a formalist at all. She was an investigator.

She met adversity with information.

Despite that impulse, she had done everything correctly that day. Although she had wanted desperately to pester Kesgrave at breakfast about his plan to confront his uncle, she had held her tongue and discussed the

Particular. She had nodded absently when he excused himself to attend to business and then had arranged an engagement with Flora, embarking on an activity that was entirely separate and apart from the dreadful affair with his family.

And having done all that—having pushed the matter emphatically to a corner of her mind, where she could think on it only occasionally—she had somehow still wound up here, at number 8 Tucks Court, in front of the building that housed the office of Lord Myles Matlock's solicitor.

It was uncanny how fate had pulled her here.

What could she do in the circumstance but submit to it?

I am an investigator, she thought matter-of-factly, and I must investigate.

It was as simple as that.

But of course it was not, and as they climbed the stairs to the second floor, she worried about how she would explain her outing to Kesgrave. Her instinct was to temper it with humor.

If she could find some way to incorporate the warships from the Battle of the Nile in her retelling, it would soften his mood.

Annoyed at herself for considering such a blatant manipulation, she decided not to think about it again until after conferring with Mr. Jordan. For all she knew, he could be away from his office or doggedly unhelpful or genuinely ignorant of any nefarious plot. There was no reason to assume he would provide her with vital information that she would need to relay immediately to the duke.

She would take it one step at a time, she thought as she arrived on the landing, which opened onto a well-lit corridor with expansive windows at both ends. Silently, she followed Mr. Caruthers down the hallway decorated with paintings of lush bouquets of flowers. They stopped in front of a gilded wall clock, and Mr. Caruthers gestured to the door opposite it.

"Ah, here we are," he said, assuring them that the slightly opened door boded well. "Jordan is most likely within. He might be engaged with a client, in which case we will have to wait, either way, I am confident he will find a moment to spare for us."

"He will find as many moments as the Duchess of Kesgrave requires," Flora announced self-importantly, thrilled, it seemed to her cousin, to finally be able to exploit the privileges of rank. "If that means he will be late returning home to his family, so be it."

Bea smiled at the haughty determination in Flora's voice and imagined the lengths to which her cousin would go to restrain the solicitor—sitting on top of him, perhaps, or binding his wrists—should he own himself too busy for a conversation with her grace.

"I am sure it won't come to that," Bea said pragmatically as Caruthers opened the door and invited her to enter the small antechamber that belonged to Jordan's clerk.

It was a simple room, with unadorned white walls and a wooden-beam ceiling. A floorboard creaked as she moved farther into the small space, whose furnishings consisted of only a desk and one narrow bookcase.

"His clerk must have stepped away," Mr. Caruthers murmured, noting the empty chair. He indicated to another door, in the far wall, also ajar. "Jordan will be right through there."

Flora nodded with approval. "Overseeing the street, no doubt. He would get plenty of daylight but also the noise of passing carriages."

Amused by her cousin's remark, which, despite its mundanity, carried the ineffable air of expertise, Bea strode across the floor, calling out a brisk hello to the solicitor as she tapped lightly on the door. It gave way to the pressure of her hand, opening several more inches and revealing Mr. Jordan lying on his stomach in the middle of the room, blood seeping onto the rug from a large dent bashed into the back of his skull.

And towering above him, his blond curls gleaming like gold in the sunlight as his fingers clutched the stem of a silver candlestick, was the Duke of Kesgrave.

Chapter Seven

I t was shocking.

Oh, yes, it was beyond astounding to see her husband standing in the middle of the light-filled room in an elegant brick building in Tucks Court, splotches of blood splattering his hand, a dead body at his feet.

And yet it was not surprising at all.

There was, Bea thought as her eyes met the duke's over the cooling corpse of Douglas Jordan, the sweet air of inevitability about the scene, as if this was precisely the way fate worked, circling back on itself, so that everything ended where it began.

If this was the moment that gave her Kesgrave, then it seemed only fitting that this would be the moment that would take him away.

Take him away, she thought, the notion causing her to pull up short.

Nothing was taking him away.

He was one of the most powerful land owners in all of England, with money and influence and an autocratic demeanor that cowed lesser men.

If anyone was able to pervert the course of justice, it was he.

Lady Skeffington had gone toddling off to Italy after cracking the skull of her victim with a candlestick. Surely, the Duke of Kesgrave could do no less—and in a style not available to a lowly baron. The shores of a foreign land were more pleasing to contemplate from the window of a majestic palazzo.

What was also familiar, she thought, was the sensation of uncertainty as she pondered the extent of his murderous rage.

Could the Duke of Kesgrave have done this?

Alone with him in a darkened library well after midnight surrounded by a silence so pervasive it felt like death, she had drawn the obvious conclusion.

Of course she had.

Next, he would snuff out her own life with the same brutal efficiency.

In those first few seconds, despite the gloom, everything had seemed so clear.

And now it was midday and sun poured in through the windows as carriages rattled by on the street below and she realized nothing was apparent.

Despite what she saw clearly, she knew she could not believe her eyes.

Kesgrave was incapable of cold-blooded murder—not because he lacked the ruthlessness required to end a life but because he would find it unnecessary. He embodied the kingdom, and the bureaucratic protocols that propped up the state had been designed specifically to benefit him and his ilk. He had no cause to appoint himself adjudicator of Mr. Jordan's guilt because the system would do that for him. All he had to do was hand him over to the authorities.

The mills of the gods might grind slowly, but a machine

devised to benefit England's oldest families turned with reassuring swiftness.

It was not a homicide, she decided.

Self-defense, then.

The duke entered the office and after a conversation—long, brief, medium length—Jordan lunged furiously at him, forcing Kesgrave to counter with a blow. The solicitor redoubled his efforts, enlisting the candlestick in his cause, and somewhere in the ensuing fight fell victim to his own weapon.

It must have been a very close thing if a man trained at the knee of Gentleman Jackson felt compelled to employ a blunt instrument to save his life.

That explained the absence of the clerk, the one whose desk was in the other room. Kesgrave would have sent him to fetch the constable.

Flora gasped, and Bea, her eyes locked with her husband's, realized barely a second had passed since she had entered the room. Buzzing wildly, her mind struggled to make sense of the scene before her, which defied explanation. Noting the immaculateness of his appearance—his ensemble as pristine now as it had been at breakfast—she could not hold to the story of a great tussle.

But if there had been no skirmish, how had Mr. Jordan wound up dead?

Truly, Bea had no idea what she was looking at.

Kesgrave, however, did not suffer from the same debilitating confusion. His lips twitched slightly, and he said with disconcerting calmness, "A man has been murdered, so naturally you appear. I believe I owe you an apology, my dear, for assuming it was your irrepressible curiosity that brought you time and again to the side of a dead body but clearly it is Providence. You may explain to me now how you arrived here mere seconds after my uncle expelled his last breath."

Blankly, Bea gaped at him, scarcely comprehending his

words, and in an act of sheer befuddlement, stared down at the victim, whose blood-matted hair vaguely resembled the duke's in color and texture. His face, however, was impossible to gauge because it was looking in the opposite direction, away from the door and toward the wall with the windows.

Could this really be Lord Myles Matlock?

Knowing the identity of the cadaver did little to clarify the situation, and Bea continued to stand at the entrance of the room, transfixed.

Her lack of response caused the duke to frown sharply, and placing the candlestick on a cabinet, he strode over to her and took her hands.

They were cold.

"Come, Bea, sit down," he said, looking around briefly, settling on the chair at the desk and leading her there. "I apologize if my attitude seemed cavalier, for that was not my intention. I grasp the seriousness of the situation. It is only that I found it so remarkable that you should be here, though I do not understand how you managed it. You are still with your cousin Flora, so I can only assume this is Mr. Caruthers."

The duke's treatment of the situation, almost as if they were welcoming guests to the drawing room at Kesgrave House, soothed Bea's nerves in a way his grasp did not and she felt her crippling bewilderment ebb.

Whatever terrible thing happened in this room, she was certain Kesgrave had nothing to do with it. He would never seek out his uncle and strike him down without compunction or clemency.

But what *did* happen in this room?

Mr. Caruthers stepped forward to introduce himself and stammer an apology for exposing the duchess to such gruesomeness. "If I had imagined for even one moment that such a thing was possible, I would never have agreed to escort her here or Miss Hyde-Clare."

"Pshaw," Flora said with an impatient wave of her hand. "It is just a dead body. Bea and I have encountered plenty before, most recently in the Countess of Abercrombie's own home. That was in the middle of a dinner party and she expressed no contrition, so I don't see why you should."

Mr. Caruthers, however, held himself to his own high standards, not Lady Abercrombie's apparently questionable ones, which he took pains to explain to the duke, using the imprecise, obfuscating language of the law. He rambled through a series of official-sounding Latin phrases, making it clear that the fault was his for not heeding the grave misgivings he had felt about leaving Lyon's Inn at all.

"No, no," Flora said firmly, "you cannot make this about reservations and premonitions. Holcroft will not be grateful to me if our outing makes you *more* of a hermit. This was a random and anomalous event."

"But you just said it happens all the time," Mr. Caruthers protested.

While Kesgrave assured the distressed man that in his experience both conditions could be true, Bea rose from the chair and approached the body from the other direction. She could see it now, the resemblance to Kesgrave, for it was not just their hair that was the same color. It was their eyes and complexion as well. And Lord Myles had the same nose, autocratic and straight.

Now that she had overcome her shock, she had a better sense of what had occurred, and interrupting Mr. Caruthers's reply, she asked Kesgrave if he had seen the killer. "Or was he already gone by the time you arrived?"

"He shoved past me as he was running from the room," Kesgrave said as he walked around the desk. "I grabbed him by the wrist to detain him, but he wrenched himself free and

I had to decide between trying to save my uncle or giving chase. Not knowing he was already dead, I chose the former."

"Of course you did," Bea said reassuringly. "It seems as though you arrived only a minute too late. How did you come to be here?"

Kesgrave shook his head. "I believe I asked you that first."

"Actually, no," Bea said, "you gave me permission to provide you with an explanation but did not explicitly ask for one. I am now thanking you for graciously bestowing your consent and explicitly asking you to explain. Perhaps in the future you should be less polite in your framing if you do not have the patience to wait for a response. In the meantime, I would like an answer to my question."

Although he was routinely objected to this kind of abuse from his wife, Kesgrave owned himself on this occasion to be relieved by the treatment. "Your unusually subdued demeanor had me worried for a moment."

Sensing an opportunity, Bea asked, "How worried?"

Cautiously, Kesgrave replied, "Why?"

"Because when I tell you we are here to interview your uncle's lawyer, I believe my likelihood of evading a tedious but well-deserved drubbing increases the more worried you are," she explained soberly. "To help you decide, do let me confess that I was so stunned to see you standing over a bludgeoned corpse again that I was incapable of processing a single thought. Dozens whirled inside my brain in a solitary moment."

"Wait," Flora said from the other side of the room. "What do you mean, *again?*"

The question, uttered with a sort of exhausted suspicion, drew a faint smile from the duke, but his tone was steadfastly disapproving as he said, "You promised to let me handle it."

Despite having already marshaled her argument, Bea lowered her head in shame and mumbled, "I know."

His only reply was to sigh, which made her feel worse than any drubbing, tedious or otherwise, for it revealed the depth of his weariness. She felt sorry to have added to it, and yet she could not wholly regret anything that brought her to his side moments after he had discovered the dead body of his uncle.

Hoping to give comfort, she linked her fingers with his and squeezed consolingly. "I'm sorry."

"As am I," he said wearily. "I dread telling my grandmother."

Of course he did. Whatever grief at the death of his murderous uncle he did not experience, he was too kind not to feel hers.

Knowing well the limited utility of compassion, Bea smothered her own sympathetic sigh and said coolly, "You were about to tell me how you came to be here when you allowed yourself to be distracted by some nonsensical comment of mine. I do not mean to be critical, Kesgrave, but I would think a man of your intellect and education would be better able to withstand my digressions. What did they teach you in Introduction to the Basics of Greek Rhetorical Philosophy?"

"It was Introduction to Greek Philosophy, brat," he said in the same straightforward tone, "and the Basics of Rhetoric, and mostly, I was taught the value of choosing a more interesting course of study because both subjects were deadly dull. But to answer your question, I came to confront my uncle because his housekeeper informed me that I would find him here. And so I did."

Bea, lowering to her knees to more closely examine the wound, asked how the other gentleman looked. "The one who ran away. Did he appear disheveled, as though he and Lord Myles had come to blows?"

Kesgrave crouched down beside her as he shook his head. "He did not appear even slightly tousled, only terrified."

"Terrified of getting caught or terrified of being killed?" she asked thoughtfully.

"An excellent question, my dear," he said with a hint of admiration in his voice. "I had assumed it was the former, but it is entirely possible that he was frightened of suffering the same fate as my uncle. I wish I had been able to restrain him."

"What did he look like?" Bea asked with a glance at her escort. "Perhaps Mr. Caruthers will recognize him from your description. He used to work in this building and is on genial terms with many of its occupants."

Flora, who had kept her distance out of respect for the uncertain exigencies of a newly married couple, decided with this question it was safe to approach, and immediately positioned herself next to the victim's head. Mr. Caruthers followed a few paces behind and remained standing, desiring to draw no closer to the corpse than courtesy required.

"He was not very tall, for his head reached only as high as my chin," Kesgrave said, "and his hair was ginger."

"That sounds like Tyne, his clerk, but I cannot be certain, as it has been many months since I set foot in the building and new lawyers might have taken rooms," Mr. Caruthers replied. "I cannot imagine that he would hurt anyone, let alone kill a peer. He is quiet and hardworking."

"We can know nothing about his actions until we speak with him," Bea said pragmatically. "Do you know his address?"

Mr. Caruthers confessed that he did not but thought it was likely he could find out by looking through the papers in his desk. "There might be an envelope or a notecard," he said, then hesitated as if seeking permission.

Happy to supply it, Bea said, "That seems promising. Would you be so kind as to take a look for us?"

As soon as he left the room, Flora announced that she had finished her initial inspection of Lord Myles. "Shall we turn him over now? There might be additional information to be gathered from his front side. It appears, however, that his attacker went straight for his head, hitting him several times until he fell. There can be no doubt that the candlestick was the weapon with which he was assaulted."

"Yes," Bea said thoughtfully, noting that the depth of the blow indicated that the assailant acted with determination and force. "I wonder if that describes Tyne."

"I imagine it does," Flora said, "considering how he ran out of the office in defiance of the Duke of Kesgrave. If nothing else, he is rag-mannered."

As this was precisely the sort of comment her aunt would make, Bea found herself swallowing a smile as she said she was not sure they could hold that against the clerk, as Kesgrave had most likely failed to introduce himself.

"No," Kesgrave agreed. "I was distracted by trying to maintain my grip on his sleeve as he wrenched it free."

Flora found this explanation inadequate, as the duke radiated importance without saying a word, as she was sure Bea would after she finished adjusting to her new station.

"Thank you, yes," Bea replied as she pressed her hands against Lord Myles's side to help Kesgrave flip him onto his back.

He was dressed simply in a tailcoat, waistcoat, pantaloons and top boots, and although nothing about the outfit struck Bea as being particularly fine, Kesgrave observed that the stitching on the waistcoat was expert.

"This is not the work of a Berwick Street jobber," he added. "Weston, maybe, or Davidson. Such excellence does not come cheaply. The quality of his lodgings did not suggest a generous income, and his debts are not inconsiderable."

"Perhaps the dowager supplied him with funds?" Bea asked.

He allowed that it was possible but did not think it likely, as she had claimed to have washed her hands of him after he lost Carfield Manor in a game of piquet. "She settled the debt and took possession of the deed, for she refused to allow the home to pass out of the family, but she warned him it was the last time. He had gambled away everything but the bricks themselves."

Mr. Caruthers, returning to the room, announced that he had found an address for Tyne. "He lives in Leather Lane, near Baldwin's Garden."

"We should go there at once," Flora said, rising to her feet as if to dash from the room.

"No, we must summon the constable," Kesgrave said, then observed how distressingly familiar that refrain had become. "In my previous life, I rarely if ever brushed up against constables, Runners and magistrates, and now it seems as though I interact with them daily."

How disgruntled he sounded, Bea thought, pressing a comforting hand against his shoulder and promising it was merely a passing phase. "The rate of murder cannot sustain or London will soon be empty of people."

At this reference to a dire future, Mr. Caruthers started and asked if she thought Mr. Jordan might have also been murdered. "He is a diligent worker, and it is unusual for him to be away from his office."

Although Bea was also curious about the location of Tyne's employer, she did not think it helped matters to jump to conclusions. Rather, she pointed out that he could be meeting with a client or consulting with a colleague. "Or he might have even dashed to the store to purchase nibs," she added, rising to her feet to look for a diary amid the papers on the desk.

In general, the office was not very orderly, with documents strewn in a seemingly haphazard fashion, with several piles on the floor next to a trunk tucked under the window and three tall stacks on the shelf above the door. Two rows of taut straps pressed worn bundles of paper against the wall behind Jordan's desk.

Presumably, having too many files was the mark of a lucrative practice.

As she approached the desk, Beatrice posed her observation as a question to Caruthers, who affirmed that Jordan indeed was quite successful in his profession.

"But all lawyers are bedeviled by documents, even the unsuccessful ones," he added. "We...er, *they*...never have enough room and are compelled to hold on to everything. In the past, the office has been neater than this. Tyne tinkered with those cabinets"—he gestured to a trio of mahogany cupboards next to the window—"to allow them to accommodate more papers. He installed a pair of dowels parallel to each other to make a rail from which to hang documents. It is actually a very clever use of space. Jordan can be frugal but even he must realize it is time for a fourth cabinet."

Bea nodded as she noted a leather-bound book, which was easy to spot on the neatly organized desk. Opening it, she saw at once that it did in fact contain a schedule of Jordan's appointments and she turned to May 12. "Here it is," she said, holding up the book for Kesgrave to inspect. "At two o'clock, it says MM. That is your uncle. Next to his initials is PH. I assume he was in attendance as well."

Stepping closer to peruse the page itself, Caruthers noted that it listed nothing else for the day. "MM and PH was his last appointment, so he cannot be meeting with a client, and it is highly unlikely that he would go himself to buy nibs. If he is not another victim, then possibly he is the perpetrator. Either him or this PH."

This prospect greatly distressed the disgraced solicitor, whose gaunt features were now pulled into an expression of grave concern, and Bea grappled for a task to distract him. She could send him to fetch the constable, although Jenkins could see to that errand easily enough.

It would be more helpful, she thought, recalling his familiarity with the occupants of the building, if he interviewed the other solicitors on the floor to see if they heard or saw anything unusual. Since the men already knew him, they would be more inclined to provide detailed answers.

Yes, she decided, that would be very helpful, for in her experience, people tended to be brusque with strangers.

Caruthers did not relish the idea of conversing with his former associates, for when she made the suggestion, he paled visibly.

Given how reluctant he was to leave his rooms in their company in the first place, Bea thought the reaction was fair. He felt his disgrace so keenly he refused to drive with them through Hyde Park in the heartening concealment of a carriage, and now he was returned to the scene of his crime, dropped right into the center of his ignominy. In all his careful consideration of every possible adverse outcome in escorting them to Mr. Jordan's offices, he could not have conceived of a more terrible one.

Nevertheless, he manfully rose to the occasion, agreeing to conduct the interviews at once.

Watching him leave, Flora sighed and murmured, "Poor Mr. Caruthers. I fear he will never forgive me for this, and I did so want to rehabilitate him. And not just as a way to ingratiate myself with Holcroft. He has value in his own right."

"Perhaps it will be good for him," Bea said, returning the

diary to the desk and perusing the top document of the neatly stacked pile. It was the lease for a building in Clerkenwell for a company called Longway & River. It was a distillery. "Strength is forged in adversity."

Kesgrave, who objected on principal to her reading the private papers of Jordan's clients but conceded it was necessary, exhorted her to make sure she returned the sheets to their original locations. Then he excused himself to speak to Jenkins about the constable.

As he left, Flora abandoned her study of the dead man and joined her cousin at the desk to look through files.

"I think it would be more efficient if you rifled through Tyne's drawers," Bea said as she smoothed the edges of the small pile containing the lease and an ownership agreement for a bookshop in Finsbury Square. "We are searching for anything that has to do with Lord Myles."

"*And* anything that generally appears suspicious," Flora amended.

"Yes, that too," Bea agreed, opening the top drawer, which held calling cards from what she assumed were various clients. Lord Myles's lightly embossed one was among the assortment, and she turned it over, hoping to find something that could be easily identified as a clue, like a cryptic series of numbers.

Alas, it was blank.

Sighing, she returned it to the drawer.

"And please call out if Mr. Jordan returns," Bea added. "I would rather not have to introduce myself whilst up to my elbow in his clients' files."

"I will be sure to explain to him very loudly whilst *my* elbow is deep in his clients' files," Flora replied amiably.

By the time Kesgrave returned fifteen minutes later, Bea felt she had a solid grasp of what kind of business Jordan conducted. Primarily, he handled contracts for companies seeking to establish or expand their businesses, but he also advised on family matters. In the bottom drawer, she found a will for a Mr. Turner, which she hastily rebounded after perusing the first page.

It was none of her business which of his children inherited their great-grandmother's ring or their father's gold watch.

Under that document was the contract for a shoe manufacturer in Bishopsgate, whose shares were divided between Mr. Eburn (sixty-five percent) and Mr. Nott (thirty-five percent). The arrangement struck her as strange, as the latter had provided the majority of the funds, and she flipped the page, hoping to see some explanation for the distribution of stocks.

"Is it very helpful?" Kesgrave asked.

Startled, Bea looked up. "What?"

"You are staring at that document with a look of intense concentration so I thought you might have found something useful," he explained.

Bea shook her head. "I did not, no. I just allowed myself to get distracted by something that intrigued me. I have looked through the whole desk and discovered nothing that pertains to your uncle," she added with a sigh. "I suppose we could go through every document in the office, but that would take a very long time and would bring us no closer to finding Jordan or Tyne. I suspect that will have to wait until tomorrow because now we must attend to your grandmother."

He nodded wearily. "After the constable arrives, I will go directly there. I have already sent a message to cousin Maria asking her to spend the evening with her. I do not like the thought of her being alone."

Having expected to go with him to inform the dowager of her son's death, Bea was momentarily disconcerted by his use of the first-person singular pronoun. But of course he wanted to speak with her alone. It was a deeply personal matter that required care and caution.

To hide her confusion, she repeated the cousin's name thoughtfully and asked if she was the one who had a bad hip or whose son had married an opera dancer.

"Hip. And it pains her dreadfully, which she is quite vocal about," he replied.

"Is that wise?" she asked. "The dowager cannot stand to listen to her endless complaints."

"If it is a choice between her being sad and her being annoyed, I would prefer the latter," he said. "And my cousin's hearing is imperfect, so she does not mind the impatient snapping. In many ways, it is the ideal arrangement."

"Do tell her how very sorry I am and that I will call in the morning, at an indecently early hour," Bea said.

"Perhaps in time for a breakfast without any hint of pineapple," he said with a spark of humor that did not reach his eyes.

Bea grasped his hand again and squeezed. "Perhaps."

The rumble of a deep voice in the other room signaled Mr. Caruthers's return from his fact-finding mission, and Bea was relieved to see he appeared to be none the worse for wear. Not only had color returned to his cheeks, but his eyes glimmered with excitement as he reported that Mr. Leach next door recalled hearing an argument at a quarter to three.

"He had an appointment with a new client that began at two-thirty and he thought the yelling from the office next door made a terrible impression," Caruthers explained. "It was unusual, and he cannot remember it happening before. Mr. Leach said it went on for quite a while, although he is not sure how long. Maybe ten minutes. He had been on the verge of sending his own clerk over to request that Jordan please modulate his voice, but just as he resolved to say something, the argument ended. There was a slam of a door followed by silence."

"And is he certain one of the speakers was Jordan?" Bea said.

"I asked him that as well and his answer was not definitive," Caruthers replied, "for all he could say is that neither of the speakers was Tyne, so who else could it be but Jordan and a client."

It was, Bea allowed, a reasonably measured reply in the circumstance because it was difficult to identify voices muffled by a wall. "How does he know it was not Tyne?"

"Tyne has a stutter," Caruthers said. "It is not pronounced, but it is persistent and gets worse when he is upset. I never experienced it, but Mr. Leach is positive that he could not have raised his voice without getting stuck in the middle of his speech."

"Jordan had a meeting at two between Lord Myles and a person identified as PH," Bea observed thoughtfully, "so the argument was likely with one of them. That is very helpful information, Mr. Caruthers. Thank you."

He nodded and seemed on the verge of saying something more. At that moment, however, the magistrate arrived with the constable in tow, and immediately began consoling Kesgrave on his loss. Although their professions brought them into regular contact with the darker elements of London society, they were excessively horrified by the treatment dealt Lord Myles and acted as though they had never seen a crime more barbaric.

Bea thought this was highly unlikely, but upon further questioning discovered that it was in fact the truth, for the brother of a duke was the most illustrious fatality they had ever overseen and their measure of barbarity correlated directly with the status of their victim.

Shaking his head sadly, the magistrate lamented the

moment Lord Myles decided to set foot in that part of town, as if Holborn were a notorious slum like St. Giles.

In fact, there was nothing objectionable about it at all.

Making objections, however, appeared to be the magistrate's singular purpose in attending the crime scene, and he performed his duty with a vigor and an attention to detail that might have been useful if it had been applied to any other goal than finding fault with the way his subordinate performed his duties.

Unaccustomed to the scrutiny of his superior, the constable stumbled his way through a series of questions to Kesgrave that Bea found baffling. He asked, for example, if Lord Myles used the Brummel method to buff his boots and if so did the duke know the vintage of champagne.

The majority of his inquiries were outlandish non sequiturs, and at first she thought he was creating a narrative so sly and complex she lacked the intellect to grasp the whole story.

Indeed, she was impressed and thought she might actually learn something instructive about the investigative process from a skilled practitioner.

It quickly became apparent, alas, that Stribley was too unsettled by the magistrate's presence for anything resembling coherence and was simply spouting queries as they occurred to him. Quantity—that was, the acquisition of great heaps of knowledge—seemed to him more important than quality, and so he learned very little of use.

As Bea had expected nothing more from a member of the local law enforcement agency, she was not disappointed by this performance and although she wanted to be amused by these antics, she could find nothing funny about the murder of Kesgrave's uncle.

The poor dowager, she thought, heartbroken for the

woman who had already suffered so much grief for her children.

Stribley's men carried the body out of the room as the magistrate pledged a speedy resolution to the difficult matter and swore to attain the justice a man of his ilk and consequence deserved.

He repeated "ilk and consequence" several times, but it was unclear to which Matlock he in fact referred.

As soon as they were gone, Mr. Caruthers announced that he would return to his residence by hack, a plan that Flora opposed because she considered it her duty to see him returned safely home.

"You accompanied me here," she said sternly, "so I must accompany you there. Bea, you do not mind if we take the carriage, do you? You can ride with the duke."

"I do not mind at all and shall in fact join you," Bea said, causing Mr. Caruthers to balk at the inconvenience to the duchess.

"A hack is fine," he insisted.

"I am sure it is," she replied placatingly, "but it is no inconvenience and I am too grateful for your assistance today not to repay you in this small way. Escorting you to Lyon's Inn is really the least I can do."

Caruthers muttered that she could do less without harm but ultimately submitted to her generosity. "You are very kind, your grace."

The matter was not settled, however, because Flora had her own reservations and pulled Bea aside to urge her to attend to her husband. "Do not make him tell this miserable news to the dowager by himself."

"That is what Kesgrave prefers," Bea replied, "and I think it is right that he and his grandmother have some time alone."

Although Flora did not look convinced, she abstained

from arguing, and a few minutes later they were en route to Lyon's Inn. Mr. Caruthers absolutely refused to allow them to leave the carriage to escort him to his door—at some point, he said, their concern for his well-being became insulting—and firmly shut the door.

Flora, watching him pass through the wrought-iron gate, with its ominous spikes, frowned sharply and said, "Still, I suppose it's progress."

"What is?" Bea asked as the horses started to move.

"Refusing to leave one's rooms out of a fear of encountering a dead body," Flora explained, "rather than mortification over one's shame. It is progress, is it not? That is to say, Holcroft should be pleased. I should send him a note."

As Bea had been giving this exact advice for two days, she immediately agreed. "Yes, you should."

"Right away," Flora added, slightly agitated, "before he hears about this from someone else. I have to send him a missive to explain that I never intended to embroil Mr. Caruthers in a murder. I seem to make a habit of it—first Holcroft and now his cousin. Do you think he will be very cross with me?"

As Bea had met Mr. Holcroft only a handful of times, she could not answer that question with any degree of certainty, but he struck her as too reasonable to hold Flora responsible for events that were beyond her control. "Now if you had bludgeoned Lord Myles..."

But her cousin was in no mood for levity and chastised her for making light of a wretched situation. Although she attributed the lapse to anxiety and grief over losing a family member ("An uncle-in-law is still an uncle-in-law even if you have never had the misfortune to meet him"), she launched into a lecture on appropriate bereavement behavior that extended well past their journey to Portman Square.

Chapter Eight

R ecalling the fear Aunt Vera had instilled in her at the prospect of overseeing a small army of foot‐ men, Bea was amused and disgruntled to discover that three was not enough to fulfill all the requirements of her current investigation.

After returning Flora to Portman Square, she had been tempted to pay a call in Leather Lane but knew it would be foolhardy to expose herself to the risk. Presumably, her life was no longer in danger, for Lord Myles's death should nullify the contract. Either the assassin had not yet been paid for the service or was free to keep the fee without performing it.

Bea could not be certain, however, for she knew nothing about the morality that governed such illicit behavior, so she contented herself with dispatching footmen. First, she sent Joseph to Tyne's address to discover if he was there.

Alas, he was not.

Fortunately, his landlady was not reticent about sharing the personal details of her lodgers and admitted that it was unusual for Tyne to miss dinner. Along with breakfast, it was included in the price of his room and he was too frugal with his money to forgo something for which he had already paid. She advised Joseph to try the young man's parents, for his father had been feeling poorly lately—catarrh, Mrs. Pitney believed—and he might have called there. Then she wrote down the address to make sure the footman did not forget it.

In hopes of intercepting the suspect should he appear at either location, Bea assigned Joseph to watch Leather Lane and Edward to keep an eye on 21 Biddlesden Street.

She also sent James to Mr. Jordan's home to inquire about his location and discovered that he had gone to Coulsdon for the night. His housekeeper, possessing the discretion that Mrs. Pitney lacked, refused to say anything more other than he was expected to return first thing in the morning. At that time, she would convey the duchess's interest.

Unconvinced of her sincerity, Bea assigned James the lookout of the solicitor's house and instructed him to pay careful attention to persons entering and exiting.

As of nine a.m. that morning, all had reported passing uneventful evenings, and she dispatched three well-rested servants—two undergrooms and one boy from the kitchens— to take over their posts.

Confident she had done everything she could to further her investigation, Bea presented herself to Clarges Street promptly at ten to pay her respects to the dowager. At once, she was distressed to see how tired the older woman looked.

Despite the faint gray cast to her feature, the septuagenarian insisted she was fine, blithely dismissing Bea's concerns.

"Come, do let us have a quiet coze in the music room," the dowager said, lowering her voice as if sharing a secret. "Maria, who will be down at any moment, would never think to look for me there. Damn Kesgrave for saddling me with such an officious relative!"

Settling in the comfortable room, which was decorated in gold and cerulean, Bea expressed her condolences, which were again brushed aside.

"Tell me how you are, my dear," her grace said. "It has scarcely been a week since Bentham attacked you. Your color is good. Are you having nightmares?"

As her hostess was clearly determined to avoid the subject, Bea could do nothing but submit to her preference, replying that she had suffered no ill effects from her encounter with the earl and launching into a comic description of her first fencing lesson.

"Carlo swore he was fine, but yesterday morning he was still limping," Bea said.

The dowager chortled and replied that she was confident the skilled instructor from Angelo's Ecole des Armes would be fine. "The numbness will pass quickly enough."

Pleased with the blush in the other woman's cheeks, Bea cast about for another topic with which to entertain her and settled on her pineapple dilemma as the perfect absurdity to make her laugh.

Here, however, Bea miscalculated, for the dowager felt strongly that her intense dislike of the fruit was merely a lack of industriousness on her part. "You simply have not worked hard enough to develop a taste for it. Do not fret, my dear. I shall have Cook send over a few of my favorite recipes and you shall see. In a month or two, you will be excessively fond of pineapple."

Before Bea could respond to this distressing communication, Maria hobbled into the room with an overly solicitous smile and said, "There you are, Gertrude. I have been looking all over for you. What a strange place to enjoy your tea. The light is not at all suitable for the morning, so garishly bright. Do join me in the breakfast room before you take your morning nap. I'm sure the duchess won't mind if you continue this visit later."

"Yes, of course," Bea said, noting again how drawn the older woman looked. "I will send a note around this afternoon and if you are feeling up to visitors, I will call again."

Although the dowager scowled at her cousin, she agreed to this plan and promised to have the first batch of pineapple recipes compiled for her return.

"*First* batch?" Bea asked with a weak smile.

Her grace nodded vehemently. "The first of many."

Initially disheartened by this inauspicious answer, Bea wondered if perhaps the dowager's presumption could be used to her advantage. Like most French chefs, André possessed a prickly ego and would almost certainly take offense at the prospect of a lesser cook advising him on the foods he should prepare. If that should somehow spark a war between the two houses, perhaps André would be too distracted or affronted to create new pineapple recipes or maybe he would be put off the fruit altogether, deeming its commonness beneath him.

Bea knew it was unlikely but nevertheless remained hopeful.

Returning to Berkeley Square, she was met at the front door by Marlow, who informed her that she had a visitor. Although his expression was as circumspect as always, she felt there was something particularly sneering in the way his heavy black brows rose as he spoke, and she wondered how she could have given offense when she was not even on the premises.

It was, she thought, a most impressive accomplishment.

Before she could inquire as to the identity of her guest, Marlow added that he had shown the caller to the back parlor.

As the dreary room at the far end of the house had previously been reserved for interrogating homicidal earls, she was surprised by this information. "The back parlor?"

"It seemed wisest, your grace, as I assumed you would not want the upholstery in the drawing room to be sullied by his person," he explained, "or the air for that matter."

Intrigued by this response, Bea wondered if Mrs. Norton had assumed yet another costume in her endeavor to fully atone for her sins. It seemed possible, for covering herself in filth was certainly one way to ensure nobody examined her too closely.

"Very good, Marlow," she said. "Thank you."

Although her tone was firm, indicating clearly that she would take care of the matter, the imposing butler followed her down the long corridor. She expected him to disappear into one of the myriad rooms along the lengthy hallway, but he was only a few steps behind when she entered the parlor, whose color scheme of brown and green was distinctly unflattering.

Bea smelled her guest before she saw him, and as a wave of nausea overcame her at the horrible rotted fish scent she decided conclusively that it could not possibly be her archnemesis in disguise. As ardently as Mrs. Norton desired to regain her position in society, she was not so desperate as to toss herself bodily into a pile of mackerel carcasses.

Truly, it was a wretched odor, Bea thought as she examined the visitor, who stood rigidly in the middle of the room staring at a canvas of a dog grasping a dead chicken in its jaw. He was compact, with narrow shoulders, a pointed nose and hair slightly darker than the rind of an orange. His clothes, though of respectable quality, were rumpled and stained, and there was a deep gash on the side of his coat.

Mr. Tyne, presumably.

Seeing her enter the room, he jumped, as if startled by her sudden appearance, dropped at once to his knees and pleaded with her to save him.

"You m-m-must, your grace, you m-m-must," he begged frantically, water pooling in his eyes, "or else I am lost."

Disconcerted by the greeting, Bea was nonetheless grateful that the man for whom she had been searching had turned up on her doorstep. Before she could address him, Marlow rushed forward and grabbed Tyne by the upper arm. Tugging him to his feet, the butler explained that the rug was Persian and could not be easily replaced.

The man's cheeks turned pink at the suggestion that he could do permanent damage to the carpet, and he stumbled through an earnest apology.

"You look as though you have undergone a great ordeal, Mr. Tyne," she said gently.

He blinked furiously, tears flowing freely down his cheeks, and nodded.

At first glance, he did not look very much like a ruthless killer, but she was far too familiar with the breed to make a judgment of guilt based on appearance. She also knew that a murderer did not have to be cruel to be dangerous. If he was feeling trapped, he could strike without thinking.

That said, she did not feel particularly endangered by Tyne. It was not only that his frame was smaller than hers but also that he had sought her out. If he had bludgeoned Lord Myles to death, then what reason could he have to desire a meeting? Thanks to her violent confrontation with Bentham, she had acquired a reputation for subduing murderers.

If he was guilty, then Kesgrave House was the last place he would be.

Thoughtfully, Bea invited him to sit down and asked Marlow to send up a tray of tea and perhaps some cold meats.

"I do not believe Mr. Tyne has had a proper meal since yesterday morning," she added with a kind look at the clerk.

He muttered that he had not.

As horrified as Marlow likely was at the prospect of treating this noisome creature with the respect commonly reserved for a guest, his expression remained impassive as he complied with her request. He did not even flinch when Tyne sat down on the armchair across from the fireplace, which led Bea to conclude that the article of furniture was of no particular value or provenance.

"I appreciate your paying this call, as I was hoping for an opportunity to discuss the events of yesterday," Bea said plainly as she made herself comfortable on the adjacent settee —at the far end, as many feet away from him as she could manage without appearing outright rude.

There was treating a guest with dignity, and then there was placing oneself in close proximity to an unbearably noxious aroma.

"You m-m-must think I'm the veriest c-c-coward," he said, his eyes darting around the room as he evaded Bea's gaze. "Running away like that! I was just so shocked b-b-by the sight of all that blood and the gash in his head and all I c-c-could think was getting away before he k-k-killed me too because Hawes is so ruthless and without c-c-conscience. I did not even realize it was your husband who grabbed my sleeve. At first, I thought it was Hawes. It was only later, when I saw you climb out of your c-carriage in front of the b-building, that I realized it m-must have been the duke, not Hawes. But I could not stop in case Hawes or his band of ruffians was nearby and saw me. If they thought for a moment I had witnessed their terrible deed, then my life would be forfeit."

He spoke slowly, deliberately, struggling, Bea noted, to control his stutter, which grew less pronounced as his confidence increased. With his ramshackle appearance, distasteful odor and lowly status, he could not have been certain of his reception at the stately home, and knowing he would be allowed to say his piece allowed him to regain his composure.

"It was disgraceful and c-cowardly," he continued as he shifted his gaze to confront hers, "but I was not thinking clearly. All I could do was run and run and run. I ran all the way to the wharf and hid in a fishmonger's shack. That is why I smell so awful. It was while I was hiding there that I realized that if I did not want to spend the rest of my life in terror, then I would have to come to you for help, your grace. You are renowned for bringing murderers to justice, even to your peril, and I hope you will do the same thing here. As Lord Myles was your uncle-in-law, I would think you yourself have an interest in Hawes's apprehension."

Although Bea had never heard of a man named Hawes, she recognized the initial from the diary and asked if Jordan had had a meeting the day before with Lord Myles and Hawes.

"Yes!" he replied excitedly. "Yes, with Phineas Hawes and Lord Myles Matlock. That is when he killed him, after their meeting. You must inform the constable. You must tell them it was Hawes."

"If Hawes had a hand in the death of my husband's uncle, then, yes, I will ensure that he is apprehended," Bea replied cautiously. "But that has yet to be established. As of now, the only thing I know for a fact is that you were in the room with the victim after he was killed."

Tyne stiffened at the implication just as Marlow returned to announce that a tray would be delivered presently. Then he added that he had sent a messenger to inform the undergrooms that their surveillance of Leather Lane and Biddlesden Street was no longer necessary.

Now her visitor gasped. "You had someone watching my parents' home?"

"Well, yes," Bea replied mildly. "I did mention that I wished to speak with you. As I could not reliably expect you to present yourself here, it behooved me to make some effort to establish your location. Thank you, Marlow, for your consideration."

Recognizing the dismissal, the butler slipped quietly from the room but did not go far. Bea watched as he paused just across the threshold to straighten a painting on the wall, then lingered to brush dust from the frame, determined, she realized, to keep an eye on the situation lest Mr. Tyne was struck by the same thirst for blood that had overcome the Earl of Bentham.

The vigilance was unnecessary, for there had been nothing impulsive about his lordship's violent attack. It had been the product of deep consideration and study, to which his success attested. Had he acted in a burst of spontaneous fury he would never have made it all the way to her sitting room without being detected by the staff.

Even so, Bea appreciated the butler's caution and the concern it conveyed for her welfare, and as she watched him idle by the doorway, she could picture him, much younger and thinner but just as imposing, hovering over a four- or five-year-old dukeling with blond curls.

Struck by it, she felt a wave of gratitude for Marlow sweep through her. If not for his intimidating presence in Kesgrave's childhood, it was unlikely the duke would have lived long enough to irritate her across the dinner table in a country house in the Lake District.

'Twas horrifying, she thought, to feel sentimental about one's butler, and yet the absurdity of it delighted her, for she knew how utterly appalled Marlow would be at the prospect.

Tyne's own expression displayed horror as he digested

Bea's sentiment, and he said with alarm, "I had not c-c-c-considered my p-p-parents. Hawes c-c-could harm them in an attempt to get to m-m-me." Anxiety sharpened his stutter, and he was barely able to get the words out. "We m-m-must do something. P-p-please apprehend Hawes at once."

Bea urged him to remain calm, and deciding she would have the best chance of getting a coherent story out of him if she was to settle his nerves, she asked Marlow to maintain the watch on 21 Biddlesden for the foreseeable future and to report back if any of the men observed something nefarious. Then she turned back to Tyne and assured him his parents would be safe.

"Now you were telling me how you came to be dashing out of the office just as Kesgrave arrived," she said firmly.

But first Tyne had to express his gratitude for her consideration, which he did so at length, for it was, he insisted, more than he had the right to expect.

"And with the house in m-mourning," he added with a pathetic shake of his head. "I assure you, c-coming here was the last thing I wanted to do. But I had no choice."

Bea replied graciously, displaying none of the impatience she felt, and reminded him that she was still waiting for an answer.

"I got there only a few seconds before his grace," he said. "Or m-maybe it was a full m-minute. I c-cannot be sure because it was such a shock and m-my m-mind was not able to think clearly. I stepped into Mr. Jordan's office and Lord Myles was just lying there, and it took me a m-moment—or m-m-maybe several—to understand what I was seeing. And then when I did understand it, I knew what had happened and I ran out as quickly as possible to save m-m-myself. That was when his grace arrived. My behavior was shameful, and I am sorry that I did not stop to prepare him for what he would see. As terrible as it was for m-m-me to see, it m-must have been a dozen times worse for him. His own uncle! I was just so terrified for my life. Of c-c-course you had one of your footman out looking for m-m-me. I am a terrible c-coward."

"If you thought your life was at stake, then you acted accordingly," Bea said brusquely, more interested in his movements than his remorse. "Why were you away from the office? Where had you gone?"

"Mount Street first to bring Mr. Nightingale a c-copy of his will, then Broadly Lane to give Mr. Owens the deed to his son's new townhouse. It is one of my duties, making deliveries. It is a good job, and I am grateful to have it. Or, rather, I was," he added as a despondent look swept across his face. "I am sure Mr. Jordan stands ready to fire me for fleeing like a c-c-coward and leaving the Duke of Kesgrave alone in the office with his m-murdered uncle."

"According to Mr. Jordan's diary, he had no appointments scheduled for after the meeting with Lord Myles and Hawes. Yet he left immediately after it for Coulsdon," she said. "Do you have any idea why he might do that or whom he might visit there?"

Tyne's brow furrowed in confusion as he repeated the destination. "That is where Mr. Bibbly lives. Mr. Jordan apprenticed with him for five years. He has on occasion taken a day away from work to consult with him on a difficult matter of the law that is troubling him, as he considers Mr. Bibbly to be a mentor, but never without informing me at least a few days in advance. It is a journey of fifteen miles, so it is unusual for him to just go there without warning."

Bea could not believe it was a coincidence—Jordan behaving oddly on the afternoon when a great oddness occurred. "What was the meeting about yesterday, the one with Lord Myles and Hawes?"

"Business," he replied. "They were business partners, you see."

"Mr. Jordan and Hawes?" she asked.

"No, Lord Myles and Hawes."

"Business partners?" Bea repeated softly. She had not expected this answer either. Kesgrave had not mentioned his uncle being engaged in any business, let alone one that required the assistance of a man who had lately been described as ruthless and without conscience. "And who is Hawes?"

He blinked at her, aghast at her ignorance. "Hell and Fury Hawes," he said, as if expecting to spark a memory. "The King of Saffron Hill."

But neither of these descriptions elicited any recognition from Bea and he continued. "Hawes directs a vast criminal enterprise, with a finger in every pie from Saffron Hill to St. Giles. There is not a m-murder, theft, extortion scheme or blackmail plot in any of the rookeries that he does not have a part in. If a ten-year-old ruffian steals even a ha'penny, Hawes gets a c-c-cut."

Insulated from the degradations of poverty by her family's situation, which was comfortable if not lavish, Bea had little personal experience with its hardships. She had read, however, several treatises on how to alleviate the suffering of the poor and many novels detailing the indignities of squalor. Although violence was never acceptable and corruption indefensible, she was too pragmatic not to comprehend their appeal to the destitute, who had known nothing but privation. Like most people who had read Jack Sheppard's account of his own life, she had found herself somewhat in sympathy with the infamous thief who managed to escape jail four times before meeting the hangman at Tyburn. It was not just the misery of a life of indentured servitude that earned her pity but also the endemic unfairness of the system that imposed it.

Even so, she was disinclined to extend her charity to a

man who participated in murder and took money from children.

"And this man does business with Lord Myles?" she asked, not quite able to suppress her horror.

"Yes, the duke's brother," he said.

"You mean the duke's uncle," she said, clarifying.

Tyne shook his head. "The Duke's Brother is the name of the establishment Lord Myles owned in partnership with Hawes. It is in Field Lane, on a generous corner plot, quite bright and cheerful inside despite its grim setting. It's very popular, which is why they are opening a second location. That was the purpose of the meeting yesterday, to sign papers on the new lease."

Because it was so shocking to discover that Kesgrave's uncle was not only in trade but in *such* a trade, Bea's gaze immediately flew to the doorway to share her astonishment with someone who would comprehend the magnitude of the revelation. But Marlow, as circumspect as ever, kept his attention staunchly focused on the wall as he attempted—or appeared to attempt—to remove a stain with the edge of his sleeve.

"You have not heard of it because the connection is not yet widely known," he continued, well aware of the impact of his words. "Rather than disclose the name of the duke too quickly, Hawes has made his identity the subject of a bet. Currently, Wellington is leading, with Manchester a close second. Kesgrave is barely in contention because he does not have a brother, which will make the revelation as surprising as it is profitable."

Although appalled by the contrast, Bea was able to distance herself from her own personal discomfort and admire its shrewdness. The longer the information was withheld, the greater the interest. "And when will that be?"

"When he opens the second gin parlor location," Tyne

said, rushing to explain that was the term Hawes used to describe the establishment. "Because its primary ware is gin in a variety of types."

This news was startling as well because after a period of heightened popularity in the middle of the last century, gin had all but disappeared from the shelves of London public houses. For several decades, the spirit, which could be distilled from a variety of grains, was enjoyed so widely by the masses that Parliament passed a series of acts in an attempt to curtail its consumption. Other factors, such as the rising cost of corn and several years of failed harvests, eventually brought the fascination to an end but not before it incited every sort of depravity among the so-called lower orders. Henry Fielding, in his pamphlet *Enquiry into the Late Increase in Robbers* blamed gin—or Madam Geneva, as the drink was commonly known—for an increase in crime and poor health.

Bea, although perceiving the persuasive aspects of his argument, thought his outlook somewhat simplistic, for it failed to consider the general misery of impoverishment and how gin-soaked intoxication, attained at a fraction of the cost of other drinks, mitigated it.

"They serve brandies and cordials too, but nothing sells as well as gin," he added. "As I said, it is a thriving business and there is talk of opening a third location after the Flockton Street building."

While it was strange to imagine any member of the Matlock family engaged in trade, it was particularly bizarre to conceive of one as a publican.

How could he have got involved in such a venture in the first place?

Tyne did not know the details of Lord Myles's arrangement with Hawes other than to insist that his lordship did not have anything to do with the day-to-day running of the establishment.

"Its management is overseen by Hawes," he said in a slightly placating tone, as if to lessen her anxiety. "Lord Myles's contribution was really just his name and a certain amount of respectability that comes from being uncle to the current Duke of Kesgrave. That is essential to the parlor's success."

"If that is the case, then why would Hawes want to kill him?" she asked.

The clerk grimaced. "He recently discovered that Lord Myles was cheating him. The overlord of the underworld gulled by a wastrel lord. That stung quite a bit."

Before Bea could ascertain the exact nature of the betrayal, Mrs. Wallace appeared with the tea service, which she placed on the table. Flinching as Tyne's intolerable odor invaded her nostrils, the housekeeper asked if her grace required anything else.

Bea assured her she did not and had the unprecedented pleasure of watching the dignified older woman all but run out of the room.

As the stench made the thought of consuming anything unbearable, Bea quickly handed a cup of tea to her guest, slid the tray closer to him and urged him not to be shy. "I know you are hungry."

He nodded gratefully as he selected a rout cake, which he promptly devoured. "You would think the smell of rotting fish would have destroyed my appetite," he said with a bashful look after he swallowed, "but it did not. It might even have made it worse because it allowed me to think of the lovely sardines my mother prepares. Her sweet and sour sauce has a wonderful tang."

Tyne gulped thirstily at his tea and Bea waited patiently for him to put the cup down before asking him to explain Lord Myles's deception.

"He owns the distillery that supplies gin to the Duke's

Brother," he replied, "which Hawes did not know when he agreed to use the firm. Lord Myles made the deal, you see."

Bea found this highly curious, for it seemed as though a man of Hawes's disposition would be inclined to negotiate his own contracts.

Eagerly, Tyne nodded. "But Lord Myles claimed that the owner's father was a tenant on his estate and would give him the better price, so Hawes deferred to him. The price Lord Myles charged was not outrageous, but that did not change the fact that he was paying himself twice and lying about it. That is not something Hell and Fury Hawes can accept without reprisal, for his power is built on strength and his lordship made him look weak."

Bea recalled the lease for a distillery in Clerkenwell that she had seen in the solicitor's office. "He owned Longway & River?"

Tyne raised his brows at this question. "Yes, that is the one. How did you know?"

"A contract pertaining to it was on Mr. Jordan's desk," she said. "When and how did Hawes discover the truth?"

"It was recent, that I know, but I cannot say how," Tyne admitted. "For that, you will have to ask him. But I don't mean *you,* your grace. It is far too dangerous for someone of your standing to venture into the dark warrens of Saffron Hill. I meant it generally, such as the constable or the magistrate. I do not know by what method Hawes discovers anything except to say that everyone in the rookery is in league with him in one way or another, either by being directly in his employ or determined to earn his good will or hoping to ease a debt. I am sure there is little he does not know, and the only remarkable thing is how long it took him to learn the truth. Lord Myles had been cheating him for four months, which, I imagine, made him doubly angry."

It was, Bea thought, a reasonable theory, for a man who

was accustomed to dominating others would certainly react adversely to finding out he had been duped. But why take his revenge in the solicitor's office when he had dozens of dark alleyways at his disposal? The blatant strike simply did not seem like the work of a villain well versed in crime.

It appeared, rather, to be the exploit of a novice acting against an enemy for the first time. It was so flagrant and ill-conceived, she thought, recalling how the sunshine had poured in through the window. The dastardly deed had been performed literally in the bright light of day.

Or maybe that was what it meant to be the King of Saffron Hill—Hawes could take his revenge whenever and however he wanted without any thought of consequences.

There was, Bea discovered, something very plausible in the brutality of such behavior.

Curiously, she looked at Tyne and wondered how he knew so much. "You said it took Hawes four months to learn the truth and yet you are remarkably well informed."

"Mr. Jordan told me," he revealed. "As he had drawn up the lease, he knew all along that his lordship owned the distillery and was scared Hawes would be angry at him for withholding the information. He had purposely kept Lord Myles's name off the papers so there would be no record."

"Do you think he is in danger?" Bea asked, aware that she had yet to confirm that the solicitor was in fact alive and well. He had only sent word to his staff that he was going to Coulsdon, not that he had arrived safely.

But if Hawes wanted to kill Jordan too, then why allow him to leave the premises and send a note to his house reporting his movements? Surely, for a man of his abilities, killing two people in cold blood was just as easy as killing one. And why leave his lordship where he lay to be immediately discovered but go to great lengths to hide an unimportant solicitor?

On every level it felt wrong to Bea, and she was certain they would get a missive soon from Jordan alerting them to his safe return.

"I had not," Tyne said, leaning forward in his chair, "but now I must admit I am a little alarmed. The way Hawes killed Lord Myles was so brutal, it makes me wonder if his rage was out of control. If that was the case, then maybe he hurt Mr. Jordan too. The one thing I know is Mr. Jordan would never have left them alone in his office. He would have considered it disrespectful to his clients."

If that was true, then Jordan's absence was even more puzzling.

As there was nothing she could do about the missing solicitor at the moment except wait for information about his return, she resolved not to worry about his fate for the immediate future.

With Tyne at her disposal, she took the opportunity to ascertain his movements during the time of the events.

"I spoke briefly with Lord Myles, who arrived early for the appointment," he explained. "While he waited for Hawes, who was a few minutes late, he asked me about my father's health because he knows he has a touch of catarrh. Our brief exchange ended when Hawes arrived and Mr. Jordan invited them to sit down in his office. Then I reviewed my errands with Mr. Jordan to make sure I had not overlooked anything, collected my parcels and left."

"And you returned at what time?" Bea asked.

"I'm not really sure. I think it was around three-thirty, probably a little before. I opened the door to Mr. Jordan to inform him of my return and saw his lordship sprawled on the floor. I remember running to his side because at first I thought he had fallen, but then I saw the blood and pulled back in horror and then ran from the room. It is disgraceful, I know, but fear took over. All I knew was that I had to get away as quickly as possible."

While Tyne finished eating his second rout cake, she wondered what else she could learn from him and, knowing whom her next interview had to be, asked for Hawes's direction.

In the midst of swallowing, Tyne choked on the cake and immediately started to cough. It was several seconds before he regained enough control to say that he could not in good conscience answer that question. "It would put your life in incalculable risk if you were to call on him at his home in Saffron Hill. He is surrounded by blackguards and villains. It is unthinkable."

Bea assured him she would be more than safe in the company of the Duke of Kesgrave, and after some cajoling— and a third rout cake—he finally provided the address.

In all likelihood he realized she would get the information with or without his help.

"Thank you," she said with a gracious dip of her head and asked him if he planned to return to his rooms.

His frame, which had slackened with enjoyment of the tea, stiffened at this question and he admitted that he did not know what to do. "If I c-c-could be certain Hawes is not looking to silence me as a witness, then I would return home. I am just too scared," he said, his stutter reemerging as his anxiety increased. "And now I am worried about m-m-my parents. If you c-c-could find out where they live, then so c-c-could Hawes."

Although she had not been tasked specifically with the goal of putting his mind at ease, Bea felt confident she could do so and began to list all the reasons she thought he had no reason to fear Hawes. The man was, after all, an experienced criminal operator and would know how to go about performing his evil misdeeds in secret. He would not have blithely slain Lord Myles with a candlestick if he believed Jordan's clerk would walk in at any minute. Instead, Hawes, knowing the deliveries Tyne was to make, would have calculated the amount of time he was likely to be gone and planned accordingly.

"The murder, if it was committed by Hawes, would have happened around two forty-five because that is when the neighboring solicitor heard an argument take place," Bea said logically. "That is more than forty-five minutes before you returned. I am sure a man of Hawes's experience would not linger at the scene of his crime. Furthermore, removing you as a suspect would only draw more attention to him, which he must know. One cannot become overlord of the underworld by making needless and obvious mistakes."

Whatever comfort Tyne drew from the cogency of her argument was undercut by the revelation that he was still considered a possible culprit. Apprehensive once again, he struggled to appear composed as he stuttered wildly that he understood. "You c-c-cannot eliminate m-m-me on m-my word, but I am c-c-confident that once you c-conduct an investigation you will see I had nothing to do with it."

Bea murmured noncommittally and rose to her feet, signaling that their interview was at an end. She was eager to proceed to the next phase of her investigation: visiting Saffron Hill. First, she would have to change into something a little less fine than the organdy walking dress she had donned to visit the dowager. Ideally, she would wear the trousers and tailcoat she had appropriated from her cousin Russell, but Flora had borrowed them to indulge in her own secret prying and she had yet to get them back.

Regardless, it would never do to enter the dark and grimy streets of Saffron Hill in a duchess's regalia.

Taking his cue, Tyne jumped clumsily to his feet, knocking the teacup to the floor and stammering an apology as he bent to retrieve it. It clattered when he returned it to the saucer, and Bea, worried that the clerk might suffer a paroxysm of anxiety, suggested that he take several deep breaths to calm himself down. No harm had been done to the cup or rug.

The observation, as sensible as it was, provoked another round of awkward apologies, this time for overreacting to a minor faux pas. It was only because he was so anxious about returning to Leather Lane.

"Do you really think it is safe for me to go home?" he asked as they crossed the threshold into the hallway.

"Nothing is one hundred percent certain, Mr. Tyne, but given the factors in consideration, I think you are more likely to be injured in a carriage accident than at the hands of Hawes," she said. "Unless there is something you are not telling me. If that is the case, then I cannot speak knowledgably on the subject without all the relevant information and must assume you are right to be so worried."

"No, no," he said, vaguely horrified by the notion. "I have bared my soul to you and trust your understanding of the situation. I will return home now and try to get some rest. I am exhausted after last night."

"Sensible," Bea replied.

Kesgrave arrived home just as they reached the front door, and if he was at all startled to find their prime suspect standing in his own entrance hall smelling of rotten fish, he revealed none of it. Placidly, he greeted the clerk, who turned an alarming shade of purple at being confronted by the man whose grip he had eluded the day before. His distress was so acute, he could barely speak a full word, and Bea, interceding on his behalf, promised to explain everything to the duke.

"You must return home so you can get that rest," she said soothingly. "I can only imagine how exhausted you are after passing the night in a fish barrel. Our carriage shall take you. Marlow, please do arrange it."

But the butler, objecting to either the quality of the rider or the rancidness of his odor, suggested that their guest might be more comfortable in a hack, while Tyne himself reiterated that he had not slept *in* a fish barrel but rather *next* to one.

"Well, two actually," he hastened to add. "Or three if you count the crate filled with bones that I sat on."

"I think we must," Bea said as Marlow called for Joseph to escort Tyne to the corner and hail him a hack.

The clerk insisted such a courtesy was not necessary but refrained from arguing further and meekly followed the servant outside. As the door closed behind him, Bea asked one of the footmen to deliver a fresh pot of tea to the drawing room while Marlow handed her a missive that had arrived during her interview with Tyne. Then he excused himself to oversee the fumigation of the back parlor.

"I am sure that is a little excessive," Bea said, unfolding the note as they entered the drawing room. Her eyes went first to the signature and saw that it was from Jordan, who apologized for missing her call yesterday. He would be at his office all day and would eagerly await her pleasure. "It is not as though the man submerged himself fully in a container of rotting fish. He only rested against it."

Kesgrave chuckled lightly as he led her to the settee and suggested that the distinction was not as sharp as she or Tyne thought. "In regards to the stench of rotting fish guts, I suspect there is something my steward likes to call a diminishing return. But more significant is how did the stench of rotting fish guts come to occupy our back parlor?"

"It did not seem advisable to have the stench of rotting fish guts occupying the drawing room," she said reasonably as she sat down next to the duke, "and I certainly was not going to let it invade the library or my office for rout cake enjoyment. How very fortunate we are to have a room so hideously decorated it is perfectly suited for entertaining noisome guests."

Kesgrave regarded her curiously. "Do we plan to make a habit of entertaining noisome guests?"

"I would have said no, but obviously one cannot fully control who enters one's house," she said, meaning Tyne but aware that it applied more broadly to determined villains such as Bentham. "But that is neither here nor there. Do tell me how the meeting with the lawyers went."

"Well enough," he said tersely.

Clearly, this abrupt reply would never do, and Bea pressed him for particulars. The duke demurred, insisting he did not want to bore her with the details.

Appalled, Bea stiffened her shoulders and glared at her husband. "*Now* you tell me this, your grace, after the knot is well and truly tied? Our entire relationship is based on your boring me with the details, and if you had intended to switch to stating only pertinent facts after our marriage, then I do wish you had had the courtesy to share *that* detail before we wed so that I could have found myself a less interesting beau."

This surly rebuke, issued with a peevish frown, delighted the duke, whose enthusiastic response left her more than a little breathless. Releasing her lips with great reluctance, he sighed deeply, ordered her to stop seducing him and shifted closer to the settee's arm to guarantee her compliance.

"My cousin was there, which made the meeting considerably more difficult than I had anticipated," Kesgrave said. "He and my uncle had a terrible falling-out only a few days ago and his last words to his father were something to the effect of: please hurry up and die so that I do not have to talk to you again. He is, as you can imagine, distraught and consumed with guilt."

"Did he mention what the quarrel was over?" Bea asked mildly.

But Kesgrave was not fooled by her matter-of-fact tone and knew at once that she had classified his cousin as a possible suspect. "He could not have done it, for he was at his tailor's at the time of the murder. I know that is true because I had Jenkins confirm his alibi."

Bea groaned as if in pain and insisted it was decidedly cruel of him to expect her to stay on her side of the settee if he was going to say such deliciously appealing things.

Amused but baffled, he asked which words in particular were the problem so that he could repeat them as often as possible.

"*I had Jenkins confirm his alibi*," she explained. "You know I find investigative competence even more alluring than pedantry."

In fact, he did not.

Bea, noting the look of fascination on his face, felt her heart flutter responsively and scooted over another cushion to ensure her own investigative competence. "Regarding your cousin's argument with Lord Myles, you were about to say what the disagreement was over."

"He had learned from a mutual acquaintance that his father planned to move from his rooms in Elder Street to a townhouse in Melcombe Street and had paid a call on him to ask how he could afford the significant improvement in his address. My uncle explained that a recent business venture that was doing very well was providing the funds. I cannot offer any more details because Mortimer insisted it was too shameful to be mentioned in my presence. He would say only that it was inappropriate for a man of my uncle's rank and breeding. Since I assume the nature of his business pertains directly to your investigation, I have scheduled another appointment with the solicitors with the intention of gathering more evidence," he said, then looked at her speculatively. "Does that not warrant another seductive moan, your grace? I did just say *gathering more evidence.*"

The words, no, she thought. But the expression in his eyes, the gleam of unholy delight and profound appreciation —that was very tempting indeed and she slid another few inches away.

They had important matters to discuss.

Bea had just launched into an account of Lord Myles's mortifying business venture when Joseph carried in the tray. She paused to confirm that Tyne had been safely dispatched in a hack, then promptly resumed her narrative. It was a lot of information to digest, and Kesgrave listened with considerable calm as she explained how deeply embroiled in commerce the Matlock family now was.

If anything, he was amused by his uncle's descent into tavern keeper, for it implied a level of desperation he had not thought possible. Clearly, his skill with cards had not improved despite decades of playing, and the fact that he would name the enterprise after the single greatest frustration of his life—always a brother, never a duke—struck Kesgrave as particularly fitting. Having expended every other resource, Lord Myles exploited the only one left to him.

Kesgrave smiled faintly and owned himself impressed with his uncle's shamelessness. "That he was able to overcome his disgust of the situation long enough to capitalize on it shows an improvement in character of which I frankly did not think he was capable. It is little wonder Mortimer refused to discuss it and is hell-bent on closing the establishment as soon as possible. I suspect he will not find that easy to do if the so-called King of Saffron Hill is in fact partial owner."

As this remark indicated an awareness of Hell and Fury Hawes, Bea feared that the duke's familiarity would hinder her investigation. Naturally, he would be disinclined to allow her to pay a call on the worst rookery in London to interrogate one of the most infamous crime lords in the country.

Fortunately, his curiosity about the endeavor and his uncle's place in it was enough to spur him into consenting to the visit without a single word of protest.

Chapter Nine

Although Kesgrave could not name a single instance in which he had confronted an unsavory crime lord on his own territory, he remained adamantly convinced he knew the best way to go about it and refused to allow Bea a single word to the contrary.

"You are lucky I am permitting you to come," Kesgrave said as the carriage rolled down Eagle Street. "Hawes is a particularly unsparing character, and I expect you to be on your guard with him."

Requiring no warning regarding the man's ruthlessness, for she understood precisely how he had risen to his position, Bea took exception to the duke's patronizing attitude.

He was permitting *her*?

The only reason Kesgrave knew about the connection between his uncle and Hawes was she had told him.

Contemplating the injustice, she curled her fingers, swathed in her finest kid gloves—yes, her finest kid gloves—into angry fists.

She was also sporting her nicest bonnet, loveliest pelisse and prettiest walking dress, all at Kesgrave's command.

Convinced that it was utterly futile for them to attempt to blend in among the regular inhabitants of Saffron Hill, he believed their only recourse was to stand out. If they addressed their audience from the center of the stage, then nothing unobtrusive could happen to them.

Holding to the shadows, in contrast, would invite all sorts of shifty behavior.

As a result of Kesgrave's theory, they were both attired as though on their way to an elegant garden party at Lady Jersey's townhouse. Bea was even wearing diamond solitaire earrings, which she thought was the visual equivalent of sauntering into the middle of a crowded road and yelling, "Hello, thieves, here I am. Please do come and rob me."

Although Bea trusted the duke in most things, conceding that his understanding of events was usually correct, in this she felt he had made a grievous misstep. Accustomed to being treated with the absolute deference owed to his station, he lacked the ability to imagine anything else.

The Duke of Kesgrave had no idea what it felt like to be worthless.

But the people of Saffron Hill did, Bea thought as they turned onto Grape Street. For them, life came cheaply.

Struggling to unclench her fists, she said, "'Tis you who are lucky, your grace, for I could have very easily withheld the information regarding Hawes's business venture with your uncle and visited on my own."

Without question, it was an empty boast. The former Beatrice Hyde-Clare was far too sensible to think she could stride easily into a thieves' den and reemerge just as effortlessly. She was stubborn, to be sure, and perhaps a little thoughtless, but she was certainly not stupid. Even if she were inclined to embark on such a foolhardy excursion, she would not do it on a day when a hired assassin might be looking for the right moment to strike.

Kesgrave, however, took her at her word, and his countenance turned stormy at the suggestion. "You would not have dared. Hawes oversees a criminal network that engages in thievery, smuggling, illegal betting, intimidation and murder. Even you would not be so reckless to meet with him on your own."

Although she took slight offense at his particular phrasing, for what did he mean by *even you,* her tone was bland as she reminded him that she had devoted all her time of late to learning various methods of defending herself.

"*All* your time, brat?" he asked, his expression lightening. "It has barely been five days."

"Five days during which I have not managed to finish a single book," she said, "so, yes, the description is accurate."

"Is that a complaint?" he said curiously. "I ask because I am sure you swore you would not complain if your lessons impinged on your reading time."

Recalling that promise as well, she explained that it was a citation. "That is, I am citing evidence that substantiates my point."

"And your point is what?" he wondered. "That a few days of training has made you excessively overconfident?"

"No, that my husband is embarrassingly easy to rile," she replied mildly as the carriage pulled to a stop in front of number 15, a four-story row house with freshly painted windows and a graceful pediment over the front door. "Now I must worry about your being maneuvered into a duel for which I will have to act your second, and that would not be at all the thing, for I have only one day's practice with the flintlock and we have yet to load the gun."

The duke was spared the necessity of a reply by Jenkins, who opened the door with unprecedented pageantry, flourishing one arm in a grand sweeping arch as he invited their graces to climb down in stentorian tones.

Clearly, he was an adherent of the Kesgrave school of ostentatious investigation.

Stepping onto the crowded pavement in her finery, Bea felt painfully self-conscious and decided that even if the duke's approach proved safer, it would ultimately be less effective because she was almost too ill at ease to think clearly.

Kesgrave displayed no undue awareness of his appearance and nodded amiably at the onlookers who slowed their steps to stare at them. Then he told Jenkins to walk the horses, escorted her up a pair of shallow steps and knocked on the door, which was promptly opened by an elderly woman in a mob cap.

Her eyes popped as she beheld them in their finery, but she otherwise smothered her surprise and invited them inside without first ascertaining their business.

With a hint of weariness in her voice, she said, "Ye be the dook, then."

Kesgrave dipped his head. "I am."

Sighing as if disappointed by the confirmation, she said, "His nibs thought ye be by, but I didn't believe him. Ye might as well come this way, then."

Slowly, she led them down a dimly lit hallway that ended in a bright parlor with red paper patterned with thistles on the walls. Wide windows admitted streams of sunlight, which poured onto a dark-painted floor and a rug the color of sapphires. In the center, at a large table with stout legs and molded corners, sat a man with black hair slightly longer than fashionable, held back from his face by a cord. His smooth features were even and pleasant, with broad cheeks, a pointed chin and eyes the color of burnished gold.

He stood as they entered, revealing himself to be an unusually tall man—well over six feet—but slender, and Bea was taken aback by his willowy frame. She had expected the

King of Saffron Hill to have a more commanding physical presence.

Marlow, with his wide barrel chest and dark heavy brows, aligned more closely to what she thought a notorious crime lord should look like.

Stepping around his desk, Hell and Fury Hawes greeted them with a bow and offered his condolences to the duke. "A death in the family is always difficult, even when the relationship is strained, and then for it to be so brutal and ugly...." He trailed off with a remorseful shake of the head before adding, "I am very sorry, your grace, that you have to go through this."

Bea thought he was apologizing.

For a moment, just briefly, she heard in these words an oblique apology for creating the pain the duke was now obliged to endure.

But that was not all, no.

It was also a confession and a boast and a challenge. He was daring them to prove his guilt.

The taunt, bare-faced and unflinching, unnerved her.

Kesgrave, displaying none of her discomfort, accepted these remarks with amiable civility and explained that they had a few questions they would like to ask regarding the nature of his dealings with Lord Myles. "I am intrigued to discover how your partnership was formed. I trust now is a convenient time for such a conversation."

"Assuredly, it is," Hawes said with a wide smile that revealed a set of white, uneven teeth. "If you had not paid this call today, I would have sent a message requesting a meeting. Lord Myles was an associate of mine and as such his murder is a personal affront to me. In Saffron Hill, I decide who lives and dies."

Bea was just disconcerted enough by this sudden change in direction—from admission to repudiation—to openly question his assertion. "You bore him no grudge, then, despite the fact that he was cheating you? In Saffron Hill, do you not also decide how one earns money and how one does not?"

"The duchess!" Hawes said in a fair approximation of delight. "I cannot properly express what an honor it is to meet you, the only other person in all of London who has stood over a decapitated chef and coolly assessed the damage! I will tell you my story if you tell me yours."

That wretched Mr. Twaddle-Thum, Bea thought, consigning the *London Morning Gazette* reporter to Hades yet again, this time for putting her on equal footing with a murderous tyrant.

Seeking to create a distinction, she said that the account had been sensationalized for the purpose of selling newspapers. "I never saw the body."

"Of course not," Hawes said agreeably with an almost comically sly wink. "I never saw it either."

Bea refused to be distracted from the original point and reminded him that they were discussing Lord Myles. "You were about to tell us why his cheating you out of hundreds of pounds was not a sufficient motive for murder. As you do not strike me as a man who enjoys being made a fool of, I am most curious as to the reason for that."

Hawes shook his head as in wonder and then let out what could only be described as a sigh of satisfaction. "You are exactly what I hoped you'd be. Too often you meet a person you have heard a great deal about and he is a mere fragment. But not you. No, you come into my home in the neighborhood over which I rule and call me a fool. Nobody else would have the audacity. Your daring will surely get you killed. Not by me," he hastened to add, his grin at once feral and sardonic. "I am an admirer, your grace. I hope before you leave I can induce you to sign Mr. Outhwaite's drawing of you from Mrs. Humphrey's shop. I see now that it does not do you justice. Your chin is more dainty and you have fewer freckles."

Bea, who had stiffened at the veiled threat, wondered what game Hawes was playing with this bewildering mix of sycophancy and menace. Truly, she had no idea now what to think, which was most likely the point of the performance. If she could not get a reliable sense of him, then she would find it very difficult to draw any conclusions.

And yet he appeared to be in possession of a copy of the wretched caricature, which had not been in the St. James window for weeks. Either he was lying about having it or some aspect of his claim to admiration was sincere.

His astute observation regarding the satirical extension of her chin indicated the latter.

It would be easy enough to discover the truth, she thought, and professed herself happy to affix her signature to his print.

"You are too kind," Hawes said, dispatching one of his servants with a pointed nod. "While Peter is fetching it, I hope you will sit down and partake of a refreshment. I can offer you anything we serve in the various taprooms and public houses I own, which includes an excellent assortment of beers, ales and porters. I also have claret, brandy, Bordeaux and madeira. Gin, naturally. Or perhaps you would prefer tea."

"Thank you, no," Kesgrave said, his tone still genial but edged now with something hard and resolute. "My wife is not here to dispense autographs, and this is not a social call. We have come to discuss your business with my uncle. If that is something you are disinclined to do in this setting, then we shall reconvene in a more congenial one. Perhaps the chief magistrate's office in Bow Street. I trust you have had dealings with Sir Edward Carling before, as have I. It will be interesting to see which one of us he fears more."

Hawes made a faint clicking sound with his tongue, as if to express his hearty disapproval of the duke's plan. "You wish to make this a contest of strength, your grace, and I must caution you against it, for you will get no satisfaction in it. I cannot compete with a man such as yourself, with all your money and influence. I have no money and very little influence."

"Ah, but you have an abundance of false humility, sir," Bea said before the duke could respond, "which my husband does not, so that puts you ahead in at least one category. You are to be congratulated. Now do please stop your posturing and tell us why we should not consider you a suspect in Lord Myles's murder."

Hawes smiled again, though not as widely, and said with convincing sincerity, "All posturing aside, your grace, I would advise you against bringing your wife to a place like Saffron Hill. It is too rough for someone so brave and foolish."

Bea resented his comment, both the words themselves and the way they were presented to Kesgrave, but she held her tongue. Protesting the insulting paternalism would only prove his point, for it *was* brave and foolish for a woman to believe she had the right to any sort of self-determination.

Kesgrave did not reply either but accepted the proffered chair and asked Hawes how he had come to form a partnership with his uncle.

"Lord Myles refused me at first, which I am sure you will be pleased to know," Hawes said, taking the seat across from Bea. "Oh, yes, he got very puffed up and insulted at the prospect of being in trade. A duke's son! But he was in deep to a moneylender who owed me fealty and did not have many options for coming up with the scratch. Despite his avocation, he was not a gifted card player. But the direness of his situation began to dawn on him, mostly, I fear, because my associate is not the most patient of men even when vast amounts of money are at stake, and Lord Myles realized he would not mind embarrassing his family with the connection. When I suggested the Duke's Brother as the name, he embraced it without hesitation. If I may, your grace, I must say that your uncle harbored a disconcerting amount of resentment for a man who was born into wealth and privilege. To be perfectly candid, I found it a little troubling because I am a man of business. I make decisions based on financial calculations, not emotions."

"And is that why you were not angry to discover Lord Myles had played you for a fool?" Bea asked. "Because it did not benefit you financially?"

Although her query was laden with doubt and suspicion, Hawes responded in the affirmative. "That is correct, yes."

How earnest he sounded, she thought. How sincere and straightforward, with neither his tone nor his posture assuming any measure of defensiveness.

'Twas a fine performance for the overlord of the underworld. She could almost believe he genuinely put little stock in the trespass.

But that could not be the way he oversaw his criminal empire. Lawlessness was an unrelenting enterprise, and if you allowed one transgressor to escape accountability, you were setting the stage to allow others.

"I understand the amount to be hundreds of pounds," Bea said. "Lord Myles, your partner, cheated you out of *hundreds of pounds,* and yet you say it did not bother you at all? I am sure you would not allow the moneylenders who work for you to pocket a few extra guineas, let alone several hundred pounds."

"That is also correct, your grace," Hawes replied, leaning comfortably back in his chair as if to deliberately annoy her with his insouciant pose. "I could never permit such thievery, but that is no more or no less of an unemotional business decision than my ignoring Lord Myles's pilfering. A money-lender serves only one purpose: to lend money at an interest rate high enough to offset the risk of losing the outlay. If the lender himself is the source of the loss, then his usefulness is at an end. Lord Myles's purpose was to add the patina of respectability to the Duke's Brother and allow its patrons to feel as though they were enjoying a more ennobling experience while drinking themselves into a stupor within its confines. He could continue to serve that function while gulling me on the sale of gin."

He still spoke smoothly, calmly, but a note of superiority had entered his speech, as if he were educating an addled peahen on the fundamental principles of managing a business. His patronization was maddening.

"You admit to being gulled," Bea said, striving to appear faintly amused by his facile effort to convince her.

"I do," Hawes said.

"And have no objection at all to being treated like a simpleton who is easily taken advantage of by his more astute business partner," she added in mocking disbelief. It had to be there, the rage and resentment. She simply needed to find the right combination of words to provoke them, and pricking a man's ego was frequently the most reliable way to get a reaction. "Lord Myles was thwarting your authority, displaying contempt for your power, and you did not mind? Truly, Mr. Hawes, I do not know whom you think you are fooling with this fiction. It is as you said: In Saffron Hill, you decide who lives and who dies. *You,* a man who has fought for everything he has, who has scraped himself off the heel of life's boot to rise to the top of the heap, not an impoverished duke's son who had lost more in a few years than you will ever earn in a lifetime. You could never allow such a spoiled worm to get one over on you and still hold your head up high."

Bea paused briefly to take another deep breath of air and to allow a moment for her words to penetrate. What she said was true: Hawes had risen while Lord Myles had done nothing but fall. Surely, the other man's sense of entitlement to Hawes's own money was beyond infuriating. The crime lord had presented him with a way to make a reasonable income and still he wanted more.

Before she could make that point, however, Kesgrave said, "Bea."

At first she thought he was issuing a warning, cautioning her to tread carefully before her target exploded in fury and retaliated harshly against her.

Since this was in fact her goal, she did not consider his assumption to be particularly outlandish. She did, however, begrudge his attempt to frustrate her efforts.

But then he continued and she realized he was mildly amused by her method. "Perhaps you would find it more effective to ask Mr. Hawes why he was not angry rather than devoting so much energy to convincing him he was."

Although she thought her own approach had merit, its utility was somewhat compromised by Kesgrave calling atten-tion to it. At the same time, she acknowledged the benefit to trying a new tactic, especially when the old one appeared to bear so little fruit.

Returning her gaze to their host, she said warmly, "Do be so kind as to tell us, Mr. Hawes, why being bested by an inept ne'er-do-well and a confirmed wastrel who was incapable of negotiating his way out of a casket of wine did not make you feel like an abject failure?"

"It is unusual for me to talk with someone who does not mince her words, and I thank you, duchess, for this novel experience," Hawes replied with seemingly genuine warmth. "My associates are too terrified of my ire to fully speak their minds. And, yes, I can see why you would expect me to react differently to Lord Myles's duplicity. But it is as I said: His value to me exceeded whatever few pounds he managed to slip into his pocket. It was not as though I was dealing honestly with him myself. We agreed to split the profits from the venture equally, and to this I have held fast. I have given my partner fifty percent of all monies earned. But as the manager of the establishment, I control where the money goes and what constitutes profit. The building, for example, is one of my properties, so the rent goes directly to me. And the barmaids—I hired them away from my other taverns, so naturally I deserved a small fee for finding them, and then I had to compensate myself for the loss."

"You were cheating him more than he cheated you," Bea said flatly.

Hawes flashed a smile. "Hand over fist."

"Did he have any idea what you were doing?" Bea asked, wondering if Lord Myles set up his gin distillery in retaliation.

"I cannot answer that question definitively, but given what I know about Lord Myles's limited intelligence and lack of curiosity, I think it's safe to say he did not," he replied, then apologized to the duke for speaking ill of his uncle. "I am sure he had many fine qualities that were not in evidence due to the nature of our relationship."

"Indeed, yes," Kesgrave murmured.

"The truth was, when I found out what Lord Myles was up to I was glad because it kept him happy and distracted. He was like a small child splashing in the shallows, amused at his own mischief," Hawes said with a faintly contemptuous sneer.

"How *did* you find out?" Bea asked.

Hawes lifted his shoulders lightly, indicating that the answer was hardly worth supplying. "How do I find out anything? I am the master of Saffron Hill and information makes its way to me through a variety of routes—sometimes circuitous, sometimes direct."

It was a vague response, as frustrating as it was obfuscating, but it was the only one he would provide. All attempts to gain specific information were thwarted by a good-natured insistence that he could not be expected to recall every last detail.

"If I had realized it would one day be of import to the clever Duchess of Kesgrave, then I would have made note of it," he added, "but I lack the ability to foretell the future. It is a deficiency I have regretted on multiple occasions. You must trust me when I tell you it makes no difference. A man does not rise to my level of success by wreaking vengeance over every little peccadillo. A restrained hand is much preferable to a show of force whenever possible. That is how I accrued power, you see, by allowing my rivals to fight among themselves over minor infractions. I merely had to wait them out."

Although Bea was intrigued by the portrait of a canny operator who remained above the fray, she was more interested in his determination to paint it. Was it for her benefit, to convince her he was innocent of this crime in particular—and perhaps others in general—or for his own?

Even if some aspect of his claim was true, she knew it would not represent the whole picture. Rising to the top of a large criminal organization required a significant amount of maneuvering, and if his rivals did in fact knock each other out while fighting over minor infractions, she had little doubt who pushed them into the ring.

"There is that charming false humility again," Bea said admiringly. "I am sure it has served you well in the pursuit of your position, but let us agree it has no place in this conversation. You are a killer, Mr. Hawes. You killed people to amass power and you kill people to retain it. It is possible that what you say is true, and you were delighted to allow Lord Myles his little mischief. But it is also possible that the stakes are much greater and you have more on the line than you will admit. A man is dead, and you are the only suspect with a history of violence and an irrefutable motive. What was your meeting with Mr. Jordan and Lord Myles about?"

Having lauded her plain speaking previously, Hawes had no choice but to appear delighted by it now and he met her remarks with a look of bland amusement. But it was an effort. Beneath the placidity she could see his temper straining to break free.

"On the contrary, duchess, false humility has a place in every conversation," Hawes replied. "But in answer to your question, we met for the purposes of signing a lease on a new property in Flockton Street. The Duke's Brother is doing so well it behooved us to open another one."

"A property that you own as well?" she asked.

This time his amusement was sincere. "Why, yes, I do happen to own it, and since its location is slightly nicer, the rent is a little higher. You see, then, how my partner's death puts an undue burden on me because now I must pay it on my own. I would much rather siphon half from Lord Myles's accounts."

As compelling as the financial argument was, Bea could not believe the money, even if it was ultimately thousands of pounds, compensated for the damage to Hawes's reputation.

Strength was his greatest asset, and that was without price.

"What was Lord Myles's mood during the meeting?" she asked.

"Buoyant," Hawes said, "and understandably so. Our enterprise, which was already lucrative, stood to make a great deal more, and he was excited by the prospect."

Bea nodded, recalling the elegant tailoring on the victim's tailcoat. Either he owed substantial sums to an assortment of creditors throughout the city or spent the money as quickly as he earned it. "What time did the appointment end?"

"I cannot say precisely because my appreciation for details is not as finely honed as yours, but I think it lasted about a half hour, perhaps a little bit longer, so somewhere between two-thirty and two forty-five," he replied. "Lord Myles was eager to discuss a third site, which I thought was premature, but I indulged him for a few minutes before going on my way."

"And to where was that?" she asked.

"To Boyle Street. I have a tavern there and since the weather was favorable, I thought I would enjoy the walk. And in fact I did."

Unfamiliar with the area, Bea could not say how close Boyle Street was or how long it should take to arrive there on foot. "Can anyone attest to your whereabouts?" Bea asked.

Briefly, Hawes's face hardened, his eyes turning cold and his mouth growing tight, and she caught a glimpse of the ruthless crime lord she had so briskly described.

And then it was gone, replaced by that familiar expression of patient good humor.

"I can provide as many testimonials to my whereabouts as you require, duchess. Just tell me the exact figure and I will supply them within the hour," he said with perfect amiability, as if not at all irritated by the question. "It is easy enough to do, you see, for not only do I decide who lives and who dies in Saffron Hill, I determine who speaks and what they say. So I do not think confirming my whereabouts will provide you with the peace of mind you seek regarding my innocence, but I believe it can be had another way. The reason you can be certain I did not kill Lord Myles is that neither I nor any of my associates would do such a slapdash job. A candlestick is the tool of a dabbler, not an old hand who has devoted his life to perfecting the art of smiting his enemies."

Hawes paused to brush his fingers against his lapel, as if sweeping away a speck of dust, and Bea was struck by the incongruity of the elegant gesture and the brutish subject. He was deliberate in his actions, drawing attention to the contrast between discordant things, and she imagined most people found the disparity quite intimidating. His nonchalance, however, was genuine, acquired through years of consolidating his power, and it was this lack of artifice that she thought was probably the most unnerving aspect of his demeanor. He was both things at once: monstrous and charming.

He continued. "And the setting—that speaks to a lack of experience as well, for anyone who has ever dealt with a blood-sodden floor knows they are the very devil to clean. Blood seeps everywhere, and even when you think you've cleaned it all, you raise the beams and find more splatters. Nature is more hospitable to acts of violence. Here, allow me put your mind at ease by explaining how I would kill someone. For the sake of simplicity, let us say, the duchess."

Chapter Ten

If Hawes hoped to disquiet Bea with this dark pronouncement, he failed miserably, for she felt nothing but mirth at the outlandishness of the attempt. She did not think her presence was so unsettling that he had to issue threats to offset it, and yet she could draw no other conclusion.

The King of Saffron Hill feared her, presumably because he had something to hide.

She did not automatically assume it was the murder of Lord Myles, for his underworld empire was complicated and vast, but there was something he did not want her to know.

Fascinated, she leaned forward and said, "Yes, let's."

Hawes inched closer as well. "Rest assured, duchess, I would never presume to attack you in your own house, for I believe in the sanctity of hearth and home. I suspect that is in part why Bentham failed, because he violated that sacredness. Instead, I would wait until you were abroad, preferably someplace out of doors. A visit to Vauxhall Gardens would be ideal, but I could make do with Hyde Park or even Bond Street. And I would not rush the moment. That seems to be another one of Bentham's mistakes, acting too quickly. I do not think more than a few hours passed between his deciding to do the thing and his doing it. That is no way to kill a duchess. First you must wait and watch—stalk your prey, in the hunting vernacular."

As he spoke, Hawes lowered his voice, intending, Bea thought, to add suspense and danger to his words. It did neither, but she would never be so churlish as to point that out.

"Naturally, I would not strike when you are with the duke," Hawes added in a more conversational tone, his eyes turning toward Kesgrave as if to include him in the discussion. "That would be a grievous mistake, for he is a respected Corinthian and generally thought to be fond of his wife. But I might seize you in a crowded ballroom while he was at the refreshment table fetching a glass of ratafia for the ladies. It all depends. Having meticulously planned your murder, duchess, I would execute it swiftly, grabbing you so fast you would not even know what had happened. Then I would drag you to the closest concealed spot, either a garden or a park or a field, and choke you to death. In this, I fear, Bentham and I are aligned because it is always best to do these things with as little blood as possible."

Hawes paused for dramatic effect, and it was all Bea could do not to break the silence with her laughter.

He wore such a look of expectation!

Truly, he thought this macabre narration would spark terror inside her, but the grisly scene with Bentham was still too fresh, too solid and real, for conjecture to cower her. Any attempt to instill an insidious sort of fear, a perpetual dread that an attack could come at any moment, was undermined by the fact that she had been assaulted in her sitting room while reading a book in a comfortable armchair while waiting for her husband to return from his business.

The Duchess of Kesgrave already bore no illusions about her safety.

There was nothing left for Hell and Fury Hawes to undermine.

Thoughtfully, she looked at Kesgrave to see how he was receiving this performance and noticed he was equally untroubled. If anything, he appeared bored by the proceedings, as if forced to endure an especially dull play.

"Having performed the deed, I would then—and this is essential—make it so your body was never found," Hawes continued with that same geniality. "I would dispatch it to the bottom of the Thames or dissolve it in lye or bury it on the Heath. And that is the most definitive evidence I can offer to prove I had nothing to do with Lord Myles's murder. If I were responsible, you would never know what happened to him. He might have been killed by an angry business partner who did not appreciate being played for a dupe, but he might just as likely have escaped to the Continent to elude an irate husband. The uncertainty is the thing. But just because the body would never be found does not mean an extensive search would not be launched. In the duchess's cause, I expect the city would be turned upside down, which would cause a rather large bother. We must be grateful, I think, that nobody has reason to wish her ill."

"We must be very grateful, yes," Kesgrave said amiably.

His pleasant reply, revealing no distress, further irritated their host, whose attempt to intimidate the duke had not succeeded as well as he had liked.

It was all a bit silly, Bea thought, for what Hawes had said earlier was true: At the snap of his fingers he could produce any number of people who would swear he had been sitting in this very room at the time of the murder even if they had personally watched him bash Lord Myles over the head with the candlestick.

He had no reason to fear her or Kesgrave.

And yet he persisted in this vein.

Clearly, he could not help himself.

Accustomed to instilling terror, he seemed incapable of accepting the duke's equanimity and felt compelled to undermine it even if his efforts made him appear ridiculous. Perhaps Kesgrave's underwhelming response felt like a violation or even an act of aggression, or maybe it was like an apple hanging from a branch just slightly beyond his grasp.

Almost close enough to touch.

Before he could extend his reach again, Bea asked for the name of the tavern in Boyle Street so that she could confirm the information he had provided. She had little hope of gaining anything useful at the establishment, but she wanted Hawes to know that she did not trust anything he had said.

Additionally, if he had the power to coerce people into lying for him, then the very least she could do was make him exert it.

"The Lamb and the Bell," Hawes promptly replied. "And you must of course talk to as many people as necessary to put your mind at ease. But I really do think your time would be better spent interviewing Mr. Jordan, my solicitor. He has been beside himself with worry of late for my partner. He was convinced Lord Myles would do something reckless that would bring disaster down on both their heads."

Although Bea knew he was pointing her in the direction he wanted her to go, she could not resist inquiring further. "Reckless how?"

Here, Hawes shrugged and blinked in blank-eyed wonder. "I do not know, but Mr. Jordan's anxiety was particularly acute during our meeting yesterday. Representing my interests in legal affairs sometimes puts him in areas that I would describe as gray. They are not necessarily unlawful, but neither can the opposite be stated. This makes his reputation fragile. I do not know what the cause of his anxiety is, but I have always found him to be a rational thinker so I can only assume it is justified. I am sure you will discover its source when you speak to him."

Responding with a noncommittal nod, she wondered if he was trying to divert her attention elsewhere or merely create problems for the solicitor, who had withheld vital information from him about his partner.

Bea rose to her feet and announced that they would allow their host to return to his business. "We have already taken up far too much of your time."

Hawes insisted that he was happy to give her all the time she required. "As I said, it is a pleasure to meet the famous investigating duchess. And I do not want to keep you from your business either. I realize how difficult this must be for you. A death in the family is always painful and a murder as well...." His voice trailed off lugubriously. "If there is anything I can do to ease your suffering now or to assist you with an investigation in the future, I hope you won't hesitate to call on me."

Glancing briefly at Kesgrave, whose expression remained impassive, Bea assured him that would not be necessary.

"Of course," Hawes said, amused by her confidence. "But if circumstances change, please know that I am here, ready and willing to serve."

Refusing to rise to his taunt, Bea thanked him again and promised to give his regards to Mr. Jordan. She wanted him to know that she was aware of the game he was playing. The rules might elude her, but she knew when moves were being made.

"So thoughtful of you," he murmured as the footman stepped into the room with a sheet of paper and his expression brightened as he took the print from Mrs. Humphrey's shop from the servant. "It is such an endearing image. I hope you are still amenable to signing it?"

Beatrice, allowing that she was, strode to the desk and picked up the quill as Hawes placed the caricature on the blotter. Dipping the pen in ink, she contemplated the picture of her holding Mr. Réjane's severed head while he begged for a private moment to pull himself together.

It was clever enough, she supposed, although perhaps a little obvious in its humor, and she quickly scribbled her name while averting her gaze from the image of her own face. Crossing the T, she took some measure of comfort in the fact that of all of Hawes's gambits to undermine her equanimity, forcing her to look at the monstrously pointy chin the artist had given her was the most unsettling.

Well satisfied with his signed print, Hawes insisted on escorting them to their carriage even though Kesgrave assured him it was unnecessary.

"But it is," Hawes replied, "for you are in a district infamous for its disreputable inhabitants. Disquieting things can happen with terrifying ease."

That he would make one last attempt to intimidate them even as he stepped onto the step in front of his house demonstrated more clearly than everything else how little he could regulate his own compulsions.

Scowling fiercely, Jenkins waited with stiff shoulders as the crime lord bid them adieu, then grumbled under his breath about unaccountably long visits with shady customers. "It has been over a half hour."

Bea contemplated the harm it would do to her standing in the household if she apologized to the groom while Kesgrave instructed him to take them to Tucks Court. Then he glanced at her questioningly and asked if she would rather return to Berkeley Square first. "We did not discuss it, and I do not want to make any assumptions."

Well, naturally, yes, she would prefer to stop briefly at Kesgrave House so she could change into a plainer dress, for she was flamboyantly attired for a visit to the solicitor. But obviously, no, for she was too practical to waste time on such fripperies and she was eager to talk to Jordan as well.

"Thank you, but that is not necessary," Bea said as he helped her into the carriage, where she settled on the bench, eager to hear his opinion of the meeting. She was inclined to believe Hawes's protestations of innocence because his point was well taken: A man of his experience would not have left such a messy scene for the Runners or constable to examine. He would have disposed of Lord Myles efficiently and discreetly, perhaps indeed to the extent that his death might not have been suspected for several days.

But pointing a finger at Jordan—that confused matters for her because it forced her to wonder what he was hoping to accomplish. Even if he actually thought the other man was guilty, why would he want to see him hanged for his crime? The solicitor represented Hawes's interests as well, so embroiling him in the murder was almost like embroiling himself. He could not want the authorities examining Jordan's business dealings too closely.

Unless that was exactly what Hawes did want.

Could Lord Myles's death and Jordan's arrest for it solve two problems at once for the crime lord?

It was possible, she knew, for that perfectly described the situation created by Bentham.

The conveyance swayed under Kesgrave's weight as he sat down across from her, and she examined him for some indication of what he was thinking. She assumed he had found Hawes's performance as comical as she did, but he said nothing as the horses began to move. Instead, he gazed at her in the way he had long ago, when it seemed as though she were a puzzle he was struggling to solve.

Leaning forward, she paused a moment to allow him to speak and when he remained silent, announced that she could not quite figure out Hawes's play. "Is he trying to Bentham me?"

Kesgrave's features sharpened at this statement, but his tone remained mild as he asked, "Bentham you?"

"Use me as an instrument against an adversary," she explained, her brows drawing together as she contemplated the possibility. "I find his determination to lay the blame at Jordan's feet baffling. Does he truly believe the lawyer is guilty or is he trying to point us in the wrong direction? Or does he just want to make trouble for him as revenge for withholding the information about Lord Myles's ownership of the distillery? Or is it some combination of the two—that is, arrange for Jordan to hang for the crime as a way to satisfy his vengeance. Tyne said that Jordan was worried about an act of reprisal from Hawes. Perhaps this is it."

"Ah, yes, I see now, the classic Bentham," Kesgrave said with a knowing nod. "It is only natural that you would wonder that after Tilly's murder mystery play, but I think you are giving Hawes too much credit. Bentham knew you would be on hand to investigate because you were a fellow guest at dinner. Hawes does not have that advantage. He could not have anticipated the unlikely sequence of events that delivered you to the scene of the murder."

"Could he not have?" Bea asked thoughtfully. "It seems to happen with such remarkable frequency, I imagine it is in the betting book at Brooks' by now: two to one odds in favor of the Duchess of Kesgrave turning up the moment a dead body drops to the floor."

"That is too vague for the betting book," he replied. "The victim would have to be identified in advance or at the very least the murder weapon. Nevertheless, your point is well taken and I understand your concern. In this case, however, I think we may take Hawes at his word. If he wanted to kill his business partner, he would have done it in a less conspicuous manner and I do believe my uncle's usefulness to him was not yet at an end. He strikes me as too practical to kill the goose that lays the golden eggs and too controlled to lash out in anger."

Although she agreed with much of his statement, Bea was not convinced that Hawes possessed the discipline with which Kesgrave credited him. "I thought he lacked restraint. All those thinly veiled threats, for example. None of them were necessary. It was comical, really, for here is this man who is master of all he surveys and yet he was still compelled to cower us," she said, smiling lightly.

But she found no answering glint in Kesgrave's countenance, which was now set in an expression of grim determination as he glared at her. Somehow she had ignited an unexpected spark of anger, and it flared furiously.

"Not us, Bea, *me*," Kesgrave said, his voice low with fury. "He knows I have the money and influence to interfere with his organization, and he wants to make sure I understand what is at stake. If I make a move against him, you will be hurt. If I allow you to make a move against him, you will be hurt. He was posturing, yes, but it was not just for show. He is genuinely annoyed that my uncle's murder has brought him to my attention. I imagine before proposing the enterprise, Hawes investigated Lord Myles enough to confirm my utter lack of interest in any of his dealings and would assume that in the unlikely event of his untimely death he would have to contend with only my cousin. But now I am knocking on his front door and asking questions about his businesses and he is extremely displeased. That is why I do not think he was involved. The King of Saffron Hill would never invite my scrutiny without another objective in mind. Do I believe he was involved in other murders and various crimes that relate in some way to my uncle? I do, yes, many in fact, and that is yet another reason why he felt compelled to intimidate me. In contrast to you, I found not a single aspect of that interview amusing, and I am greatly troubled to discover that you could sit through a disquieting performance like that and have not an inkling of the danger you are in."

Suddenly, everything was still, and it seemed to Bea, staring in stunned amazement at the duke, as though the world itself had come to a stop.

Then Kesgrave shifted forward, and she realized it was just the carriage. They had arrived at Jordan's building.

Confused, she wondered when that had happened and watched as the duke opened the door to leave. He dropped to the ground just as Jenkins stepped around the conveyance, and Bea felt an overwhelming urge to tug him back inside. She did not want to talk to the solicitor, not yet, not before she could apologize for being flippant and thoughtless and oblivious to the current that roiled beneath the surface of the conversation.

Truly, she felt awful, and yet she thought the misunderstanding was not entirely her fault.

By design, the full force of Hawes's coercion had not fallen on her. She had been in the room, yes, and participated in the conversation, but another discussion—a parallel one that excluded her—had taken place at the same time.

As a result, she been unable to properly assess its weight.

Ignorance, however, was no excuse for obtuseness because she had known what Hawes was before setting foot inside his home. His bona fides as a killer had been neatly established, and just because his demeanor did not align with her expectation of a ruthless crime lord did not mean his notoriety was unearned.

If anything, she thought now, it implied the opposite.

Real brutishness did not pound its fist in a bid for attention.

Only those who could not hold the focus demanded it.

She had glimpsed it herself only a half hour ago, when Hawes swept his fingers silently across his lapel and yet failed to comprehend what she saw.

It was little wonder Kesgrave was so furious. The situation was already difficult, what with his grandmother's grief to navigate and whatever mental anguish accompanied discovering one's uncle's bludgeoned corpse, and her blithe disregard for her own life only made it harder.

Her utter lack of consideration was appalling.

"Damn it," she muttered, rising from the seat. 'Twas not as though she had any more experience negotiating the feelings of a spouse than the duke. Living with her aunt and uncle had taught her only two things: silence and irreverence. She could no more employ the former with Kesgrave than she could restrain the latter.

It made for a rather challenging state of affairs, she thought, and wearily climbed out of the carriage.

Chapter Eleven

The hum of conversation greeted them as they entered the building, and Bea observed two men speaking in the doorway of an office halfway up the hallway. The pair nodded in greeting as they passed, and she wondered what they thought of having two such august personages in their midst.

For her part, Bea felt ridiculous.

The diamond solitaires were as distracting as the unexpected marital strife, and although she could do nothing about the inappropriate extravagance of her earrings, she could at least address the matter of her dimwittedness.

As they approached the landing at the top of the staircase, she laid her hand on his arm to halt their progress. "I want to apologize for my glibness in regards to Hawes. He did not meet my expectations of a fearsome criminal, which led me to underestimate him. Even finding him comical, I should have remembered that he is dangerous. But if I failed to properly grasp the threat he might pose to you in particular it is only because I know you are capable of handling yourself in all situations and would, if necessary, flick him to the side like an irritating fly."

Kesgrave regarded her silently for several moments before loosening his clenched jaw. "That is to be your approach, flattering me out of my anger?"

"Absolutely not, your grace," she replied firmly, "for a man of your intelligence and experience would never succumb to such a facile manipulation. If I wanted to flatter you, I would praise your handsome features and athletic build and sigh girlishly over your masterful ability to take control of every situation."

"I am certain you have never sighed girlishly in your entire life," he said.

"On the contrary," she insisted, "when I finally found Charles Nicholson's *Introduction to Aerial Navigation and the Heavens* at the lending library, I positively swooned."

"Well, naturally, yes," he said as a fleeting smile crossed his lips, "for its print run was small and the Vatican destroyed as many copies as it could get its hands on. The specialist who oversees the library at Haverill Hall despaired of ever obtaining it."

Confident that amends had been made, Bea resumed her ascent up the staircase and asked what success his librarian had had in acquiring Nicholson's next work, *A Treatise on Flight,* which had so far eluded her.

Kesgrave could not say but resolved to inquire about it right away.

Bea thanked him as they arrived on the landing, where they were met with the sound of creaking floorboards. It grew louder the closer they drew to Jordan's door.

When they were a few feet away, a figure suddenly darted into the hallway and strode purposely toward the clock on the opposite wall, which he glared at angrily for a few seconds. Then he turned sharply on his heels to march back into the office.

He gasped mid-spin.

"Your graces!" he cried with what could only be described as relief. "You got my note!"

Jordan was a stocky man with a thick waist, plump cheeks and a full bottom lip. His dark hair, which had begun to turn gray, tumbled into his eyes as he rushed to greet them, and he exhaled sharply in an attempt to blow the strands away.

When that did not work, he brushed them back over his ears. Promptly, they spilled forward again.

On an awkward chortle, he thanked them for coming and eagerly led them through Tyne's small antechamber to his own spacious office. "I did not know if I should expect you this afternoon, but I was determined to stay here until well after dark to ensure that I did not miss you," he explained, beckoning them toward chairs arranged beside his desk. A third was positioned across from them, and he waited for his guests to take their seat before lowering his considerable girth into a bergère. "We have so much important business to discuss. Are you comfortable? I do hope you are! I have only those two to offer, but I can pop next door and nab some from Mr. Leach. He has a pair of comfortable leather armchairs that I am sure he won't miss."

Although she understood from Caruthers that the residents of the building were fairly relaxed in their interactions with each other, she thought taking each other's chairs was a bit more informality than the circumstance required. "We are very comfortable, thank you," she said, noting the room looked slightly larger without the woolen carpet, whose removal had revealed an unscuffed swath of wooden boards underneath.

And the stack of papers were gone as well, she realized.

Somehow Jordan had found a place for all those documents.

Had he straightened up in anticipation of their visit or out of a need to keep himself busy?

Given the enthusiasm with which he had greeted them, she assumed it was the latter.

"I am happy to hear it," Jordan said with a nod, his manner sedate and dignified. Then he stamped his feet, slapped his thighs with the palms of his hands and expelled what could only be described as a high-pitched whoop. "My goodness, your grace, but it is wonderful to see you looking so well, so robust and alive. Look at your cheeks! They are so rosy, so glowing, so breathtakingly alive!"

Bea could not say which surprised her more—his words, his excessive giddiness, the shout that seemed to topple out of him inexorably like a rock tumbling down a cliff—and before she could decide, Jordan bestowed the same treatment on Kesgrave.

"And you, my lord duke, are the very picture of health, so fit, so vigorous. You could go a dozen rounds with Jackson and remain on your feet, I am certain of it! It is a joy and relief to me," he said with an absurdly wide smile. "I was so afraid it would be otherwise."

As the significance of his words struck her, Bea's stomach lurched with fear.

Hers was not the only life that had hung in the balance.

Did it surprise her?

No, it did not.

And yet it had seemed plausible to her that Lord Myles would have contented himself with a small victory. Eliminate the immediate threat of an heir now and worry about the next hurdle later.

Calmly, she said, "Your client was conspiring to kill his nephew as well?"

Jordan gasped, turning to gape at her as if she had just performed some remarkable feat such as divine the thoughts that were in his mind, and Bea could see what Mrs. Norton meant about his droopy left eye appearing perpetually lowered in a wink. It was particularly disconcerting now, given the gravity of the topic, and she had to remind herself that he was not teasing her.

"You know?" he said.

"That Lord Myles planned to hire someone to murder me?" Bea asked calmly. "Yes, we know. That he also wanted to hire someone to kill Kesgrave? No, that is news to us."

Jordan winced as he shook his head vigorously. "He was beyond the planning stage—well, well beyond it! He had paid the wretched creature and had only to wait for the deed to be performed. The only reason Mr. Trudgeon did not proceed with the commission was Lord Myles decided he wanted him to murder the duke as well and that required another negotiation. Obviously, I could not be a party to such madness and left the building as soon as I learned that milord had arranged to meet with Mr. Trudgeon here."

A lot of information was conveyed in these few brief sentences, and Bea struggled to make sense of it. It seemed as though the solicitor was admitting to knowing the details of Lord Myles's nefarious scheme and doing nothing at all to alert its intended victims.

But could a solicitor really be so remiss in his duty or so indifferent to a woman's life?

To clarify, Bea asked when that conversation had taken place.

"After the lease on the building had been signed and Mr. Hawes had left," he replied, his agitation growing as he recalled the exchange. "I expected Lord Myles to leave as well, but instead he sat down and informed me that Mr. Trudgeon would be here in fifteen minutes to discuss the fee for killing the duke and that we should establish a top rate to ensure we were not taken advantage of. I trust I do not have to explain my horror at this information, for any feeling human being would be utterly appalled. I tried to talk him out of the madness, and the argument grew quite heated. He was, unfortunately, entirely lost to reason, so I left the office before Mr. Trudgeon arrived."

"And went immediately to *Coulsdon*," Bea said pointedly, putting particular emphasis on the destination to draw attention to its strangeness. Then, to make her critique even clearer, she added, "Without paying a call in Berkeley Square or sending us a note."

Perceiving none of the disapproval in her tone, Jordan swore he could have done nothing else. "My situation was utterly wretched, and I had no other choice. Obviously, I could not allow Lord Myles to go forward with his plan to kill the duke. That would create such an uproar! This is England, is it not? We cannot allow our citizens to be treated like mongrel dogs. Every magistrate, constable and Runner in the city would be called upon to ensure the swift execution of justice. They would find Mr. Trudgeon almost at once and he would confess that Lord Myles hired him and the whole dreadful business would come out, embroiling me in its web and destroying my practice. I had to do something to prevent that awful fate! But Lord Myles was my client and as such I owed him my loyalty, especially as the information came to me in confidence. And of course there was Mr. Hawes to consider because it was he who introduced Lord Myles to Mr. Trudgeon, and if Mr. Hawes found out that I had told the authorities about his associate, he would be quite irate. Already, I had earned his ire by failing to disclose the truth about the distillery. I feared for my life *and* my firm because Mr. Hawes has so many businesses and pays well for my services. It was an impossible quandary and wringing my hands would accomplish nothing, so I went to Mr. Bibbly."

It was a remarkable speech, astonishing in its egotism and inability to consider anything that did not directly relate to its speaker. Comprehending fully the miserliness of the human heart, Bea did not expect a man of his nature to fret more deeply for the safety of a pair of strangers than his own welfare, but she and the duke were sitting mere inches away. Surely, for the sake of propriety, he could muster a little anxiety for their well-being?

"Mr. Bibbly?" she asked.

"Leon Bibbly," he replied at once. "My former tutor and current mentor. There is nothing remarkable about my seeking his counsel, for I have been doing so for years, although this was the first time I arrived unannounced without a servant to attend me. You understand, I trust, how the situation was too dire for niceties."

Indeed, Bea did, for apparently warning Lord Myles's victims of the threat to their lives was a fussy detail for which he had no time.

"I'm sure it appears overly dramatic to you, but I swear it was not!" he continued fervently. "Lord Myles was ranting about killing a duke and Mr. Hawes was angry at me for withholding the information about the distillery and I was trapped in the middle with no clear way out, so I sought the counsel of a trusted adviser. It was my only option."

Although the solicitor worked himself up into a convincing lather as he recounted the intolerable predicament in which he had found himself, Bea doubted the sincerity of his performance. It was simply too implausible to believe any rational person could behave with such depraved apathy.

He had to be lying.

In a stroke, Jordan bounded to the top of her list of suspects.

Bea asked what Mr. Bibbly advised.

"That I outwardly support Lord Myles in his endeavor while working secretly to undermine it by having Mr. Trudgeon arrested for a lesser crime such as burglary," Jordan explained. "He knows a Runner who could arrange it for a fee and volunteered to coordinate it so that my name would not be part of the procedure."

"A kind offer," Bea noted satirically.

Once again, the solicitor did not rise to the provocation, answering without a hint of defensiveness. "Oh, yes, Mr. Bibbly is very kind."

"Did you accept it?" she asked.

"I considered it, but it is not really a solution, is it? It would remove Mr. Trudgeon from the situation, but what was to stop Lord Myles from seeking another recommendation from Hawes and another and another?" Jordan said, visibly upset at the prospect of a never-ending supply of brutish murderers. "But Mr. Bibbly thought that the delay would be enough to allow Lord Myles to come to his senses. He did not understand how sharply his mental acuity had declined. Lord Myles inveighed frequently against the duke, complaining at every turn that he had usurped his inheritance, but he never said a word about causing him physical harm. He would just rage and fume until he wore himself out. It was harmless, was it not? Only the impotent ravings of a second son. But then your betrothal was announced and his mind seemed to crack and then break. He began to rant about removing the duchess. I did not think he meant it. How could I? Only a madman would actually consider it. I learned yesterday that he had hired Mr. Trudgeon to kill the duchess. Money had actually changed hands! But Lord Myles decided he wanted to append the agreement to include the duke, and he wanted *me* to negotiate the additional expense. That was when I realized how unmoored from reality he truly was. There were other indications that had greatly concerned me, but I thought I could manage him. In retrospect, I see that my understanding of the situation was unduly optimistic."

Bea felt her jaw drop. "Lord Myles wanted you to negotiate the price of killing his nephew?"

"Precisely," Jordan said, satisfied with her response. "You see the problem. Lord Myles's mental faculties had degraded to such an extent he thought this was a reasonable request to make of his solicitor. I disabused him of that notion as quickly as possible, which made him quite angry. Negotiating the fee for the duchess had been a very trying experience for him and he had no desire to repeat it. And he had very firm notions about how much it should cost! He insisted that the duke should only be half again, as killing two people was not twice as difficult as killing one. Both murders could be performed at the same time, he argued. He expected Mr. Trudgeon would have a different opinion and insisted a man of the law would be better suited to making the argument. I trust by now you can see how broken Lord Myles's mind had become. I had no choice but to consult with Mr. Bibbly. What other options were available to me?"

He paused briefly, either for dramatic effect or to allow Bea to supply an answer, and when she did not speak, he continued. "I could not stay and allow him to embroil me in that devilish plan. I am a man of the law and know well how rarely justice is fairly dispensed. If the choice was between stringing up a man of noble blood or a lowly solicitor, there is little doubt whose neck would wind up in a noose. I could not allow that to happen. I have worked too hard to build a respectable practice to allow an unhinged former duke's heir to take it away from me. So I left, yes, as quickly as I could and raced to Coulsdon to seek Mr. Bibbly's help. I defy anyone to act differently."

It was, Bea thought, a particularly fatuous thing to say, for it drew even more attention to the utter implausibility of his tale. Any other person in the world would have chosen to seek help for the intended victims, not himself.

She wondered if this half-cocked tale of pathological self-preservation was the best Jordan could do in the situation. Did he really expect her to believe it?

Presumably, no.

As a lawyer, he understood that the only suppositions that mattered were the ones that could be unequivocally proved. Everything else was just speculation—and as things stood, that was all she had. She could not convincingly demonstrate that he had left for Coulsdon *after* slaying his client. Fifteen miles was too great a distance to establish a conclusive time of travel. If it took him two and a half hours, then he had had a swift and untroubled journey; if he arrived within three, then he had contended with the usual travails of the road.

The solicitor next door, Mr. Leach, had reported hearing the argument at two forty-five and Jordan insisted that Trudgeon arrived at three. That meant he had stormed out of his office somewhere in that fifteen-minute interval, most likely at two fifty-five because the neighbor thought the argument had lasted about ten minutes. If he remained in the building to eavesdrop on the conversation and heard the assassin agree to Lord Myles's terms after a short skirmish, then Jordan could have disposed of Lord Myles and still left Tucks Court with plenty of time to arrive in Coulsdon at a reasonable hour.

It was, Bea thought, a viable sequence of events. After making one last attempt to persuade Lord Myles from his course, the solicitor had responded in a deadly and decisive manner.

Perhaps spurred by panic.

Perhaps spurred by calculation.

If it was the former, then he might not have even known what he was doing while he was doing it. If he picked up the candlestick in a haze of fury at Lord Myles's intractability....

Swinging it wildly, he might have struck without thinking.

Then, horrified by his actions, he ran from the room and raced to Coulsdon to establish his alibi and beg his mentor for help.

Deciding this theory had considerable merit, she glanced at Kesgrave to gauge his thoughts, but his expression again revealed nothing. She paused, allowing him an opportunity to speak, and when he remained silent, she resumed her questioning.

"Several times now you have mentioned that Lord Myles's mental faculties were diminished," she said. "In what way?"

"Good God, he hired a man called Thomas 'the Bludgeon' Trudgeon to slaughter you in cold blood!" he exclaimed. "Do you really need further evidence?"

In fact, she did, Bea thought. As abhorrent as such a violent death was to her personally, she knew there was nothing irrational about seeking to eliminate an obstacle that stood in the way of acquiring a vast fortune.

"You must understand that Mr. Trudgeon is literally a blunt instrument. He *clobbers* people to death with whatever tool is handy. He pounds and pounds until all life is extinguished. This would be no pleasant evening gone tragically awry, no unfortunate accident. The brutality of the murder would cause a public outcry. People would demand that the monster be brought to justice, for if the Duke and Duchess of Kesgrave could be slaughtered in the street like animals, then no one is safe. An exhaustive investigation would follow, and when the truth came out, we would all be ruined. And yet Lord Myles was committed to this disastrous course," Jordan said, revealing that his objection was not so much to the deed itself as to the man who had been selected to perform it. "Surely that conveys to you how greatly his thinking had degraded. But it was not just that! In recent weeks, he had begun drawing random scribbles and calling them the greatest invention of the century. He insisted I must patent it for him even though he could not explain to me how it worked other than to say it would make the world new. And his affect—so secretive and suspicious. He was convinced someone was following him around the city, changing his clothes and appearance to make him think he was several different people. And the wart! No tenant of Bedlam has ever rambled so incoherently as Lord Myles's nonsensical blather about warts. He insisted his mysterious shadow had a wart that moved all about his face, and whenever he saw someone on the pavement with a wart, he would accost them and pull at it. He was quite, quite deranged."

Oh, but it was not deranged at all, his fascination with warts, and this time when Bea glanced at the duke she knew he was thinking the same thing.

"Do you have the papers?" she asked.

Mr. Jordan stared at her in confusion. "Which papers, your grace?"

"The invention Lord Myles wanted you to submit to the patent office," she explained. "Do you still have them?"

He drew his brows together as he stood and walked around his desk. "I must still have some because I have been using the sheets for taking notes on other matters," he murmured, sifting through the pile of papers on his desk and shaking his head. Then he chewed thoughtfully on his top lip and strolled to one of the cabinets near the window. "I think it was Rudin. Yes, yes, it was Rudin."

Confident now, he opened the door, revealing neatly ordered documents, and extracted the file in question.

"Here it is, your grace," he said as he handed Beatrice two pages with exuberant swirls and circles. "I trust you see what I mean."

She did, yes, for the drawings were chaotic, with their frenzied markings, but it was not quite the amorphous jumble of scribbles the solicitor had described. In the middle was a tall oval, which contained coils and semicircles inside it.

Patently, it was trying to be something.

Lord Myles simply lacked either the skill or the understanding to express it.

Baffled, she handed the drawing to Kesgrave, who identified it almost at once. "It is a still."

Jordan gaped at him in astonishment, wondering, Bea thought in amusement, if the mental defect that beset the duke's uncle bedeviled his nephew as well. "Well, it *is* a drawing, your grace. I have yet to see one that is not still."

Bea, scooting her chair closer to Kesgrave's to examine the image more closely with this information in mind, clarified that he meant it was a still for the distillation of spirits. "Presumably gin, given his ownership of Longway & River and his partnership in the gin parlor. I must confess that I myself am not overly familiar with the contraption, although I have seen renderings of the pot still. That, however, looked more like an onion, with a wide bottom. This is much different."

"The pot still has been recently supplanted by the column still," Kesgrave explained. "It was devised by a Frenchman called Jean-Baptiste Cellier-Blumenthal, who replaced the lye pipe and worm with a series of perforated plates arranged in a vertical column. It has the advantage of allowing you to feed the wort continuously and is therefore more efficient. The pot still has to be cleaned after each batch, slowing down the process considerably."

Mr. Jordan pressed his hand to his forehead and groaned

as if in great distress. "Yes, that is exactly how Lord Myles sounded, always going on about worms and worts and mash and daff and rectifying plates. Yes, yes, the rectifying plates! As if the dishes off which we eat our meals could have any bearing on our morality."

Ignoring this outburst, Kesgrave professed that he had never seen a still with what appeared to be internal compartments. "It looks like a series of chambers, one on top of the other. This drawing has no dimensions, so I have no sense how tall the machine is. Perhaps as high as twenty or thirty feet? It is strange, yes, but not nonsensical, Jordan, and you may be assured my uncle was not out of his mind. I am surprised you did not realize it yourself, for you drew up the lease for the building in Clerkenwell, near the New River."

For several long moments the solicitor's expression did not change, remaining twisted in the agonized confusion spurred by the duke's observations regarding the still. Then it slowly transformed to comprehension followed by embarrassment, which was accompanied by an awkward and stilted laugh. "Yes, but the other strange behaviors...the secrecy... increased obsession with violence...accosting strangers on the street. Those cannot be explained by the distillery."

"They cannot, no," Bea agreed, "but you may trust me when I tell you his concern about being followed was actually justified."

But Jordan could not trust her and immediately turned his attention to figuring out the identity of the mysterious stranger. "Was it Hawes?" he asked with a thoughtful lilt. "He could have instructed his men to keep an eye on Lord Myles to make sure he did not betray him further. He was quite put out with him for lying about the distillery."

"Was he?" Bea asked, leaning forward with interest, for she had found Hawes's claim of indifference to be highly unlikely. He had been duped by Lord Myles, and no amount of compensatory thievery would be enough to offset the blow to his vanity.

"Oh, yes, very. He was none too pleased with me either when he found out I had arranged the lease," Jordan replied. "He is the one who introduced me to Lord Myles in the first place, you see, and feels that I owe him my loyalty. And I do! I mean, I *am* loyal to him. But I am a lawyer and am obligated to respect my clients' privacy. If they cannot speak to me in confidence, then I cannot pursue objectives that are in their best interest. Hawes sees it differently and believes he deserves a portion of any business that comes to me through association with him. I had not looked at it that way and found his understanding of the situation very helpful. I am much gratified that Mr. Hawes feels he can speak so freely with me about difficult subjects. Now that I understand his perspective, I will of course comply with his expectation and will refuse any business that might cause another conflict. I have no desire to stir his ire again. With all the resources at his disposal, I am fortunate to have received only a severe tongue lashing, and I cannot assume I will be so fortunate in the future."

Struck by the curious blandness of the word *resources* to describe the assortment of violent rogues at Hawes's disposal, Bea asked if it was a reference to Mr. Trudgeon.

"Mr. Trudgeon and men of his kind," he replied.

"So you think Hawes sent one of his henchman to kill Lord Myles in reprisal for lying about the distillery?" she asked.

Abruptly, Jordan pulled back his shoulders and in a moment his posture was as straight as a rod. "Absolutely not, no," he said emphatically, his volume increasing as he spoke. "I do not in any way think, believe or suspect that Phineas Hawes had anything whatsoever to do with Lord Myles's death."

It was funny, Bea thought, how assertive he was in his denial, how strident and loud, as if the crime lord were somehow nearby listening. Obviously, it was impossible, for the room was sparse and contained few places for concealment—nary an accommodating wardrobe or voluminous drapery to be seen. She supposed the trunk could do if the situation was critical, but the fit would be uncomfortably tight. A human male of average size would have to curl his legs under his chin and pull in his shoulders.

It was incredibly difficult to imagine Hawes contorting himself in such a way.

There was also the window, but she found the notion of someone teetering on a ledge two stories above the ground, assuming there was a ledge, just as implausible.

Even if Hawes could devise a way to eavesdrop on her conversation with the solicitor, she had no reason to believe he would. Desiring to know its substance, he would pull up a chair and readily participate.

A crime lord who oversaw a shadowy organization was able to roam freely in the light.

Jordan's anxiety made sense, however, for having given offense once he was terrified of doing so again. No aspect of this conversation would be conveyed to Hawes, and yet the lawyer was determined to make sure his behavior could withstand scrutiny.

"Noted, Mr. Jordan," she said solemnly. "You do not believe Hawes was responsible for Lord Myles's death. But you *do* believe Hawes was angry enough to have someone like Mr. Trudgeon trail him around London?"

Although his posture did not change, he no more appreciated this question than the last one and insisted that he had only been trying to understand her meaning. "When you said that Lord Myles was being followed around London by a mysterious stranger, I thought you were implying that Mr. Hawes was involved. I have made it clear from the beginning that I know nothing about his murder, and just because you believe the victim was in possession of all his faculties does not make it true. I continue to believe he was unbalanced. Even if the drawings are of something in particular and not merely the scribblings of an unhinged gentleman, his insistence that securing a patent for the device would make him a wealthy man was obviously unsound."

As Bea knew little about the challenges of alcohol distillation, she could not judge the accuracy of his statement, but she thought it was possible that Lord Myles's conclusion was in fact quite sound. The pot still, with its onerous cleaning demands, was tedious and slow. By Kesgrave's description the column still improved on that by functioning in a continuous fashion. If Lord Myles's changes further increased yield, then his altered still would be worth a great deal of money.

Could Hawes have got a glimpse of Lord Myles's drawings when he was in the office to sign the new lease and agreed with her assessment?

A man of his proclivities would assuredly know the value of an efficient distillery, and it would provide a motive separate and apart from revenge, which he had taken pains to refute.

Certainly, it was something worth considering.

And it was also possible, she thought, that Jordan was merely pretending to dismiss the scribbles as nonsensical. Perhaps he agreed with Lord Myles's assessment of the device and seized an opportunity to make a fortune. Given that he conducted business for an infamous criminal, he could not claim to have a rigorous moral code or be above venality.

The timing was curious as well, for Hawes had only just found out about Lord Myles's connection to Longway & River. If Jordan had been in the process of devising a scheme to steal ownership of the invention, then perhaps that discovery forced him to act quickly—and recklessly.

Bea had only the solicitor's word regarding the nature of his argument with his lordship. In actually, it could have been about any number of things.

If only Mr. Leach had heard specific words, not merely raised voices.

While she wondered if there was information to be found at the patent office, Jordan continued to insist on Lord Myles's diminished mental capacity, speculating that it had been precipitated by his involvement in the gin parlor. "It is called blue ruin for a reason, your grace, and he would certainly not be the first man to fall prey to its effects. If you could hear him talking about the wart, I promise you, you would have no doubt. His erraticism was growing worse by the day, and it was only a matter of time before he brought ruin on us all. He had to be stopped."

It was not a confession of murder, but it had the tinge of culpability and Jordan heard it immediately, how guilty he sounded. His face pinched as his cheeks lost color, and he drew a sharp breath before adding, "Through rational intervention! He had to be stopped through rational intervention such as persuasion or analysis or trickery such as the type Mr. Bibbly proposed. Even if Lord Myles was lost to reason, *I* am not. Murdering a man of his standing in my very own office would be an act of madness. Audacity on that scale requires a stalwartness I do not possess. I am, in fact, quite cravenly. See how I am pleading for your understanding? If necessary, I shall beg. Would a criminal hardened by life do that? This conversation alone is more stress than I can bear. I do not understand why you are devoting so much attention to me when Mr. Trudgeon met with Lord Myles after I did—Mr. Trudgeon who is *famous* for bludgeoning people. Why are you not hurling your accusations at *him*?"

Bea did not think she was hurling accusation at anyone so much as asking pertinent questions, but she understood the solicitor's defensiveness. Despite his business dealings with the overlord of the underworld, his reputation was mostly pristine, and the idea that he could be a suspect over a man whose name contained the word *bludgeon* must be deeply frustrating.

"As that does not appear to be enough evidence for you," Jordan added, "I trust you will contact Mr. Bibbly for corroboration. He will attest that I arrived at his residence at approximately half past six, just as his housekeeper was laying dinner on the table, and did not leave until seven the next morning. I could not have killed Lord Myles while on the London Road."

"The journey to Coulsdon can be done in two and a half hours, yet it took you three and a half," Bea said, aware that the former estimate would require ideal conditions, such as a good road and a sturdy horse. "Instead of leaving right away you could have remained on the premises and listened to the conversation. As you have pointed out several times, Lord Myles's decision held grave consequences for you and it would be understandable if you wanted to hear how Trudgeon responded to his offer."

"It is true, your grace," he admitted, his cheeks turning a bright shade of pink. "I am a plodding traveler and have never regretted it more than now. But I cannot bring myself to risk laming my horse the way a dashed goer might. I take my time. You can confirm that with Mr. Bibbly as well, for he often pokes fun at my cautious pace of travel."

Bea assured him that they had every intention of confirming his story with Mr. Bibbly, which caused him to flinch even though it was his own suggestion.

"But you must not mention his association with an

untrustworthy Runner," he added, "for he would be very cross with me if he knew I told you about it."

Although she promised to be discreet, Jordan was far from satisfied and grumbled at length at what he described as the fundamental unfairness of her investigation. "I am a well-respected solicitor and Mr. Trudgeon is a famously violent miscreant who works for the greatest crime lord in London. The two situations are not comparable."

Intrigued, Bea leaned forward. "So you *do* think Hawes is responsible?"

The query startled Jordan, who silently reviewed his statement for evidence of the implication, and finding none, insisted that the duchess was putting words in his mouth.

"Trudgeon works for Hawes and Hawes resented Lord Myles," she replied. "You said both things yourself."

His demeanor turned bellicose for several long seconds before he took a deep steadying breath and allowed that there may be some slight connection between Hawes and his lordship's murder. "But only in the sense that Mr. Trudgeon acted on a belief of what he assumed Mr. Hawes wanted. Mr. Hawes is not responsible for the conclusion the men who surround him draw."

He raised his voice now, as before, to ensure that the unseen spectators who reported back to Hawes conveyed the fullness of his faith.

The persistent fear that Hawes had spies everywhere, even in this room two stories up, was the most persuasive part of his argument, for it conveyed to Bea just how deep his cowardice ran. Possessing neither courage nor moral clarity, he seemed precisely the type of person who would flee London rather than warn the Duke and Duchess of Kesgrave of the immediate danger to their lives.

"Tell us about Trudgeon," Kesgrave said.

Jordan started at the command, his muscles tightening as

his eyes blinked in alarm. "I do not know what to say other than he is a brute, a vicious brute who beats his victims to death with whatever heavy instrument is at hand, delivering strike after strike until the skull is crushed and the brain is expelled and blood spatters cover the floor and the walls," he said before suddenly covering his hand with his mouth as he realized he was describing their deaths to them.

It was certainly gruesome, and the pristine cleanliness of Bentham's attempt to smother her seemed almost quaint in comparison.

And that was his mistake, Bea realized, trying to set the scene. If he had taken Trudgeon's approach and not worried about what her corpse looked like, she would have been buried days ago.

It was chilling to think about, and no matter how hard she tried to analyze the subject from the detached perspective of an investigator, she kept picturing a hammer arching furiously in the air, cracking her skull on the down sweep and splintering her chin on its way back up.

That was the fate Lord Myles had arranged for her.

Cautiously, she looked at the duke, noted the tight clenching of his jaw and feared briefly for the lawyer's safety, for she knew of what he was capable. On more than one occasion, she had seen him knock a man unconscious with a single blow.

Suddenly aware of how depraved his own indifference must appear, Jordan rushed to add that it would never have come to that for them. "Mr. Bibbly had a plan! You would have been perfectly safe. I only descended momentarily into morbidness to draw attention to the obvious similarities, for Lord Myles's murder bears all the hallmarks of Bludgeon Trudgeon's work. Well, not *all* the hallmarks, for usually his victims are found in a field, but I think even he had enough respect for Lord Myles not to leave his noble carcass exposed to the elements to be gnawed on by rats."

This image, alas, was no less grisly than the last, and realizing it, the solicitor let out a frenzied giggle that swiftly turned into a cough. Grappling for a benign subject, he shouted, "Tyne!"

"Tyne?" Bea asked.

"My clerk who works for me," he said with the same frantic energy. "You must interview him as well. He will not be able to tell you much about Lord Myles, for he had minimal contact with him, but he knows Mr. Bibbly well. Tyne has had the pleasure of meeting him on several occasions and can attest to how I rely on his wisdom. I had a note from him earlier that he is home recovering from yesterday's events. I can give you his direction."

"We have already spoken with Tyne," Bea said. "And he did mention your consultations with Mr. Bibbly. He also noted that your dashing off to see him without warning was unprecedented."

Feeling vindicated by this testimony, Jordan nodded exuberantly. "Yes, yes, and this was an extraordinary situation. As I said before, there was nothing I could do but seek my mentor's immediate counsel. I am confident your conversation with him will continue to convince you of the truth. Just do please recall that we agreed you would not mention the Runner."

Aware that further discussion would yield nothing more of interest, Bea thanked him for his time and rose to her feet.

"We will take the drawings as well," Kesgrave said as he stood.

Confused by the request, Jordan wrinkled his brow. "The drawings?"

"My uncle's scribbles," he clarified, "as well as any patent forms you or he filled out. I will take them with me now."

As he had used the sheets with Lord Myles's meaningless

scrawls to record notes about important business he was pursuing, Jordan was extremely disconcerted by the request and stammered incoherently before announcing that he could not in all good conscience give the duke private information about his clients.

Kesgrave's forbidding expression lightened at this display, for he found the solicitor's utter lack of faith in his honor and decency vastly amusing. "I assure you, Mr. Jordan, whatever terrible straits in which you imagine the Matlock holdings to be after your dealings with my uncle, the situation is not so dire that I must peruse the documents of strangers in hopes of finding a minute advantage I can exploit. Your concern for retaining the possession of the information contained on the pages is legitimate, and I invite you to present yourself to Kesgrave House at your earliest convenience to copy them down on fresh sheets that my steward will provide. I trust that arrangement is to your satisfaction."

By the expression on his face, Bea judged that it was not, but the lawyer was by his own admission a cravenly man and accepted the offer with a brisk nod. Then he spent several minutes gathering together the pages, of which there were six in total. He handed them to the duke with a look of deep regret, and she wondered again if he comprehended their true value.

"We are returning to Berkeley Square now, so the papers will be available to you immediately as I have no wish to cause you any inconvenience," Kesgrave said graciously. "That will change, Mr. Jordan, if I find out an application has been submitted to the patent office for a contraption bearing a resemblance to the one depicted in these drawings."

"Your words are well heeded, your grace," Jordan replied, "and unnecessary. The drawings are your property now, or, rather I should say, the property of your cousin. As you instructed, I will sort out the matter with your solicitor. You need not bother with it further."

Kesgrave thanked him as Bea strolled over to the window to satisfy her curiosity regarding the ledge.

As she had suspected, there was not one.

Chapter Twelve

Once they were settled in the conveyance, Bea requested the drawings and asked Kesgrave to explain the mechanism as he understood it, for she found the scribblings almost as incomprehensible as the lawyer did. "Truly, I do not blame Jordan for thinking your uncle was unstable for these pictures do look like nonsense and something like Mrs. Norton's migrating wart is rather difficult to conceive," she allowed, then added on a more thoughtful note. "But I think he is wrong to cite Lord Myles's plan to kill us as further proof. That decision makes perfect sense, for you are the only thing standing in the way of his son inheriting the title. Eliminating you is a highly rational decision. And as your wife, I could be carrying your heir, so naturally I must be disposed of as well. I suppose if one wanted to be slightly less homicidal, one could wait a few months to see if I am with child first, but that does not appear to be a concern of your uncle. Anyone who would hire Bludgeon Trudgeon to clobber us to death does not care about how much blood is spilled."

On a strangled note, Kesgrave said, "Bea."

Or maybe it was an agonized groan.

Either way, she was tugged across the carriage and pulled onto his lap with his lips crushing hers in a matter of seconds. It came so quickly, the passion, the prickly heat of desire, that she could not catch her breath. Burning with helpless need, she slid her fingers from his broad shoulders to the nape of his neck, urging him closer. When his lips trailed downward, she tilted her head back to grant him access to her neck and she thought she would dissolve into a puddle of pleasure when he laid gentle kisses on her collarbone.

Tightening her grip, she thought, We cannot do this here.

Oh, but could they not, she wondered, his fingers skimming the edge of her bodice. Surely, there was some way to ensure privacy. Writhing against him, she slipped her fingers to the front of his shirt and applied herself to the button.

A desperate moan tore from Kesgrave as he pulled back, his breathing as heavy as hers but perhaps his thinking not as dulled.

Gently, his rested his forehead against hers and murmured, "I'm sorry."

"Don't be," Bea said, struggling for sense, for it was difficult to think with her head spinning and the feel of his lithe body against hers. "These curtains are flimsy, to be sure, but if we are both judicious with our movements, I am confident nobody will notice anything amiss. I am game to try if you are."

Now it was his laugh that was strangled as he momentarily tightened his hold on her. Then he sighed and dropped his head against the back of the cushion. "No, I am sorry for thinking you were the problem."

Although her thoughts were still muddled, she did not require complete coherence to perceive the accuracy of his statement. Graciously, she accepted his apology, then added,

"I trust in the future you will remember that I am never the problem."

But her levity did not amuse him and he said with disquieting seriousness, "I thought it was your infernal investigating that put you in mortal danger, but it is I. It is marriage to me that imperils you. First Tavistock, now my uncle. I shudder to think what will come next."

His tone was flat, almost disinterested as if discussing a particularly dull book he had read, and yet he could not quite smother the note of bitterness, the hint of self-pity. He was determined to take full responsibility for the dishonorable deeds of others, which was absurd. Even if he could see into the hearts and minds of other men, he still could not control their actions.

He was just as subject to the vagaries of fate as everyone else.

It was hardly surprising, though, that he would consider himself impervious. His wealth and privilege had insulated him from the worst the world had to offer, turning the roiling ocean into a placid sea, and it seemed inevitable that he would assume that what had merely been good luck was in actuality the subordination of fortune to his will.

Although she could understand the conceit, Bea was still annoyed by it and peevishly reminded him that she had confronted Lord Taunton on the terrace at the Larkwells' ball all by herself. "I had my suspicions and blithely followed him out there to conduct an interview. And at the Particular, I again had an inkling and marched into Latham's dressing room to confirm it. In both instances I acted without any thought to my safety—or yours, I'll remind you, in the case of the theater. And then there is Bentham. Now on that occasion, I called on the jeweler, not my suspect, but I gave no thought to my personal safety. It did not occur to me to ask Mr. Kimpton to refrain from contacting his client to apologize for his shabby work even though he explicitly said he would contact his client to apologize for his shabby work. So really, your grace, if anyone is putting my life in mortal danger, it is I, and I would advise you to add lessons in self-preservation to my daily schedule because that is evidently the area where I require the most training."

Kesgrave's lips tightened as she made her recital and as soon as she finished, he said sternly, "This is not a joke, Bea."

"I do not recall laughing," she said.

"I did nothing," he replied heatedly. "I knew well my uncle's resentments, for they were long-standing, and yet I did not pause to wonder what he thought of my marriage. I did not think of him at all."

"You are not omniscient," she pointed out.

Ah, but the Duke of Kesgrave did not consider himself bound by the laws of nature and insisted he should have known. "A healthy suspicion is not omniscience. Mrs. Norton thought of it."

Oh, dear, Bea thought in amusement, the situation must be quite dire indeed if he was comparing himself unfavorably to the spiteful heiress who had conspired with Tavistock to destroy her reputation. "Neither are you desperate."

"That is true," he conceded, joining his hand with hers and raising them to his lips, "but something must be done, for relying on the desperation of your archnemeses is not a reliable way to ensure your future safety."

"Archnemeses, plural?" she asked. "Just how many people do you think I have managed to offend during my six seasons of wallflowering?"

"Given how readily you abuse me, I can only assume the number is legion," he replied.

"Yes, of course, your grace," she said with a laugh, "for if I could overcome my awe of you, then I could overcome my awe of anyone. It had nothing to do with circumstance, only my impertinence. It is a wonder I had not charmed another duke to the altar well before you."

"You jest," he said tenderly, pressing a soft kiss against her temple, "but it *is* a wonder to me."

"You see, that is another service Mrs. Norton has done us," she said, "which I believe you thanked her for previously. If she had not ensured my social pariahdom, I would have been saddled with a husband and a parcel of children by the time we met. Clearly, she is the long-term solution you are searching for."

"Archangel, not archnemesis?" he asked, his lips loosening into a smile.

"The hand of fate in its most unlikely form," she added.

"Is it enough to reinstate her vouchers to Almack's?" Kesgrave asked.

"It would be churlish to deny her," Bea said.

He readily agreed and promised to send a note to Lady Jersey. "But do not think you have managed to distract me from my negligence in this matter. If not for my uncle's venality somehow rebounding to bring his own life to an untimely end, you might have wound up in a field being consumed by vermin because of my thoughtlessness."

Aware of how stubborn Kesgrave could be, she had little hope of convincing him he was wrong. He was determined to hold himself responsible, and all she could do to ease his worry was devote herself to her lessons. The more proficiency she gained, the less anxious he would be.

But that was a process—a long, arduous and seemingly illiterate one, if her first few days of instruction were any indication—and his mind was troubled now. Determined to take another pass at providing a distraction, she feathered kisses along his jaw as her fingers returned to the buttons on the front of his shirt.

He growled in response, and Bea, shifting position to

press herself more fully against him, thought she might just succeed in diverting him yet.

She did.

Oh, yes, she did, so well in fact that it was not until Kesgrave disappeared into his study with Stephens to discuss his uncle's patent application that she realized they had failed to establish the next step in their investigation.

Interview Trudgeon, obviously.

Rarely had a suspect presented himself as a more likely candidate. His reputation and chosen profession certainly indicated that he had the skills and stomach required for the act.

Even so, she could not bring herself to trust anything Jordan said, for either he was lying about his own movements or he was deeply immoral. Or perhaps both were true, in which case he might have decided that a slain uncle to a duke was preferable to a slain duke.

Arranging an interview with the known killer, however, would be difficult. A man of his temperament and experience would be exceedingly reluctant to discuss his avocation with a pair of potential victims and would have to be cajoled into complying.

Well, not cajoled, Bea conceded.

Coerced.

And Hawes was just the man to apply the pressure.

Kesgrave would argue. Deeply resentful of the other man's repeated efforts to cower him, the duke would never agree to seek his assistance.

She understood his objections, of course, and was prepared to bow to them if he could propose a reasonable alternative. The problem was, she simply did not see any other way to compel the suspect to submit to her questions.

Presumably, a man with the sobriquet "the Bludgeon" did not submit to many things.

As she was anticipating an argument, Bea decided it was prudent not to interrupt Kesgrave's conference with the steward. Instead, she sent Joseph with a missive requesting he meet her in the back parlor. The ugly room was, she thought, the perfect setting for a heated exchange.

That was an hour ago.

When he finally appeared, Bea was finishing her second cup of tea and tearing up her third note card. She was so confident her logic would prevail that she had begun composing the missive to Hell and Fury Hawes. To her frustration, it was not as easy to write as she had anticipated. Putting herself in the crime lord's debt was intolerable, and striking a balance between asking for a favor and not sounding as though she was asking for a favor required a particular agility.

Kesgrave, she felt certain, would know precisely the right phrasing to gain Hawes's assistance without promising anything alarming in return.

One's family did not consolidate power for five centuries without an innate understanding of how to retain the upper hand in a negotiation.

"Ah, there you are," she said, smiling as she collected the assortment of scraps into a neat pile on the silver tray. "I have been struggling over the wording of this note for a half hour and could well use your help."

"Asking me to meet you in the ugly room without specifying which one that refers to is not the most efficacious way to arrange an assignation," he said chidingly as he crossed the threshold. "If you have been waiting an age for me to appear, you have no one to blame but yourself."

Bea stared at him blankly for a brief moment before glancing pointedly at the unappealing decor all around them: the gloomy color on the walls, the disagreeable pattern of the rug, the unsettling painting of a dog snarling at a small child who was clutching the neck of a flapping chicken. "It is your home, of course, and you may describe as many rooms as you like as ugly, but obviously this one is the *most* ugly."

"I see Mrs. Wallace has not consulted you on the new curtains for the Versailles room," he said with amusement as he crossed the floor.

"She might have tried, for I have a vague memory of her showing me fabric swatches and my brushing her off with a fortifying comment about trusting her judgment implicitly." She asked curiously, "And how does this seeming non sequitur relate to your tardiness?"

"The Versailles room is a bedroom on the second floor styled after the Hall of Mirrors, complete with Rouge de Rance pilasters and chandeliers with multiple tiers of leaded glass. Imagine Tilly's drawing room but twice as lavish and half as large. It is hideous," he explained, sitting down next to her on the settee. "We can go there now, so you may judge for yourself and perhaps form an opinion about which color best suits the drapery. I am sure Mrs. Wallace would still welcome your thoughts."

"No," Bea said with a laugh. "I do not think she would, for the options ran the dizzying gamut from pale yellow to light straw, and my only comment would be to suggest she put her time to better use. But that is neither here nor there, for I will not fall for your ploy to remove me to a room with a bed. Really, your grace, I would think a man of your experience could come up with something a little more enticing than curtains."

A smile played at the corners of his mouth as he leaned forward to smooth a shiny lock that had escaped its hairpins, his blue eyes vibrant despite the dimness of the room. "I assure you, your grace, a man of my experience does not require a bed, as I have taken pains to demonstrate on multiple occasions this past month. If I have failed in that endeavor, I stand ready to rectify the oversight."

Her breath hitched—of course it did—for the look he gave her was a marvel, as serious as it was mischievous, embodying all that he was and yet somehow distilling him down to his essence.

Utterly enthralled, she tilted her head to the side, leaning into the gentle tenderness of his fingers as they swept her forehead. His lips were so close, she could almost feel the lovely press of them on her own.

Alas, they had business to discuss.

With a regretful sigh, she rose to her feet and stepped several paces away from the duke. She would not be diverted again.

"Considering the inherent difficulties of locating a man of Thomas 'the Bludgeon' Trudgeon's proclivities *and* convincing him to answer our questions, I believe the most practical course is to gain Hawes's assistance. I understand you might be uneasy with my suggestion and am eager to discuss it with you as well as listen to other ideas you may have."

Calmly, Kesgrave assured her that no such conversation was necessary because the matter had already been handled.

As this was among the last things she had expected him to say, Bea blinked in surprise and asked, "What do you mean *handled?*"

"What one typically means when one uses the word," he replied with a mildness she could not help but think was deliberately provoking, for it implied he had done nothing remarkable or untoward, but he had. Obviously, he had. "That is to say, the issue has been resolved. Since Trudgeon is almost certainly the man who murdered my uncle, I alerted the constable who attended to the scene yesterday, Stribley, who will see to his arrest. If you would like to interview him once he is in their custody, that can be arranged."

It was his nonchalance, she thought, her stomach sinking with anxiety, that was especially devastating, for it communicated more clearly than any words ever could how little he understood the implication of his actions.

How little he thought there was to comprehend.

Confer with his wife before making a decision?

Scoff!

It was, she thought, a devastating blow, for they had just had this conversation not two days ago, when she persuaded him to tell her about his childhood. In the starkest possible terms, she had made it plain how important it was to her that he regard her as a true partner.

Ardently, he had sworn that he did.

And yet here they were, in the same place, not a full forty-eight hours later.

Somehow she was surprised.

She should not have been.

It was inevitable that this was how their marriage was to be conducted, with Kesgrave doling out equality at his discretion. It was how *all* marriages were conducted. The source of the disagreement was specific to them, but the existence of a persistent point of discord was as common as dirt. Her aunt and uncle had been having the same argument for twenty years, and although it took a variety of forms, it was always about his lack of interest in domestic affairs.

Of course Kesgrave had granted her request for equality in the matter of his family history. The concession suited the occasion, and even the most ignoble husband would respond with proper gallantry when emotions were heightened to such an irresistible degree.

Grand moments, she thought cynically, called for grand gestures.

But life was not lived in the grand moments.

No, it was lived in the banal little exchanges that occurred day after day, and it was the accumulation of these insignificant interactions that made up a relationship.

That was where the truth resided—in the cracks between grandiosities.

Comprehending how she had allowed herself to be misled —his response to Bentham's attack, for example, had been breathtakingly open-minded—did nothing to ease her sorrow.

Be grateful, she told herself, to know the truth now. Imagine the crushing pain if the delusion had been allowed to persist for months.

It was a mercy, really.

But it did not feel like a blessing, and Bea rose to her feet to console herself in private.

Console herself? she thought in mocking disdain.

She had not lost anything.

Precisely the opposite, for she had gained a better understanding of her husband as well as indispensable knowledge of where his boundaries lay. Just because his goodness did not extend indefinitely did not mean he was not still the best of good men.

Even so, she felt an overwhelming desire to be away from the back parlor, with its ugly walls, angry rugs and vicious paintings, and to return to the comforting warmth of her office.

Regardless, she had too much to do to linger there indolently. She had promised the dowager she would call again that day. Mrs. Norton was no doubt on tenterhooks, waiting for word regarding the status of her vouchers. Bea could certainly take a few minutes to dash off a note assuring the other woman of her success, and a missive to Flora would not go amiss either, for she had no idea how her cousin's plan to earn Holcroft's forgiveness had fared. She would send one to

Caruthers as well, inquiring about his welfare and reiterating her offer to drive in the park.

And the pineapple conundrum remained just as pressing and vexing as always. If she did not come up with a feasible scheme soon, afternoon tea would be permanently marred by the wretched fruit.

The list of responsibilities soothed her, and with a matter-of-fact calm of which she had not believed herself capable only a few seconds before, she thanked Kesgrave for bringing the unpleasantness to a satisfying conclusion.

Did she sound bitter?

Perhaps a little sullen?

Neither was her intent, and yet it was difficult to interpret the word *satisfying* in any other way, for there were few things less satisfying than leaving the apprehension of a murderer in the incompetent hands of a constable.

To compensate for the inadvertent surliness, she smiled broadly as she excused herself. "I will be in my office if you would like to consult with me further."

Oh, dear, she thought, that sounded sarcastic as well.

No matter how determined she was to deal with her disappointment graciously, a mutinous part of her brain was bent on revealing the truth.

It was funny, she thought, for she had spent two decades suppressing her resentment toward her family, and here she was, newly married, and could barely stifle it after little more than a few weeks.

Surely, Kesgrave deserved at least as much consideration as she extended to Aunt Vera and Uncle Horace.

The idea amused her, although in a perverse sort of way, but it was humor nonetheless and she was grateful for its glimmer. She had always found laughter to be consoling.

Murmuring that she would send Joseph to collect the tea

tray, she strode toward the door, her movements remarkably smooth for the agitation she felt. She could be as clever and rational about it as she wanted, but a part of her was as hurt now as it had been when he had refused to talk to her about his uncle.

It was madness, truly, the way she kept expecting to be the equal of a duke.

She was almost at the entrance to the room when Kesgrave called her name, and he said it so mildly, almost absently, she assumed he was going to remind her of something minor she might have forgotten, such as his plan to have dinner with his grandmother.

Smothering an impatient sigh, for she was quite eager to be out of his presence, she turned slightly to acknowledge the comment and was shocked to see his face set in anger. His jaw clenched tightly and his eyes seethed as he briskly crossed the floor to stand next to her. Firmly, he shut the door, barring her exit.

Despite his furious expression, his tone was calm when he said, "I fail to comprehend why my reluctance to share the painful details of my appalling childhood portends terrible things about our relationship and yet you are allowed to withdraw from me as if it bears no significance. Something has distressed you greatly, and I will not allow you to leave the room until I know the whole of it. If you require some time to figure out how to articulate your thoughts, I am prepared to give a five-minute dissertation on the production and application of false mustaches. My valet received a full tutorial from Mr. Fairbrother at the Particular."

It was such a thing to say, oh, it was, calculated to make her grin and even sigh at the reminder of their first kiss—that awful, absurd, wonderful thing. If she closed her eyes, she would be all but back in the carriage with everything ahead of her.

Smiling faintly, she said, "The difference, your grace, is that I did not cause your pain."

Somehow, it surprised him, the distinction she drew, for his eyebrows flew upward as a look of utter bewilderment descended.

The sincerity of his astonishment did nothing to lessen its infuriation. Indeed, it only increased it, for it revealed plainly how little he had thought about the consequences of his actions. He had simply done as he pleased, which was his prerogative.

It would always be his prerogative, and that was the beating heart of it.

Troubled by her words, Kesgrave said her name with a hint of exasperation, as if pleading with her to reconsider. But he did not specify what in particular he would like her to reexamine and she shook her head.

"No, your grace, it will not do," she said, feeling more than a little exasperated herself, "for your *handling* of the situation gives away the whole game. You see what I did there, I trust, drawing attention to the word *handle*? I am aping your ways by being provokingly coy. I am sure you find it just as charming as I did."

Thinking he understood the source of her ire, he straightened his shoulders and announced that he would not apologize for discharging a distasteful duty as swiftly and efficiently as possible. "And it is irrational for you to expect me to."

"Yes, your grace," she replied stiffly, for there was nothing left to say. He had asked why she was upset and insulted her when she explained. "If that is all, I would please like to leave the room. It is after five, and I have several letters to write before dinner."

But that was not all, no, for perceiving the coldness of her tone, he pressed himself more firmly against the door and said with weary confusion, "Damn it, Bea."

Blandly, she stared back at him.

"Very well, yes," he said with a frustrated sigh. "I sent Jenkins to alert the constable as soon as we returned because I suspected you would suggest we ask Hawes for help and I wanted to remove the possibility from contention. To be fair, it was a logical suggestion, but I found the prospect of your having further contact with him intolerable. At this point, I will remind you, my dear, that I was correct. You did want to seek Hawes's assistance."

"You are right, yes. Being prone to logical suggestions, I did want to secure Hawes's assistance," she conceded easily, "but that was why I asked you to meet me in the back parlor. So that we may discuss it."

"Well, no, you asked me to the ugly room," he said with a hint of levity, "and I still contend there are several rooms in Kesgrave House that meet that description. There is also the bedchamber in the east wing that is decorated with my great-great-grandmother's amateurish daubs. She was inordinately fond of landscapes but also dreadfully nearsighted, so her works are mostly splotches of green, brown and blue paint, more vague impressions of trees and waterfalls than actual representations. Everyone who has spent the night in the room has found it most unsettling. The Chevalier d'Éon reportedly called it an abomination, although my great-grandfather insisted he was talking about the Treaty of Paris, not his mother's artwork."

He said this spryly, blithely, endeavoring to elicit a laugh or a giggle or at the very least a lightened expression. It was not an outrageous tactic, trying to draw a smile from her in the middle of a weighty conversation, for it was one she regularly employed. That he would attempt it now, at a moment when she could not muster a smidge of response, was another small tear in her heart.

Sadly, as if he had not said a word, she continued, "I asked you here to *discuss* it, to present my plan and listen to your objections and, yes, try to overcome them because we are partners pursuing a goal jointly. I would never would have acted without your approval and expected the same from you. I know the situation is difficult because the victim is your uncle. I understand that it is harder to consider ideas objec-tively when your emotions are entangled and would have taken those factors into consideration if you had come to me and said, 'This is what I want to do and here are my reasons.' I am not unreasonable and can perceive that sometimes the logical suggestion is not the right one. But you did not come to me with your plan. You did not allow me the dignity of rising to the occasion or even the ignominy of sinking beneath it. The only way you could do that, the only way you could discount my opinion entirely, is if you do not consider me your partner. If we are equals only when you deem it, then we are not equals at all. And that, your grace, is why it is different when I withdraw from you. Because I need a few quiet moments to adjust my expectations of our marriage without harming myself further. When that condition applies to your situation as well, I do hope you will do me the cour-tesy of explaining so that I may grant you the privacy you require."

The amusement on the duke's face dimmed during this speech, slowly giving way to impassivity, and he regarded her now with an almost neutral curiosity. Bea, who examined him for some indication of what he was thinking, found herself deeply unsettled to realize she had no idea at all.

He could excuse himself to dress for dinner or announce he was off to New South Wales to discover a new species of orchid—both options seemed equally possible.

"I was supposed to get you with child and then leave you to embroider samplers in the drawing room," he said in a tone that was striking in its insouciance. He slid one hand into his pocket as his shoulders, visibly loosened, drew away from the door. "I was supposed to show you off at the theater and then visit my mistress. I was supposed to laud your hostessing skills and then play whist at my club while discussing horseflesh."

He took a step forward with the same casual grace, his eyes faintly amused as he contemplated how drastically his life had diverged from its expected path. Bea understood perfectly, for her own life had gone wildly off course the moment she met him, and although she could not conceive what this observation had to do with her concerns, she was relieved to be taken seriously.

It was always so easy to dismiss a woman's complaints.

"That was the marriage I was supposed to have," he said softly, so close to her now she could feel the flutter of his breath on her cheek. "That was the union into which I was raised from birth to enter. You know it well, for you delight in reminding me of the beautiful porcelain figurine who would have decorated my home if I had just made the correct choices."

It was a dizzying sweep for Bea, the arc from despairing to hopeful, and she felt oddly lightheaded. Flustered by the sensation, which was as unusual as it was disquieting, she strove for the familiar and, recalling the exchange to which he referred, exhorted him to remember the children. "And the perfect little cherubs she would have produced. I frequently mock you for them as well."

Kesgrave's lips twitched—ah, yes, now *that* was familiar—as he swore he had not forgotten anything. "I am counting on you, Bea, to provide me with the least cherubic children in all of Christendom."

Breathless now, she said, "Feisty devils, your grace, who track mud into the drawing room and slurp their soup."

"And a fiend of a girl who will petition Oxford for admission," he added with steady confidence that made Beatrice gasp.

How was it possible that his vision was so much bolder than her own? She was the upstart who did not know her place, and he was the avatar of an entrenched aristocracy stretching back centuries.

It should have been the other way around.

Or should it, she thought, contemplating the solidity of roots that dug into the earth five hundred years deep.

What a sturdy tree that would produce.

"Truly, Bea, how could I have imagined this?" he asked with curiosity and wonder, as if genuinely baffled by the turn that had tilted him toward an inexplicable fate. "With everything I am and everything I was raised to be, how could I have ever conceived of a marriage between equals and having attained it, how could I know the correct way to go about it all the time? I am sorry for sending the note to the constable without discussing it with you first and will send a second letter at once explaining I made a mistake."

"Thank you," Bea said with a calm nod, although in fact her heart was thumping and her blood was pounding and her arms were trembling slightly with relief and happiness. Although she possessed no greater understanding than he of the strange events that had delivered them here—to this ugly room in his stunning home, yes, but also to a union forged in love and respect—she no longer believed the duke was an unfathomable anomaly.

He was merely the fruit of a very sturdy tree.

"Of course, Stribley will think me mad when I send him another missive ten minutes later reversing my mistake," Kesgrave added pensively, "for that is how long it will take me to persuade you that allowing him and the magistrate to sort out the matter is the correct course of action."

But Bea was not convinced of even this minor point, for

she felt certain his calculation had failed to take into account several significant factors, including her obstinacy and skill at mounting a cogent argument.

Also overlooked in his estimate, she thought, as she pressed her lips gently to his, were the minutes lost to the expression of her gratitude. Given how ardently he returned the sentiment, clutching her shoulders with a hint of desperation as he pulled her closer, anything under an hour might be grossly inaccurate.

"I believe someone was boasting earlier about not needing a bed," she murmured, with a meaningful glance at the settee.

Kesgrave chuckled lightly between kisses, and spinning her around so her back was against the door, said, "I believe he is prepared now to boast about not needing a sofa."

Her excitement rising to an unbearable pitch, Bea deepened the kiss and when she felt a vibration course through her, she assumed it was the effects of desire before she realized it was a knock on the door.

If the duke heard it too, he was just as determined to ignore it, and when Joseph called out, Kesgrave ordered him to come back later.

And still the footman persisted, apologizing profusely while asking if his grace was sure he wanted to refuse the caller without at least speaking to him briefly. "Jenkins insisted you would want to talk to him immediately."

Sighing with regret, Kesgrave lowered his forehead to Bea's and said, "I'm sorry, my love."

But she assured him there was no need to apologize. "I am curious to see whom Jenkins considers an urgent visitor. He is too sensible to waste your time with a flower seller."

Kesgrave conceded this was true but still resented the interruption to a very pleasurable activity, which his grumbling made plain as Bea stepped to the side to allow him to open the door. There, on the other side, was a large man, not in a tall or towering way but like a barrel, wide and deep. His shoulders were stout, his arms were thick, and his chest was broad. His clothes were neat, slightly worn but well cared for, but his body was scuffed. He was missing a nail on his left hand, a recent scratch ran the column of his neck, and his nose was an ill-shaped knot in the middle of his face. His eyes were pale, almost a nonshade of blue, and they stared at her with ardent dislike.

It was, Bea noted, extremely disconcerting to be confronted with such vicious malice in the hallway of her very own home. After all, the visitor had presented himself at Kesgrave House voluntarily. Nobody had dragged him there by the ear.

Joseph, taking half a step forward, said, "This is Tom Trudgeon."

"No, me lad," he growled, annoyed by the introduction. "Tom Trudgeon is me father. I am Thomas 'the Bludgeon' Trudgeon, but most folks call me Bludge. Now I understand we need to have a chat."

And so saying, he stepped forthrightly into the room.

Chapter Thirteen

Bea wanted to run.

Truly, watching the man who had been hired to bludgeon her to death enter the back parlor terrified her in a way she had never before experienced.

It was visceral, to be sure, as if she understood the threat on some primal level, and yet utterly baffling. He could not hurt her, not with the duke next to her and Joseph nearby and the whole staff alerted to his presence, and it was not as though a man who lived by his wits and his fists would be so blank-brained as to seek out his quarry via the front door.

He meant her no harm, at least not now, and if something in their conversation should cause him to change his mind, his success was not assured. Even without Kesgrave et al. at the ready, she had managed to defend herself against a determined killer while depriving him of sight in one eye.

She was not an easy target, and after besting Bentham, she confronted him fearlessly here in this very room, demanding answers while he glared at her malevolently.

Perhaps that was the difference, Bea thought, for she did not know if she would have triumphed in a confrontation with Trudgeon and felt with sickening certainty that she would not.

Not with those fists, already like hammers.

And he was younger than Bentham by a good fifteen years —quicker, she thought, and stronger.

Because the desire to flee was so intense, Bea tightened the muscles in her legs as if to make movement impossible, rooting herself firmly to the spot. Considerably more difficult was compelling her eyes upward to meet the seething hatred in his unsettlingly light eyes.

If Kesgrave felt any disquiet at the sudden appearance of his uncle's killer, he gave no indication as he greeted the man coolly. Then he dismissed Joseph with an equally brisk nod, although the footman was disinclined to leave and Trudgeon closed the door in his face.

'Twas a shocking act of presumption, Bea thought, and then jeered at herself for being so facile. The man was a murderer, for God's sake, and would have little compunction about violating the customs that regulated polite society.

"Ye got to call off yer dogs," Trudgeon said.

A plea for leniency was not what she was expecting from the hardened criminal, and her fear diminished as she became aware of his agitation.

He was afraid.

"Excuse me?" she asked, glancing curiously at the duke.

Could he be referring to the constable?

Had the usually inept law enforcement official actually discharged his duty with competence and skill?

It was an astonishing idea.

"Ye dogs," he said again, his voice rising sharply with impatience. "The constable and Hawes. Ye got to tell them I didn't do it. Because I didn't. I swear on me father's grave, milord was alive when I left that lawyer's office. I didn't touch him, not even a little bit. Why would I? He done nothing to me. But everyone thinks I killed him."

"We have nothing to do with Hawes," Kesgrave announced. "As I am sure you realize, he is law unto himself. But I am surprised to hear that he thinks you are guilty. He made no mention of you during our interview."

Trudgeon shook his head, slowly at first and then with increasing speed. "No, no, Hawes is convinced it was me. He had Nunley threaten me mam if I don't go surrender meself to him by noon tomorrow. You have to tell him it wasn't me. He'll believe it if he hears it from Quality. And it's the truth. I ain't lying. I never touched him. I had no reason to. Our business was done. We parted ways. No hard feelings."

Bea, recalling how eagerly Hawes had dangled Jordan as a suspect, wondered if he had intentionally misled them to keep the field clear for himself. If their next interview was with the solicitor, then he could pursue the real culprit without interference.

Well, obviously, yes, she thought, for the King of Saffron Hill could not allow one of his subjects to kill his partner without reprisal. To hold his territory, Hell and Fury Hawes had to keep an iron grip and demonstrate that nothing was beyond his control.

If that was the case, then Trudgeon's appearance at Kesgrave House was not remarkable. There were few people in the world with the power to counter the threat Hawes posed, the Duke of Kesgrave being among them, and securing his assistance, even if he had to beg for it, was a shrewd solution.

It would only prevail, however, if he was telling the truth, and Bea found it very difficult to believe that the man who went around London introducing himself as Thomas 'the Bludgeon' Trudgeon did not in fact bludgeon Lord Myles.

Just as he had been hired to bludgeon her.

Again, her eyes drifted to his hands, so large and thick, and further unsettled by his presence, she grappled for a way to regain her composure.

Inexplicably, Aunt Vera's voice popped into her head, as inconsequential as ever as she pontificated on the importance of decorum. It was an echo, Bea realized, of the endless lecture she had given during their sojourn in the Lake District.

Good, old-fashioned English courtesy would not cow a murderous brute, she thought, but perhaps taking refuge in the familiar might soothe her own nerves.

Consequently, she invited her guest to take a seat.

The first time she had taken her relative's advice and it was with a vile homicidal miscreant.

Aunt Vera would be horrified if she knew.

Trudgeon flinched at the suggestion and insisted that he was fine to stand.

"No, please, do sit," Bea insisted, "or I shall begin to think you are afraid of a settee."

An ornery expression swept across his features, and she felt his dislike keenly, which gave her an odd sense of control. Wielding it, she sought to make him angrier by assuring him the sofa was quite harmless. "It will not bite, I promise."

Although his face grew even darker, he held on to his temper, stomped over to the settee and threw himself onto the cushion with an almost comical petulance.

Taken aback by the peevishness, for it was staggering that one could be a ruthless murderer and recalcitrant child at the same time, she said, "I am sure you are regretting that you did not bludgeon me to death when you had the chance."

Softly, warningly, Kesgrave said her name and she acknowledged his concern with a fleeting smile. He was right. She had taunted Trudgeon enough.

Bea sat down in the armchair a few feet away and

explained that her only concern was seeing justice done. "If you can convince us you are not guilty of this particular crime, then we will call off the constable. We have less influence with Hawes, which I am sure you know, but we will send him a note informing him of our opinion. That is the best we can do."

Trudgeon, his fingers curled at his sides, narrowed his eyes as if expecting a trick. "Ye swear to it?"

"I do, yes," she said.

"And ye won't change yer mind?" he asked warily. "Even if ye don't like me answers or I says something that offends ye, ye'll still call them off?"

"I promise to hold fast to our agreement, Mr. Trudgeon, no matter how personally repulsed I am by your intention to kill me," she said with blithe indifference.

Kesgrave frowned at this comment but remained silent as he took the seat next to her.

"But you must tell us the truth or our agreement is nullified," she added, "and I fear that might be a challenge for you. Already, you have lied to us about your business with Lord Myles. You claim it was at an end, and that is patently not true."

At the charge, his knot of a nose twitched and a pugnacious look entered his pale eyes. "Who have ye been talking to? Who told ye that? It ain't true. Our business was over. Ain't no two ways about it."

His voice was low and growly, snarly and coarse, and Bea found it too easy to imagine its rumble ringing in her ears as he delivered blow after blow to her skull.

Grasping her hands together to keep them from shaking, she told him her proof was incontrovertible. "I am alive. If your business with Lord Myles had been concluded, then I would be dead. Can you deny it?"

"Yes, I do deny it! If it was just ye, then I would have

eagerly done the job. The Bludge always fulfills his contracts. Twenty years in the business, and I have never missed a single one. But after hiring me to kill ye, milord comes back with *him* too," he sneered bitterly, pointing a finger at Kesgrave as if the duke had personally ruined the agreement by inserting himself. "And now I got a problem on me hands, don't I, because *he* is directly related to milord. Yer just a woman from a nothing family, nobody cares what happens to ye, but milord's nephew, the current duke? That's gonna draw attention, and mebbe people start to think Hawes is behind it. Mebbe it's a warning or a reprisal or mebbe he just wants to remind his partner who's in charge. I dunno for sure what everyone will think, but I can see it being a problem. Because the duke is a duke and now Quality cares, and the Runners poke their nose into the Hill's business and Hawes is furious. I'm brave but not reckless. I know when to back off."

If Kesgrave felt anything—rage, horror, disgust—at hearing his wife's death discussed in such matter-of-fact terms, it was not in evidence as he asked Trudgeon how his uncle responded to his refusal to accept the offer.

The ruthless killer sneered at the question and explained with marked condescension that a man of business such as himself never refused an assignment. "Ye need to keep your options open because ye never know when something is gonna change. A setback can become an opportunity. So I didn't refuse. I just raised me price. By rights, killing two people should cost twice as much as killing one, but I quadrupled the fee. But that was fair, wasn't it, because the both of ye is more dangerous for me. A husband and wife and Quality too, that's gonna draw heat. I can take it. Don't ye doubt that. But it comes at a price and if milord had met it, I would have gone through with it because that's the requirement of the job. I knew he wouldn't have the money, though, because he argued with me over the price for the duchess," he said, and turned to Bea with an apologetic look. "I thought ye were worth ten pounds, yer grace, but he insisted on five and wouldn't agree to one farthing more."

It was not contrition, Bea realized as he tilted his eyes downward, but embarrassment. Having discussed her brutal murder without flinching, the Bludge was mortified to admit that he had accepted a lower rate for its commission.

"Ordinarily, I would have told him no deal," he added in a subdued tone. "That's just good business because customers only value yer service as highly as ye do, and I can't let it be known that I'll work for less. Ye gotta have standards. But me mam is sick and needs money for medicine. I can't give me mam money for medicine if Hawes kills me, though. So I raised me fee. I said it was four times as much for the two. That did not make milord happy. No, he was incensed and seethed that it was robbery of the worst kind. Adding the duke should only double the cost—and that was at most. He thought it should be only a portion of what he paid for the duchess. That was outrageous! Because the duchess had already been marked down. So now he wanted me to do two people for three-quarters of what I usually charge for one!"

Here, again, his face pinched with shame as a light flush shaded his cheeks, and Bea braced for another apology. He merely shook his head, however, and fixed his gaze on hers.

"I stood firm this time," he said with a trace of pride and she wondered if he expected her to congratulate him. "I had to, didn't I? The rate was already so low that adding the duke would almost be like throwing him in for free. I couldn't let *that* get around, could I? Ain't good for business. I refused, and milord swore up and down he would get me the money. He was about to come into a great fortune, he said, and promised to pay me fee with interest if I extended him credit."

Trudgeon all but spit out the word, shaking his head in

disgust. "Credit! As if I was a fishmonger or a linen merchant in Covent Gardens. I ain't no clunch, performing a service on the expectation of getting paid one day. Ye want me hammer, you pay for the swings."

Bea commended him on remaining true to his principles. "You cannot go around London killing people for free. That would be a terrible business model."

Detecting the sarcasm in her tone, Trudgeon nevertheless insisted that her observation was correct and reminded her of his mother. "Ridicule me all ye like, yer grace, but I have obligations. Me poor mam is suffering."

Although Bea was not entirely convinced of the woman's existence, she imagined every villain required a mitigating factor or two to make himself slightly less villainous in his own eyes. If it was not an ill parent, then it was a sickly child.

But of course her understanding of the situation was far too simplistic, for no small boy ran around the slums of London thinking he wanted to be a hired killer when he grew older.

Young Thomas Trudgeon had probably had other dreams.

And yet look at him now, Bea thought, her eyes drawn again to the misshapen nose. How many blows had it sustained to end up so deformed?

Returning her attention to the topic at hand, she asked if Lord Myles mentioned the source of his anticipated wealth.

The question drew a cackle from her visitor, who tittered in genuine amusement as he answered, "A gin machine. He was going to make a great fortune on a new and improved machine that distilled gin faster than anyone had ever seen. Going to change the way gin was made, it was. Ye never heard a man yammer on with such fawning wonder about some pipes and coils. Ye'd think it was a lightskirt the way he talked about its parts. It was embarrassing. I couldn't look at him because it was so hard to hold in me laughter."

"You did not believe his invention had any value?" Bea asked.

Trudgeon belittled the query. "I didn't care, did I? I work for cash and cash only. If ye want to hire me for a job, then hand over the blunt or be on your way. Don't rattle on about patents and stocks and huge profits that will take years to earn. That's what I said to him. I says, either pay me the amount we agreed to for the duchess and I'll get on with it or allow me to leave. He did neither."

"Neither?" she asked sharply.

"He stood in my way, didn't he? Planted himself in front of me like a tree and said we weren't done yet. I said we were and shoved him aside," he explained, then quickly amended the sentence to say it had been a push. "A light push. A brush like I'm walking past ye in a crowded street. If milord had a mark on his shoulder, that's only because his skin is weak, not because I hurt him. He was fine when I left, I tell ye. Perfectly fine. Cursing at me while I walked to the door. Ye gotta tell Hawes that. Yer Quality. He'll believe you. You have to. Please. I can't die. Who would take care of me mam?"

The irony was not lost on Bea, the man who had been happy to kill her for five pounds—less than the maid in the scullery was paid for a year of work—begging her now to spare his life, and she took her time evaluating the situation. Although she could not permit her feelings for her would-be murderer to affect her judgment, she readily allowed them to draw out the moment as she considered the trustworthiness of the man before her.

He certainly did not have a lot to recommend him except for the fact that he was here, pleading his case, when he could have been long gone from London. Having identified himself as a practical man of business, Trudgeon hardly seemed likely to linger in the city if he was being pursued for a crime of which he was actually guilty. Surely, his calculation in that case would be to cut his losses and flee.

Ah, but there was his mother to consider.

Could concern for her welfare convince him to play a desperate game that might end in his ruin?

And even if his poor mam was merely an invention to earn her sympathy, he would have other ties to Saffron Hill, for it was the place in which he had built his successful career as an assassin. If he was forced to abscond to an unfamiliar city he would have to start over from the beginning, painstakingly establishing new connections until he was once again deemed a reliable resource for the termination of one's enemies.

He could not relish the prospect of beginning anew, and earning the Duchess of Kesgrave's support might preclude the necessity.

This was true, Bea thought, and yet she could not deny there was something persuasively candid about the way he spoke of her murder. If he was acting out of clearheaded manipulation, then he would have realized the value of rounding the rough edges of his story—claiming, for example, that Lord Myles had tricked him into taking on the job of her murder or that he was only pretending to go along to earn his trust.

There were any number of stories he could have told to make himself look like less of a blackguard than admitting that the value of her life had been bargained away.

His honesty felt like the result of panic, as if the threat of Hawes so undermined his ability to think he simply could not come up with a more calculating story. Confessing every detail, no matter how unsavory, and throwing himself on their mercy was the only approach his terrified mind could devise.

It struck her as more likely than the other option—that the disagreement between the two men grew so heated that

Trudgeon bludgeoned his former employer to death in a fit of anger. She simply could not conceive what Lord Myles could say that would move the professional killer to irrepressible fury.

And of that, Bea was convinced. Trudgeon was too much of a professional to ply his trade for free without proper provocation. The situation, for all the dark menace of murder for hire, was actually relatively benign. Lord Myles was simply a customer trying to secure a deal on terms most beneficial to him, which was something Trudgeon would understand. He might resent the implication that he was no better than a fishmonger or a linen merchant, but he certainly would not bludgeon a man to death for suggesting he accept credit.

It was bad for business.

With that in mind, Bea decided his description of events was probably accurate—with the exception of the light push on his way out. She had no doubt that was in fact a very hard shove.

Sighing with reluctance, she moved Trudgeon to the bottom of her list.

"What time did you leave?" she asked.

"Three thirteen," he said immediately.

"That is strikingly precise," she observed.

His features curled defensively as he replied that it *was* striking. "I thought I'd been bracketed in with him for more than an hour listening to him yammer on about his stupid contraption and then I open the office door and the clock is staring me in the face. Only thirteen minutes had gone by," he said with a shake of his head, as if confused by it still. "Damned thing must be broken."

Bea, who had noticed the sparseness of the small antechamber, with its lone desk and bare walls, found this statement curious. "You mean as soon as you opened the door to the corridor?"

"No, the office door that leads to the small room," Trudgeon said. "I saw the clock in the hallway."

But that did not make sense.

"If you saw the clock in the entry from Jordan's office, then the door to the antechamber was open," she said.

"It was," Trudgeon confirmed.

When he remained oblivious to the implication, Bea was forced to remind him that he himself had closed that door.

Shocked by this comment, he stared at her in awe for several long seconds. "I *did* close it. How did you know that?"

She enjoyed a few brief moments of being perceived as omniscient before providing the explanation, which was considerably more prosaic. "You closed the door to this room, which indicates to me that it's a deeply ingrained habit."

Startled again, he allowed that this was true. Yes, indeed, it was, for a man of his vocation must employ as many precautions as possible. "You never know who might be listening."

"True," Bea conceded.

Despite taking measures, Trudgeon had not been careful enough in Jordan's office, for it was clear that someone had been in the antechamber and left without closing the door— either because they forgot or did not have time for such niceties.

Tyne, of course, was the most obvious contender. He returned to the office at three-thirty, but that was by his own account. In truth, the time could have been twenty minutes earlier, making him privy to the conversation between Lord Myles and Trudgeon. It was easy to imagine the timid clerk feeling terror at the discovery and running away.

Jordan, of course, was the other, more likely possibility, for it aligned with her prevailing theory. Having decided to listen to the conversation, he might have been taken aback by how abruptly it ended. Unprepared for Trudgeon to come striding out of the office, he might have scurried away quickly to evade discovery. Then, after he was sure Trudgeon was gone, he would have crept back into his office to assault Lord Myles.

Although it made sense to Bea, she could not allow personal enmity to influence her reasoning, so she also constructed a case for Tyne as well. It was difficult because she could not imagine what antipathy he might hold against Lord Myles, a man with whom he had minimal contact, according to Jordan. A lack of interaction, she reminded herself, did not mean an absence of judgment, and perhaps the clerk had good cause to resent his lordship. The victim might have been cruel to him in a million little ways.

Oh, but the list of candidates did not end with Tyne and his employer. The informality among the solicitors who worked on the floor meant that any one of them could have entered the antechamber unseen. Overhearing the shocking conversation, the lawyer might have seized the opportunity to blackmail Lord Myles in exchange for his silence or tried to dissuade him and despite his intentions the scene spiraled wildly out of control. Before he knew it, Lord Myles lay sprawled on the rug with his skull shattered.

Or maybe he loathed his lordship for an as-yet-unknown reason and seeing an opening, acted impulsively.

Either way, she felt certain Lord Myles's murder had been spontaneously committed, which made Trudgeon even less likely to be the culprit. A man who openly admitted to ruthlessly haggling over the value of a duchess's life would not succumb to an impulse.

He was simply too much of a businessman to act without a plan.

Removing him as a suspect did little to whittle her list, for she now had the entire floor at number 8 Tucks Court to consider if not the whole building.

It was, she thought, disheartening to acquire new suspects.

Seemingly just as disconcerted as Bea by the revelation of an interloper in the office, Trudgeon insisted that he had not heard a sound. "I have very sharp ears, ye know. I'm always alert. It's necessary in me business to know what's happening around me. I didn't hear him at all. Quiet as a mouse, he was."

Bea expected him to insist that she discover the intruder's identity so she could prove his innocence to Hawes and the constable. But having lowered himself to begging repeatedly, he appeared determined to leave with a modicum of dignity and thanked her for receiving him. Then, as if embarrassed by the whole ordeal, he bowed in Kesgrave's general direction and opened the door to leave.

Marlow himself was hovering just outside the room, which was, Bea allowed, not at all unexpected. Obviously, he would be disinclined to trust anyone but himself to successfully escort a known assassin from the premises.

"Thank you, Marlow," she murmured, closing the door to explain her prevailing theory to Kesgrave. Clearly, they would need to interview all the solicitors at Tucks Court as suspects, not just witnesses, which was how—

All thought was halted the moment she turned, for there was Kesgrave, his hands clutching her shoulders as he pressed her back against the door and his lips reclaimed hers, determined to pick up the activity exactly where they had left off.

No, she realized, not resuming.

This was different, she thought, as her bones weakened in response, her stomach quivering with desire as he deepened the kiss. He was more intent now, more fervent and determined, fiercer and stronger, in the wake of the threat.

She understood, yes, why he would react with such fire, having spent the past twenty minutes listening to a ruthless killer calmly discuss her death as a business proposition. The theorizing tenor of it, the fact that it existed as an untested hypothesis, was daunting in a way Bentham's actual attack was not. She had felt it herself.

After several wonderful minutes, Kesgrave's intensity lessened and his kiss gentled. Eventually, he lifted his head and looked at her with a disapproving frown, which she found comical in light of their recent activity. She was reasonably sure she had not given offense by yielding so eagerly to his ardor.

"I would be grateful if the next time we entertain a murderous brute in the back parlor, you could refrain from provoking him," Kesgrave said mildly.

Naturally, she thought this charge was highly unfair, as she had only discussed various aspects of the man's business that were relevant to the topic, including but not limited to his intention to kill her. But rather than quibble over what was really a very minor point, she took issue with his aggressively fatalistic stance. "I am certain we will never again entertain a murderous brute in the back parlor."

"In the drawing room, then," he immediately amended, "or the library, conservatory, bedchamber, office of rout cake enjoyment—"

"Consumption," she interjected with a sad shake of her head. "As long as chef André insists on inserting pineapple chunks in my rout cakes, I will derive no joy from them."

His lips twitched in faint amusement. "And yet you will continue to consume them?"

"I am disgruntled, your grace, not deranged," she replied.

He acknowledged the distinction with a nod and said, "Nevertheless, my point remains. Regardless of which room we happen to be in the next time a murderous brute pays us a call, do try to be a little less provoking."

As the inclusion of the word *try* meant she had to make only the most meager of efforts to be in compliance with his request, Bea readily agreed. Then she added that she believed Trudgeon was innocent of Lord Myles's murder because it would never do for a professional assassin to go around killing his clients. "He is a levelheaded if conscience-less man of business who makes decisions based on his own interests. Bludgeoning your uncle because he was annoyed at him for negotiating his fee is not a sound business practice."

Kesgrave, leading her to the settee and retaining posses-sion of her hand as they sat, agreed with her conclusion. "I will send Jenkins with a note to Stribley alerting him to my mistake, but I do not think we can do anything about Hawes. In fact, my prevailing theory is that Hawes is responsible after all and merely laying the blame on a convenient target."

Bea allowed it was possible, for although Trudgeon appeared to be among Hawes's legion of eager minions, there was no telling what caprice lay at the heart of a powerful crime lord's actions. Maybe Trudgeon had pricked Hawes's ego with some insignificant offense, or perhaps he was just conveniently expendable.

"I fear now we must also consider the various lawyers who work on the same floor in Tucks Court," she said. "As Caruthers noted, they wander in and out of each other's offices freely. Any one of them could have entered the antechamber, overheard the discussion and decided to act for reasons we have yet to discern. Lord Myles showed himself to have been a highly dishonorable person and is no doubt responsible for a half dozen other betrayals of which we remain ignorant. Our next step must be to interrogate every occupant of the building."

"I am not sure the open door is quite as significant as you think," he said. "Given that my uncle was arguing over the price of our death, I think any solicitor who overheard the conversation would leave as quickly and as silently as he had arrived. No man wishes to be caught eavesdropping on a murder for hire."

"Or he was excited by his unexpected good fortune and promptly concocted a scheme to extort money from your uncle," Bea countered.

"Extort money from the man he just heard crying poverty —and to some length if Trudgeon's version is to be believed?" Kesgrave asked doubtfully. "I would think any reasonable-minded solicitor would be clever enough to know you cannot draw blood from a stone."

"But your uncle's invention," she reminded him. "You yourself said it is an ingenious device, and if the interloper believed it would bring the great wealth Lord Myles swore to Trudgeon it would, then blackmail would not be inconceivable. Consider it, Kesgrave. He hovers in the hallway until Trudgeon leaves and confronts Lord Myles, swearing to reveal the truth to you or the authorities if he does not add his name the patent. Lord Myles refuses and picks up the candlestick, intending to kill the witness who could ruin everything, but after a brief struggle—brief because his clothes were not disheveled—he is disarmed and is bludgeoned himself."

A faint smile hovered over Kesgrave's lips as he contemplated her theory, which he considered outlandish from top to bottom. "I can no more see my uncle waving a candlestick threateningly at a grown man, as he much prefers terrorizing small children, than I can conceive of him inventing anything but excuses."

Taken aback by this observation, Bea shifted her position so that she could look him in the eyes. "You mean to say, you do not think the modified still is his invention?"

Further amused by the query, he replied, "You mean to say that you do?"

There was something about his tone that mortified her—

the cynicism, perhaps, or maybe the certainty—and she foundered for a response that did not make her appear entirely without wits. "Given Lord Myles's agility in evading his creditors and responsibility, it seemed possible that he possessed the mental acuity to tinker with the existing structure just enough to improve...its ... functionality...and..."

Bea trailed off as an unsettling sensation overcame her and she realized she had heard those words before.

Not them exactly, no, but something similar that expressed the same idea.

Closing her eyes, she tried to focus on a voice.

It was male and admiring.

Caruthers!

That was it, yes, the disgraced solicitor from Lyon's Inn commenting on Tyne's ingenuity in creating an improved system for filing documents in Jordan's office. *He tinkered with those cabinets to allow them to accommodate more papers. It is actually a very clever use of space.*

Now, at once, it was startlingly clear who the inventor was.

Of course it was Tyne—ingenious tinkerer, relentless fiddler.

How absurd to believe for even one moment that a man of Lord Myles's temperament was capable of anything so meticulous and precise as the modified column still. He did not possess the patience for painstaking minor improvements.

He preferred broad strokes, not subtlety, she thought, bounding to her feet as the meaning of the distillery's name struck her.

It was so clear now: Longway & River.

Long way meaning "miles", and *river* referred to the Tyne, the waterway in Newcastle.

And the catarrh!

Despite Jordan's insistence that the victim had minimal contact with his clerk, Lord Myles knew Tyne well enough to ask after his father's health.

What had he said?

Because he knows he has a touch of catarrh.

Agitated by the revelation, she paced across the room, applying this new information to the crime and seeing how that changed its complexion.

The eavesdropper, she thought. Assume it was Tyne.

Returning from his errands, he entered the antechamber in time to hear Lord Myles swearing that his patent on the modified column still would bring in thousands of pounds.

How infuriating that must have been—an entitled nobleman who had wasted every advantage he had ever been given stealing the invention an impoverished law clerk had labored over for weeks.

Or possibly months.

Bea had no idea how difficult it was to improve the column still.

The longer he listened, the deeper his fury grew until he felt an all-consuming rage. Hearing Trudgeon approach the door, Tyne scurried from the office, waited for the other man to leave before returning to confront Lord Myles.

Perhaps they argued.

Perhaps Tyne picked up the first thing he saw and struck.

Either way, when it was over, Lord Myles lay dead on the floor, blood from his bludgeoned skull seeping into the woolen rug.

It must have hit him then, the gravity of the situation, and with wild, desperate eyes he looked around the room, seeking something...anything...he could use to extricate himself.

Bea did the same now, reviewing the items in Jordan's office: desk, chairs, cabinet, trunk.

The trunk!

It was the perfect size for storing a human body.

She had noted that herself, picturing Hawes within its narrow confines, his knees tucked under his chin to make his long body fit.

And its contents had been strewn across the floor as if someone had emptied it in a hurry.

Good lord, how oblivious could one woman be?

Obviously, it was the trunk. Tyne intended to use it to remove Lord Myles from the premises.

The plan, Bea allowed, was reasonable. It required someone to help him carry the heavy chest out of the office, presumably in the dead of night, but it was easy enough to find that kind of assistance on the docks with a few shillings. The bigger challenge was figuring out where to stow all those sheets of paper.

Perhaps he had planned to shove them all under his desk and behind the cabinets.

She wondered if he had even progressed that far in his planning.

Shoving the body into the trunk would have been his first and most pressing goal.

Everything else would be fine if he could just hide the bludgeoned corpse.

What relief he must have felt to have concocted a scheme.

And then in walked the duke.

Of all the rotten turns fate could have dealt him!

Imagining his terror at Kesgrave's presence, Bea wondered how Tyne had timed the encounter so precisely. Somehow, he managed to run out of Jordan's office at the exact moment the duke entered it.

Something alerted him to his presence.

Pacing wildly across the room, she paused for a moment

and closed her eyes, recalling the antechamber, with its square table, plaster walls and dark-painted wooden planks.

Yes, yes, its dark-painted wooden planks that *creaked*.

Tyne knew well the groans the floorboards made, for he tread them daily. As soon as Kesgrave stepped into the antechamber, he would have recognized the sound of a visitor and dashed from the office as quickly as possible.

His next move was probably not as clear to him, she thought.

Having escaped the scene of the murder with his freedom intact, he must have considered taking permanent leave of the city. He had been lucky so far, wresting his arm from the duke's grasp, but he could not rely on that to sustain.

He was guilty, and a guilty man had no business remaining in the capital.

Oh, but he had such a good life here: a sufficient income, a comfortable home, the solace of family.

And what could anyone prove?

An inkling was not evidence, and why would anyone look at him with suspicion—an efficient, harmless, timid law clerk —when the most ruthless crime lord in all of London bore a grudge against the victim?

Bea wondered if the idea to blame Hawes had occurred to Tyne while he was actually hiding behind barrels of fish or if he had deliberately sought out the pungent filth of the docks to make his story more convincing.

Ultimately, it did not matter, for she had been persuaded by the picture he presented.

She rather thought anyone would, for Hawes was the better villain by every measure. Tall and commanding, he was already guilty of dozens of crimes, including murder, a fact to which he proudly attested. With his vast underworld empire of rogues and thieves, he could have arranged Lord Myles's demise with barely the flick of his wrist.

In contrast, Tyne was small, meek and terrified.

Sending Bea and the duke into the murky filth of Saffron Hill was the only smart thing to do, for it would all but guarantee that clarity would elude them.

There, Tyne had made a misstep, perhaps his first one since concocting his clever scheme. Not only had he underestimated her tenacity but he also overestimated Hawes's brutality. The likelihood of the Duchess of Kesgrave sitting down for a chat with the King of Saffron Hill must have seemed vanishingly small to him. He would have naturally assumed there would be aversion on both sides.

Instead, they had had a productive if uneasy discussion.

Bea had left the meeting with new questions and another suspect to pursue, which had, through the familiar circuitous path of a murder investigation, brought her back to the beginning.

Of course the killer was the man caught fleeing the side of the dead body.

Her agitation settled as she acknowledged the necessity of the process, of the investigation itself, with its requisite twists and turns, for Tyne had been correct in his presumption: An inkling was not evidence.

Even if she had been convinced of his guilt from the outset, she had no proof.

Now she had a theory that could withstand scrutiny.

The rest would follow.

Drawing a deep breath, she stopped pacing and looked up to find the duke watching her. His expression displayed no impatience, only curiosity.

Absently, she wondered how much time had passed since she had realized Tyne was the inventor of the modified column still.

Mildly, he said, "I am relieved to discover we will not have to conduct interviews with almost two dozen occupants at

Tucks Court. I know you consider me an affirmed pedant, but there are some levels of thoroughness to which even I take exception. I would have lent my assistance, of course, for I know how tenuous my position is and that Flora stands ready and eager to supplant me, but I would have begrudged the effort."

Shaking her head placatingly, Bea returned to the settee and assured him Flora would never dare such a presumption. "She is a Hyde-Clare, after all, and would insist on only temporarily replacing you."

"You put my mind at ease," he said, reaching for her hand. "Now do tell me whom I should instruct the constable to apprehend, so that we may put this matter to rest. I would like to pay a call on my grandmother before dinner."

"It was Tyne," she said, wondering if knowing the circumstances of her son's brutal murder would provide the dowager with any comfort. "He was your uncle's business partner in the distillery and the one who invented the modified still. Recall, if you will, it was he who devised Jordan's clever filing cupboard. Presumably, overhearing Lord Myles's plan to patent his invention sent him into a murderous rage. I suppose he did not put in the application himself because he could not afford it. I believe you said it was a lengthy process requiring two dozen signatures, stamps, warrants and seals."

"Well beyond the means of a clerk who does not have a benefactor," he said with a thoughtful nod, as if all this information made sense to him. "I should have realized the connection sooner given the names. I knew *long way* meant 'Myles' because my father liked to say that their parents named him 'miles' because he was a long way from the dukedom. But I attributed *river* to the New River in Clerkenwell, near the distillery. Knowing my uncle could never devise anything so clever, I naturally assumed one of his workers did, which would have conferred ownership rights on him. I seem to be in possession of several facts that would have made your investigation easier, and I apologize for not sharing them sooner."

"Given that barely twenty-four hours have passed since your uncle was murdered, I think we can both agree that *sooner* is a relative term. No harm has been done, except to Trudgeon, whose pride took a drubbing when he was forced to request help from his would-be victims. And even he is satisfied," Bea pointed out, and as she made the observation she found herself struck by the ruthless killer's sanguinity. The simple fact of a witness in the antechamber did not absolve him of guilt. All it did was imply there was a way to prove his innocence. Before that could happen, however, the person would have to be found and questioned. If the eavesdropper was the killer himself, that process would be quite arduous, especially as there were so many solicitors in the building to interview.

But these potential challenges had not weighed on Trudgeon, who had walked out of the room as if his problem had been resolved.

Only now did it occur to Bea to wonder about his attitude.

If he was confident his problem had been resolved, then none of the perceived difficulties of the situation applied to him.

That was to say, he saw a simple solution.

Deciding that the simple solution was the obvious one, she realized Trudgeon knew the interloper was Tyne. Aside from Jordan, he was the only person who would have been in the antechamber in the regular course of events, and the solicitor's well-aired indignation at meeting with a killer in his own office removed him from contention.

Harder to figure out was if this information had any significance.

What did it mean for Trudgeon to know the witness's identity?

The fact that he had come to Kesgrave House seeking their help indicated that he knew Hawes would not simply take him at his word. He required substantiation.

Tyne would be his proof.

His proof, she thought, vaulting to her feet again in agitation as yet another thought occurred to her. If Trudgeon was in fact the killer, then Tyne was a threat that had to be eliminated.

Was it really possible that events had unfolded precisely as Tyne had insisted that very morning?

If that was the case, why did he not mention that he had personally observed the terrible event?

Because he was too scared?

Possibly.

Or was she now making the situation more complicated than it was?

Desperately uncertain, she turned to the duke, who had also risen, and said, "We must find Tyne. There is no time to waste."

Although his brow furrowed as if he wanted to disagree, Kesgrave nodded sharply and called for Marlow to fetch Jenkins.

Chapter Fourteen

❧❀❧

Bea and the duke were still discussing the relative merits of Tyne's guilt versus Trudgeon's when they arrived at 24 Leather Lane to see the law clerk leap from a second-story window onto the low roof of the building next door. The descent was steep, about eight feet, and there was a three-foot gap between structures. Tyne's legs flapped in midair, as if he were running, and he landed on the hard surface, his knees collapsing beneath him. He lay still for a moment, then rolled onto his stomach and bounded to his feet.

A few seconds later, Trudgeon poked his head out of the window and blanched at either the drop or the distance. Then he climbed out onto the sash, and after two false starts, forced himself to make the jump. More nimble than Tyne, he remained upright, teetering slightly upon landing.

By the time he regained his balance, his quarry was hanging off the edge of the roof. Tyne released his grip and fell to the pavement, alighting in front of a flower seller, who shrieked in surprise at his sudden appearance and dropped an armful of roses. Tyne crushed them underfoot as he spun around, his gaze flying left, then right, before darting into the road. Evading a curricle, he crossed to the other side.

Baffled by events, compelled by instinct, Bea ran after him. Without pausing to look, she dashed into the street. A horse neighed loudly as its rider tugged its reins abruptly, and Kesgrave's shout of alarm was drowned out by the rattle of a carriage that passed behind her as she stepped onto the pavement. She caught a flash of Tyne's gray coat to her left and gave chase, dodging pedestrians and carts. It was not easy, for her half-boots were ill suited to the task and she had to lift the hem of her dress to widen her stride and avoid tripping. Still bedecked in her Saffron Hill finery, she cut an absurd picture, barreling down the narrow street, her elegant gown hitched and her diamond earrings flailing.

Rounding the bend onto Greville, she felt a fresh gust of wind as Kesgrave flew past her followed a few paces behind by Trudgeon, who was surprisingly swift for a man of such heft.

Her lungs burned as she redoubled her exertion, raising her skirt even higher so that now she could feel the breeze on her calves.

Tyne's gray coat disappeared around another corner, and she promptly lost sight of the duke.

Gasping painfully, she looped around the curve and almost smashed into Trudgeon, who was standing in the middle of the pavement. She pulled up sharply, twisting to the side to avoid contact, and struggled to regain her equilibrium as momentum carried her shoulders forward even as her feet stopped. Holding her arms out for balance, she found herself clutching the fawn-colored superfine of Hawes's tailcoat. She stared at him with confusion, which only deepened as a man marched up to Trudgeon, seemingly out of nowhere, grabbed him by the scruff of his collar and called out, "Here you go, your grace, Mr. Thomas 'the Bludgeon' Trudgeon, apprehended by the constabulary precisely as you requested."

Bea, her astonishment so acute she tightened her grip on Hawes's arm, swiveled her head to the right to where Kesgrave was standing over Tyne. The law clerk, trapped on two sides by a vegetable cart and a building, stared pugnaciously at the duke.

Trudgeon, either oblivious to the constable's presence or merely unconcerned by it, focused his attention on Hawes and professed his innocence. "It wasn't me, boss. I swear it. I never harmed a hair on milord's hair. It was that man. The clerk. The duchess will tell you. She knows it."

"Does she?" Hawes murmured, examining Bea with interest.

Mortified to realize she was still clutching his coat, she immediately dropped her hand and took several steps back. The constable scoffed dismissively at the claims of innocence and assured her grace that she did not have to answer to the riffraff.

"Indeed, this is an inhospitable part of town and I would urge you to depart from it at once," he added. "I will have one of my deputies escort you and the duke home safely."

Hawes, who had not risen to the top of a vast criminal enterprise only to be classified as disreputable by a law enforcement officer, protested the description. "You will find that in this part of town, *you* are the riffraff."

The constable's expression darkened as Trudgeon twisted free of his grasp and, walking over to Bea, begged her to corroborate his claim to Hawes. "Tell him what you told me. Someone was there, in the other room. Tell him it was Tyne. I know it was Tyne, the weaselly miscreant, aping my ways. He wanted you to think it was me. It's worse than murder, it is, setting someone up to take the blame."

Previously uncertain, Bea was convinced now of Tyne's

guilt. His motive was simply the more compelling one. Trudgeon, despite his eagerness to thrash the law clerk for daring to employ his methods, would never slay a patron in a bout of professional pique.

"I believe he returned to the office in time to hear your partner promising to pay Mr. Trudgeon's fee from the proceeds of his patented new invention," she said, addressing her explanation to Hawes. "The invention, in fact, was of Tyne's devising, and discovering that Lord Myles was trying to steal the proceeds, he responded with murderous fury."

The constable stepped heavily forward, gripping Trudgeon by the wrist to recapture his prisoner, who was too distracted to notice. Then he explained to Bea that her thinking was confused, which was understandable, given the unhealthy physical exertion in which she had just engaged. "Exercise muddles the female brain. It is a known fact. If you doubt it, you may ask my wife, for she is a prime example of its debilitating effects on a woman's ability to think clearly. She will, for example, come inside after working in the garden and say all sorts of inexplicable things to me, such as I do not work hard enough or I am an albatross around her neck. But you may put your mind at ease. This man is responsible for Lord Myles's murder. I have it directly from the duke himself, and he is infallible."

Kesgrave's lips twitched at this description, while Bea suggested the constable try his hand at weeding to mollify his wife. He blinked at her in confusion, apparently incapable of comprehending why mollification would be required of any husband.

Indeed, he was so puzzled by the prospect, he loosened his hold on Trudgeon, who inched several steps to the right without the constable noticing.

Hawes also took issue with Bea's conclusion because Tyne had known about the deception prior to overhearing the conversation. "It was the reason he sought me out last week. He needed money to fund his own patent application, and in exchange he informed me of Lord Myles's ownership of Longway & River, of which I had previously been unaware. He said his invention decreased the cost of gin production to a mere fraction, which meant that my partner was soaking me for more money than I could imagine."

To say Bea was baffled by this information would be to severely understate her level of confusion, for she was in fact utterly flummoxed. Her argument for Tyne's guilt hinged on the anger that overtook him when he discovered the truth about Lord Myles. If he had not been astonished by his lordship's deceit, then what spurred him to act? What was his motive if not irrepressible rage?

According to Hawes, Tyne had already come up with a satisfying measure to counter Lord Myles's duplicity. Swooping in and securing the patent first would certainly scotch his lordship's plans, especially since he possessed a far more comprehensive understanding of his own invention. Lord Myles's scribbling significantly misrepresented the complexity of the device.

Bewildered, Bea shifted her gaze to Kesgrave to see if he also found this revelation difficult to reconcile. Not surprisingly, his own eyes were focused on Hawes, whom he was examining with suspicion. Given his deep mistrust of the crime lord, his feelings were hardly surprising. Nevertheless, she took his response seriously and entertained the possibility that Hawes was lying about Tyne. The problem was, she could not conceive what he stood to gain by insisting Tyne had the information earlier than he actually did. All it did was help make the argument against the law clerk's guilt.

What end did that serve?

Maybe it was simply that Hawes wanted the other man free so that he could administer justice himself. Tyne had overstepped by killing Lord Myles. The King of Saffron Hill was judge, jury and executioner, and the law clerk had denied him the pleasure of deciding his lordship's fate. He had done it before, casting suspicion in Jordan's direction when he thought Trudgeon was guilty.

To a certain extent that made sense, for it aligned as well with Trudgeon's concern about drawing too much attention to Hawes's dealings by killing both the duchess and the duke.

Perhaps Hawes was simply angry that, thanks to Tyne's precipitous actions, he was now forced to endure the company of the Duke of Kesgrave and the parish constable.

Thoughtfully, Bea looked at Trudgeon, who had sidled so close to Tyne he now stood directly behind him. His expression intent, he raised his clenched fist in the air above the law clerk's head and began to lower it with the obvious intent of doing grievous harm.

She called out just as Kesgrave, realizing something was amiss, jerked Tyne to the side, removing him from Trudgeon's trajectory. Deprived of his victim and propelled forward by momentum, the ruthless assassin stumbled forward and tripped, falling to the ground and landing hard on his knees. He snarled viciously and glared daggers at Tyne as he rose to his feet.

It was stunning, his anger, she thought, that he was so incapable of containing it even though they were all right there—she, the duke, Hawes, even the constable.

And then it struck her: It was his rage that was significant, not Tyne's.

While Stribley apprehended his prisoner for the third time in ten minutes, Bea said to Hawes, "You were supposed to kill Lord Myles. That was Tyne's plan. He told you the truth about Lord Myles on the assumption that you would have him killed for his duplicity. Not only was he cheating the King of Saffron Hill, he was playing him for a fool, and surely that was enough to warrant his death. In a single stroke, Tyne would gain sole ownership of the distillery and eliminate the threat to his patent. But Lord Myles was actually worth more to you alive than dead, and being a dishonest dealer yourself, you had been operating your own deceitful schemes to gouge your partner. So you were content to let him live."

It was amazing, she thought, how neatly the events arranged themselves into an orderly line in her head.

Turning to Tyne, she added, "You could not stand it, waiting day after day for Hawes to make his move. What could possibly be the delay? Why was Lord Myles still drawing breath? How could Hell and Fury Hawes allow this trespass against him to stand? It must have driven you mad. And then yesterday, you return from your errands and there is Lord Myles bracketed in Jordan's office with Thomas 'the Bludgeon' Trudgeon! It is happening, you think. Finally, it is happening. But as you listen, you realize the Bludge has not been sent by Hawes to end him. He is there on a completely unrelated matter, and that is when you decide the circum-stance is too good to be denied. Trudgeon and his lordship in the very same room! If Lord Myles was found in a field blud-geoned to death after meeting with Trudgeon, then no one could doubt what had happened. It would be obvious. That was why you were emptying the trunk, to transport him to a field, and when you heard Kesgrave enter the antechamber, you panicked and ran out. But as soon as your head cleared, you realized it was still possible to point the finger at Trud-geon. That is why you implicated Hawes. You knew an inves-tigation of Hawes would reveal his many unsavory associates, including Trudgeon, whose methods matched the crime. You figured it was so easy to implicate Trudgeon there was no reason to leave town. You could stay and operate Longway & River and accrue a tidy fortune."

Trudgeon growled furiously and took a threatening step

toward Tyne. The constable, trying unsuccessfully to constrain him, tugged on his sleeve.

Calmly, Hawes said, "Thomas," and the ruffian responded at once, stiffening his posture and smoothing his features.

Bea looked then at Kesgrave, uncertain what was supposed to happen next. Tyne, to be sure, would be arrested for the murder of his uncle and made to stand trial. That was straightforward enough.

But what about Trudgeon?

He had agreed to murder her in cold blood in exchange for five pounds and had only failed to do so out of regard for his own well-being. If Lord Myles's ambition had remained safely limited in scope, then she would be at that very moment lying facedown on the Heath with her skull bashed in.

Surely, they could not allow such a dangerous man to simply disappear into the dark warrens of Saffron Hill to continue plying his trade.

But seeing him pay for his crimes would not be as simple as affixing handcuffs to his wrists and bringing him to Newgate, for he was an associate of Hawes's. A negotiation must be made so that the crime lord did not feel as though some boundary had been transgressed.

The expression on Kesgrave's face indicated that his thoughts ran along a similar line and perhaps out of concern for the thorniness of the situation, he sought Hawes's opinion.

Stating it plainly, the duke said, "From our prior conversation, I know you are aware of the regard with which I hold the duchess and I am confident you can see the dilemma in which we now find ourselves. Mr. Trudgeon accepted a contract to murder my wife, which he backed out of only when the stakes became too high. I cannot allow a trespass of that magnitude to go without punishment. There must be consequences."

Stribley, perceiving now the depth of his prisoner's iniquity, assured the duke that he would make sure he got the noose for daring to even think of harming the duchess.

Trudgeon started in surprise and protested that treatment was very unfair. "I apologized, didn't I?"

"Did you?" Kesgrave asked coolly.

In fact, he had not. Insisting repeatedly that his taking on the commission to murder Bea was only a matter of business, for he bore her no personal grudge, and under that circumstance, an apology was not appropriate. One did not offer one's regrets to a chicken before lowering one's cleaver.

"I threw myself on yer mercy," Trudgeon added with increasing anxiety. "I sought yer help. It was parley! Ye respect the rules of parley, don't ye, yer grace? Ye promised to call off the constable!"

Before Bea could point out that their deal was in regard to Lord Myles's murder, not her own, Tyne cried, "You owe m-m-me her life, your grace! He was going to do it. I heard every word exchanged between him and Lord M-Myles, and after it was clear that Lord M-Myles did not have the ready to p-p-pay for the two m-m-murders at once, he convinced him to p-pay for the duchess first. He said it would eliminate the immediate risk of an heir and then Lord M-Myles could come back in six months when he had more blunt to pay for the duke. He insisted it was the better business decision."

A feral sound rose in Trudgeon's throat as he leaped at Tyne, intending to knock him onto the pavement, but Kesgrave, sufficiently warned by the howl, jerked Tyne to the side while angling his elbow upward. It connected with Trudgeon's windpipe, sending the brute to his knees, gasping in agony.

Tyne, sensing an opportunity, added with heightened

fervor, "She'd be dead now if it wasn't for me. He planned to do it last night, at Mrs. Summerton's rout, which he said was sure to be a crush. I saved her life, your grace. I saved her for you. She'd be dead right now."

Seething with anger, struggling with pain, Trudgeon called from his crouched position, "Ye can't take his word. He's a murderer."

"*You* are a m-murderer," Tyne said, shaking his head as he smiled faintly without humor. "I admit it, your grace. I k-k-killed your uncle. He was a greedy, horrible, deceitful man who would not hesitate to sell his own son if it would earn him another shilling. I had no idea what he was truly like when he approached m-me about starting a distillery together. He had noticed how clever I was with my hands and thought I would be adept at building a still, which I actually was. I should have realized his duplicity because he led me astray from the very beginning. The papers that established our partnership—he had his steward draw them up because he knew Mr. Jordan would protect my interests. But he swore it would be cheaper for me if we did it that way, so I agreed. Once I realized how dishonest he was, I did come up with a plan that I hoped would free m-me from our agreement. And, yes, I did beat him with the candlestick when I realized Hawes would take no action against him. But I only did it because I knew Trudgeon was a vile k-k-killer who deserved to hang for his crimes. I would never have implicated an innocent person. The fact that he has a m-method to ape says all you need to know."

"Ye all heard it," Trudgeon replied wildly, wincing as he rose to his feet. "Ye all heard him admit to murder. He's the murderer, not me. The duchess is alive, isn't she? That's because of me. I delayed Lord Myles's plans when I accepted the assignment. If I hadn't he would have found someone else and the deed would've been done by now. I saved her life, yer grace. If it weren't for me, she would have been dead long before by another man's hand."

Sparing only a fleeting glance at his associate, Hawes stepped forward and disavowed all knowledge of Trudgeon's activities. "I am shocked to discover that a man whom I've hired to transport casks of wine to my various establishments is also engaged in such immoral business. That he would target the duchess is especially horrifying to me because I hold her in such high esteem and would be very upset if any harm came to her through someone in my employ. As it is, I am deeply grateful to her grace for exposing a weakness in my entirely law-abiding organization. Mr. Stribley can handle the matter from here. My interest in this episode is at an end," he said, before looking at Bea and aiming an elegant bow in her direction. "It has been a rare treat to observe your deductive skills firsthand, duchess. Thank you for the pleasure."

Since assuring him he was welcome did not seem like an appropriate reply, Bea held her tongue and merely tilted her head in acknowledgment. She imagined, however, that he was sincerely grateful, for she and the duke had neatly rid him of an associate whose poor decision-making skills made him more of a liability than an asset.

Trudgeon emitted a snarl deep in his throat, but his awe of Hawes was enough to restrain any invectives that might have been straining to pour forth.

Stribley, pleased to have his sovereignty over his prisoner affirmed, fastened one handcuff to Trudgeon's wrist and another to the gate in front of a nearby building. Then he gave a young boy a ha'penny to fetch a deputy from the magistrate's office.

Taking possession of Tyne, the constable told the duke he had everything in hand and that he should feel free to proceed with his day—although, he immediately acknowledged, it was now approaching seven o'clock and so he should feel free to proceed with his evening. "Or whichever suits you best. Regardless, you have performed an important service for your family, and I am sure your uncle would be grateful to you for bringing his killer to justice."

Tyne, demonstrating remarkable composure given the direness of his situation, kindly asked Stribley if he was a complete dunderhead. "Have you no understanding of what information has been disclosed here today? Lord Myles hired a man to slaughter his wife. Trudgeon was contracted to kill the duchess and would have performed the service had I not interfered," he said, directing his words now to Kesgrave. "I will not try to gull you into believing I acted out of anything other than my own self-interest, your grace, but the result is nonetheless the same. Lord Myles was vanquished before your wife was hurt. Surely, that has value to you. I do not expect you to allow me to go free, but banish me to the Indies. Anything other than the noose."

Kesgrave did not respond to this plea. Instead, he surveyed the general vicinity, settled on a shopkeeper who met his requirements and solicited his assistance in ensuring Tyne did not escape the constable's custody.

Eager to help even before being promised generous remuneration, the man, who towered over Stribley, grabbed Tyne firmly by the upper arm with both hands and said, "Is this good?"

The duke assured him that it was, thanked the constable for his quick response and asked Bea if she was ready to depart.

"I am, yes," she said as eager as ever to remove herself from the aftermath of her investigation. The circumstances wildly diverged, and yet somehow the feeling they engendered in her chest was always the same. It was sadness, yes, usually for the victim, mixed with a sort of weariness for the desperation unleashed on the world by violence.

Nothing ever seemed fixed by death.

And yet that was essentially what Tyne was arguing—that by murdering Lord Myles, he had solved her "uncle" problem.

Bea was unsettled to realize she was sympathetic to the clerk's point of view because the truth could not be denied: His actions saved her life.

She and Kesgrave might have managed to intercede before any harm had been done based on the information Mrs. Norton provided. But it was just as likely Trudgeon would have struck before Lord Myles could be compelled to nullify the agreement. And even if they thwarted this attempt on her life, there was no guarantee they would succeed against the next.

Possibly, it would have never ended, with Lord Myles's conspiring constantly against them like a villain in a gothic novel.

That Kesgrave would not feel weighed down by her continual exposure to danger through him was a relief in ways she could not even begin to articulate.

At the same time, she could not dispel her disquiet at Tyne's self-possessed determination. It would be one thing if he had acted in the rage of discovery, but instead he had coolly assessed the situation and decided that killing Lord Myles in the style of Trudgeon was in his best interest. Even after he had been forced to flee the scene, he continued with his calm evaluations.

But he had not acted with premeditation, she thought. He had not returned to the office intending to kill Lord Myles.

No, he had been content to leave that to Hawes.

Around and around Bea went in her head, considering his guilt from every perspective, and no matter how much the violence repelled her, she kept returning to one inconvertible truth: She was safe.

As they turned the corner, she realized she would lobby on Tyne's behalf. Banishment to an obscure colonial outpost seemed like a fair compromise and she was sure Kesgrave would agree after she made a case for it.

But not now, she thought, as Jenkins came into view. It had been a long day and she was exhausted and Kesgrave had already contended with enough. She would make light conversation during the ride home and suggest dinner in their bedchamber. In the morning, they could both call on the dowager to tell her the news.

Jenkins grumbled as they approached, peeved at being left behind to attend to the horses when an exciting chase was afoot. "And running into the road with no thought for your safety. Don't know if you're alive or dead, do I?" he muttered as he opened the carriage door. "The dowager would box my ears if anything happened to you."

As this was the second display of petulance from the loyal groom in a single day, Bea could not overcome her impulse to feel contrite and apologized for leaving him in the lurch.

Kesgrave, however, reiterated the necessity of someone remaining with the horses. But if Jenkins wanted to ensure that he was free next time to give chase, then he would be happy to engage another driver who could keep the groom company on the bench.

Blanching, Jenkins declined the offer and mumbled that the more practical solution was to eschew mad dashes altogether.

"I will see what I can do," the duke said noncommittally as he climbed into the conveyance.

As the door shut, Kesgrave settled on the cushion next to Bea, pressing gently against her side, and took her hand in his own. Then he rested his head against the back of the seat.

He looked tired, Bea thought, aware that it was the first time she had seen exhaustion on his face.

Suddenly, she was unsure how to proceed.

Light conversation or silence?

"If you have no objection, I am going to send a note to the magistrate advising transportation," he said without inflection. "I am not convinced it is kinder than the gallows, but I cannot deny him his request. He is right. I do owe him."

Grateful to be able to dispense with the issue at once, Bea assured him she had arrived at the same conclusion herself. "And I agree that it is barely a life. But I suppose some life is better than no life."

He sighed heavily, then squeezed her hand so hard she feared he might bruise it. Then he said with more sorrow than she could stand, "I am sorry."

It would never do, she thought, no, not at all, for him to bear the weight of things he could not control, and she felt a surge of hatred for the man she had never met—the man who had done so much to ensure that she would never meet *this* man beside her.

Wonderful, she thought, now they were both angry and sad.

Determinedly, she searched for a topic that was as frivolous as it was engrossing.

The stock certificates her parents left her certainly met the latter requirement, and if she asked if she could exert a measure of control over the company based on the percentage of shares she had inherited, she knew the duke would enjoy lecturing her on her presumption and general lack of understanding of how ownership worked.

Or perhaps Mrs. Norton's wart. The way it traveled from the tip of her nose to the edge of her jaw was sure to elicit a laugh.

Yes, she thought, lighthearted and silly was the better direction. But it had to be more absorbing than her arch-nemesis's pasted-on blemishes.

It should be easy, for making patently absurd conversation was her particular talent.

Think, Bea.

And then it occurred to her: those horrible pineapple chunks in her rout cakes.

Shifting slightly in her seat so she could see him clearly, she said, "Tell me, Damien, does the pinery have full-time attendants?"

"Excuse me?" he asked, tilting his head to look at her.

"The pinery at Haverill Hall," she explained. "I understand heat is used to cultivate a tropical fruit, and I assume some sort of furnace is necessary to maintain the temperature. Does this furnace require constant attendance?"

"Actually, tanner's bark is used," he replied, "which is bark from the oak tree, commonly employed in leather tanning. It ferments slowly, which keeps the temperature in the tan pits even for two to three months, or up to five if stirred regularly."

"How regularly?" she asked.

Unable to smother his curiosity, he straightened his shoulders and asked why the sudden interest in the pinery's care and maintenance.

"I am devising a secret plan to sabotage it," she explained.

It was faint, just a slight twitch of his lips, but it was enough to lighten his expression.

Having tread this ground before, she expected him to urge her again to confess her aversion to the staff, but instead he told her the dimensions of the tan pits—large cold frames that housed the young sprouts, which were called succession plants. These he identified as the most vulnerable part of the process and where she would want to strike. "It is not attendants to the pinery you need to worry about, however," he added, "but the stable boys, for the pits are behind the barn stalls, and they are about from dusk till dawn."

"So I would need a distraction," she said.

"Yes, a distraction," he said softly, fondly, tugging her hand and drawing her closer. "Fortunately, you excel at them."

Delighted by his improved disposition, she pulled back and observed that he appeared to possess some skill in that arena as well. "But I will not be diverted from my mission. Tell me, your grace, what is the best way to distract a stable boy? Would firecrackers be sufficient or would they scare the horses?"

"I cannot speak for the horses," he said, "but I am terrified."

But he did not look it, no, not at all, and as he leaned down to kiss her, she saw laughter on his face and pleasure in his eyes.

My Gracious Thanks

Pen a letter to the editor!

Dearest Reader,

A writer's fortune has ever been wracked with peril - and wholly dependent on the benevolence of the reading public.

My endless gratitude to the gracious reader for rewarding an intrepid author's ceaseless toil.

Keep reading for an excerpt of the next Bea installment: An Ominous Explosion

An Ominous Explosion

Although Vera Hyde-Clare was not a particularly large woman, possessing the gently rounded figure common in a matron of six and forty, she was still too big to disappear into the wingback chair she currently occupied.

She made a noble effort, however, pulling her shoulders together as tightly as possible as she scrunched one side of her body against the leather. At intervals, she closed her eyes, like a small child who thought she could not be seen if she herself could not see, and opened them wide, incapable of not gaping at the spectacle of the Duke of Kesgrave arguing with his grandmother.

Noting her aunt's discomfort, the duchess—formerly Miss Beatrice Hyde-Clare—thought the reaction did not accurately reflect the events currently unfolding before her. In particular, the disagreement, which hardly rose to the level of spectacle. During the quarrel, which had grown quite heated in the twenty minutes since Bea's aunt Vera had arrived, the dowager maintained an expression of polite good humor and Kesgrave kept his tone smooth and even.

Without imbuing his voice with undue emphasis, the duke informed the septuagenarian that he would escort her to Cambridgeshire to attend the burial of his uncle. As her other grandson, Mortimer Matlock, had already left the capital in the company of his father's body, the duty fell to him, and even if he did not desire the responsibility—which, to be clear, he did—it was morally incumbent upon him to assume it.

Firmly, her grace disavowed the existence of any such obligation.

Kesgrave frowned.

The dowager grimaced.

Mrs. Hyde-Clare cringed.

Poor Aunt Vera!

Having allowed herself to overcome four decades' worth of reticence and awe to pay a condolence call on the highest-ranking peeress of her acquaintance—no minor feat for a woman who genuflected before finely veined marble—she was now forced to endure an exchange best conducted in the privacy of a secluded room, preferably one with very thick walls so that not even the servants could overhear.

It was the very devil, for the situation had already been so awkward, what with the deceased getting himself bludgeoned to death for behavior unbefitting a gentleman.

Bea's aunt would never go so far as to imply that Lord Myles Matlock deserved the ill treatment, for nothing justified murder, especially not the sort administered via candlestick, but his lordship *had* descended into trade. What else did one expect to happen when one sullied one's hands with the ownership of a drinking establishment?

And then to sink further into degradation by setting up an operation to *produce* the liquor oneself.

The scion of one of the oldest families in England making gin!

'Twas a wonder Kesgrave House was still standing, for, in truth, the walls should have disassembled themselves stone by stone in shame.

The fact that the duke and his grandmother were quarreling in front of a personage of Mrs. Hyde-Clare's ilk—gentry, yes, but in possession of only an indifferent plot of land in some unheralded corner of Sussex—testified to the insidious effects of iniquity, for clearly it corrupted everything it touched, even these exalted beings who had seemed as impervious as oak trees.

"You must consider your bride," the dowager said, and although this seemed like a benign enough statement to Bea, it caused her aunt to press her cheek against the fine upholstery of the chair. "You have been married so briefly, and your leaving town would cause tongues to wag. People will say you have abandoned her, and at such a time. She has barely recovered from a monstrous attack on her life. They will consider it a harsh judgment on her activities."

In light of the circumstance, this claim was patently false, for even the most zealous gossip could not entirely dismiss the reality of a dead uncle. Lord Myles's brutal murder had reverberated throughout the beau monde, and even people who knew the enmity between the two men had felt compelled to offer their condolences.

Nevertheless, Kesgrave addressed the concern as if it were a legitimate worry, assuring her that Bea would accompany them on their journey as well. "She has never seen Haverill Hall and has lately developed a keen interest in its pinery."

But this reasonable solution dismayed the dowager as well, for she could brook no interference with Bea's rigorous training schedule. "Her fencing skills are so deplorable, Carlo still walks with a slight limp, and I comprehend her speed could withstand considerable improvement. During your foot pursuit on Wednesday, she fell well behind you and some hefty log of a man easily overtook her."

Kesgrave narrowed his eyes suspiciously. "Comprehend from whom? My groom? Have you taken to gossiping with the servants?"

"Nothing of the sort," the dowager replied blandly. "I served tea to Jenkins. I believe my granddaughter calls that an interview." She turned to Bea for confirmation. "Or was it an interrogation when you entertained the Mayhews' house-keeper in the drawing room at Kesgrave House during your investigation into Mr. Réjane's death? I am not yet conversant in the subtle distinction."

Although this tidbit was already known to everyone in the room, for it had been contained in Mr. Twaddle-Thum's extravagant account of the new duchess's investigation, which had been published in the *London Daily Gazette,* Aunt Vera tightened her features as if discovering a new unsavory detail about her niece's proclivities.

Indeed, her shock appeared to be so great she actually straightened her posture and pulled away from the corner into which she had been burrowing.

Bea, anticipating a sharp rebuke, marveled at how deeply Aunt Vera's disapproval ran. Truly, the only thing that would allow her to forget her mortification at the scene unfolding before her was condemnation of her former ward's behavior.

She simply could not help herself.

As if to prove Bea's point, Vera scooted to the very edge of her seat and said, "I shall go with you."

At this announcement, three sets of eyes turned to look at her.

All displayed surprise.

Only Bea's goggled with utter befuddlement as she sought to make sense of what her aunt had just said.

It *sounded* as though she was offering to accompany the dowager.

But that could not be right.

Clearly, Bea heard it wrong.

Her aunt had said *high* or *sigh*.

Or maybe she meant *aye* or *eye*.

Quickly, as if aware she had said something untoward, Vera added that the dowager could not go alone. Then she flinched at the unwieldy confidence of her own tone and stammered that of course the dowager could go alone if that was what she wanted. "I do not mean to tell you what you should do, for you are an old woman...that is, a woman who is old enough to know her own mind. If you genuinely desire to go on your own, then you must. But it is a difficult circum-stance, and you would want family with you," she said, imme-diately shaking her head as she rushed to correct a potential misunderstanding. "Not that *we* are family. Obviously, I know that I am not *your* family. I would never presume to claim a kinship with a family as illustrious as yours...or, rather, any family not my own. I do not mean to present myself as the sort of person who goes around society rooting about for relatives, for that would be vulgar. And strange. Yes, that would be quite strange. But we are *like* family, for my niece is married to your grandson, so there is a connection, and I would like to be of service if I may. I comprehend that there are quite a lot of family members who could attend to you, but it appears as though most of them annoy you. No...no...no, not *annoy* you. But try your patience. Yes, they appear to try your patience because you know your own mind."

As articulate as this explanation was—and representative of her relative's harried, self-conscious thinking—Bea still could not fully comprehend the words she was hearing. Aunt Vera *wanted* to spend hours and hours alone with the Dowager Duchess of Kesgrave? Given the older woman's age, the pace of travel would be slow, with the sixty-mile drive spread over two, possibly three days.

Aunt Vera would have to *put up* in a posting house with her.

She would have to eat her meals at the *same* table as her.

She would have to sit across from her in the *confined space* of a coach.

Surely, Mrs. Hyde-Clare would disintegrate from all that exposure to grandeur.

Aunt Vera could barely sit in a drawing room with the newly minted duchess without swooning from nerves and she had spent years treating the girl like an unpaid companion.

The dowager, taken aback by the offer, looked at her granddaughter-in-law as if to ascertain her opinion, and it was all Bea could do not to lift her shoulders in a shrug.

Truthfully, she had no idea what to make of the proposal.

Vera, either noting the dowager's confusion or feeling as though still more needed to be said, added that she would also like to see the pinery, for she could not imagine anything more indulgent than growing a tropical fruit on English soil. Then, fearing she had insulted either the duke or the lavish splendor that was his birthright, she explained that pineapples were obviously a necessity for someone of his wealth and position. "*I* would not like it at every meal because my palate is plain and undeveloped and suited only to simple English fare such as roast beef or plum pudding. I do, of course, enjoy a nice ragout when it is served to me, but I find nothing so favorable as a humble bowl of stewed meats with an assortment of sturdy vegetables."

Anticipating an ode to boiled mutton to swiftly follow, Bea was surprised when her aunt paused in her speech to allow the dowager to respond.

Verily, she affirmed the worthiness of turnips, carrots and onions, and asserted the ingenuity of the pinery. "You will be very impressed, I think, when you see how pineapples are cultivated. And your understanding of the fruit is correct. It does require an effort to be liked, as I recently explained to your niece. I am confident by the time we return to London, you will like them as much as I do. My chef is particularly adept at preparing dishes incorporating pineapple and I will have him send an assortment to Portman Square for your own cook."

Vera, intrepidly bearing the weight of this oppressive generosity, dipped her head in a dignified nod and owned herself grateful for the opportunity to acquire a taste for the exotic delicacy. "I shall devote myself to the task."

And that was all she said.

Despite her habit of rambling through a seemingly endless supply of caveats, she made no attempt to clarify the extent of her proposed devotion or provide its precise dimensions. Bea, observing her restraint, thought Aunt Vera might indeed be the solution to a rather thorny problem, for the dowager was determined to go without Kesgrave and no amount of cajoling or coaxing could convince her to relent.

It was baffling, her refusal, for she was fond of her grandson and Bea assumed she would desire his consoling presence at such a painful time. Lord Myles had been a terrible human being in every way imaginable, seeking the removal of his own nephew to clear the line of succession for himself, but he was still her child. No matter what he was, she could not help loving him, if only for the small, endearing, innocent little boy he must have once been.

His death was a terrible blow.

Surely, Kesgrave could help soften it.

And yet, Bea knew, it was impossible to account for the vagaries of grief, and even if they could not comprehend her wishes, they could at least abide by them.

The duke's understanding of the situation varied greatly from hers, however, and he remained ardently opposed to any outcome that did not involve him. With a brisk nod, he thanked Mrs. Hyde-Clare for her kind offer, then firmly rejected it.

At his curt rebuff, Bea expected her aunt to redouble her efforts to disappear into the furniture, for Kesgrave's tone had been brusque if not harsh, but she held her position at the edge of the seat. Then, in what her niece considered an unfathomable event, she replied that the right of refusal belonged to his grandmother.

Her courage held for one breathless moment.

Doggedly, she kept her eyes steady as if daring the duke to disagree.

Then her pluck seemed to desert her, and she rounded her shoulders as she added in a quivering rush, "I am sure your counsel is invaluable to her. You are so wise and learned, she could not possibly make a decision without taking your thoughts and opinions into consideration, for they are known to be better than everyone else's. Your intelligence and discernment are widely admired, and her grace is fortunate to have you to advise her. But in the end, we have to trust that she knows what is best for herself and allow her to make that decision. I hope it goes without saying that *I* believe your companionship is vastly superior to mine and I would be delighted for the opportunity to accompany you on your travels."

But that would never do, for Vera Hyde-Clare to invite herself on a journey with the Duke of Kesgrave, and she explained that she was speaking only in hypothetical terms. "Our actually traveling together would be highly irregular and inappropriate. I cannot imagine what the *ton* would say if such a thing were to occur. And where would we be going? Not abroad, I hope, because I cannot stand foreigners, with their incomprehensible languages. It is bad enough when Flora and her father speak Latin. Regardless, anywhere we went, Bea would come with us, even if it meant she would have to miss her fencing—"

Abruptly she broke off and looked at her niece in confusion. "I am sorry, but did the dowager say you are taking *fencing* lessons?"

"She did, yes," Bea said, amused and relieved by Aunt Vera's return to form. The digression into coherence and kindness had been as shocking as it was unsettling and forced her to entertain the highly disconcerting notion that she had underestimated her relative. For years, she had assumed she knew every frivolous and disapproving thought that flitted through the other woman's head, and to allow now for the possibility that she might have been wrong was almost more than she could handle.

It was not only the obligation of a sweeping reappraisal that unnerved Bea but also the horrifying possibility that Aunt Vera might be the victim of a grave disservice. Having endured gross misjudgments herself, she was appalled at the prospect of inflicting them on someone else.

Fortunately, her aunt's gasp at the confirmation of her fencing lessons indicated that a comprehensive overhaul was not in order.

Perhaps only a slight reevaluation.

"And what did she mean about your being overtaken by a

lug of a man?" Aunt Vera asked. "Were you *running* in a public street?"

"'A log of a man' is the term she used," Bea explained, "and she was referring to Mr. Trudgeon, who was also chasing the man who killed Lord Myles."

Now Aunt Vera pressed against the leather of the chair as if too exhausted to hold herself upright. "Does Mr. Twaddle-Thum know about this foot race of yours?"

Although Bea could have objected to the use of the possessive, for she did not consider the pursuit of justice to be her exclusive domain, she chose not to belabor the point. Rather, she confessed that she had no idea what the scurrilous reporter did or did not know. "But considering how resourceful he has been in the past, I imagine it is only a matter of time before we read about it in the *London Daily Gazette*."

Appalled at the prospect of yet another newspaper report detailing her niece's ghastly activities, Vera fanned herself with dramatic vigor, as if trying to ward off a faint. Although her intent clearly had been only to further censure the unruly young duchess, her theatrical display eased the tension in the room, and instead of issuing the cutting set-down that had been on his lips, Kesgrave told Mrs. Hyde-Clare that she was correct.

"It is for her grace to decide," he agreed, before turning to look at his grandmother and asking her why she would not allow him to accompany her. His tone was mild now, more curious than hurt, as if he was seeking merely to understand her intransigence, not overcome it. "I assure you, it is not an inconvenience to me or Bea in any way. He was my uncle, after all, and it is right that I should be there, and even if he were not, I am very fond of you and wish to provide my support."

Ordinarily forthright, the dowager lowered her gaze to

her hands, which were clasped tightly in her lap, and stared silently at her clenched fingers for several long moments. Despite these signs of agitation, her voice was matter-of-fact when she finally replied.

Even so, she kept her eyes tilted resolutely down, unable, it seemed, to respond while looking at her grandson. "It is because he *was* your uncle. He was *your* family, *my* blood, and I could exert no control over him. He was horrible in every way, without a drop of decency in the end, and there was nothing I could do about it. Every attempt I made to dissuade him from his course, whether threats of penury or pleas for integrity, only further entrenched his hatred. He blamed me for every setback he suffered going back to the day he was born, for he deeply resented being a second son. Your father did not make it any easier on him, but I do not hold him responsible for Myles's spitefulness—for other things, yes, but not that," she said, continuing in the same mild tone, as if making a vaguely interesting comment about that evening's diversion. "I was given two opportunities to raise honorable men and I failed on both accounts. I feel that failure always, and nothing I do makes it better. But having you there, with your surfeit of decency, will make it worse, and that is more than I can bear."

Kesgrave wanted to quarrel.

Oh, yes, Bea could see it in his eyes, the determination to make the counterargument that his presence could provide his grandmother with solace and succor, that his surfeit of decency, as she called it, was nothing more than affection and concern for her well-being.

It was, Bea thought, an understandable impulse—and a lovely one at that—but she could not allow him to indulge it. The dowager had enough with which to cope without having to console the wounded vanity of her grandson.

Consequently, she announced that it was the shoes.

All three occupants in the room turned to look at her, but only the duke's face twisted with irritation at the heavy-handed attempt at diversion.

He did not appreciate her changing the subject.

Undaunted by his disapproval, she said, "During the chase to apprehend Lord Myles's killer, I was encumbered by a pair of silk booties while Kesgrave and Trudgeon had the advantage of sturdy boots. I am confident that if they had been forced to contend with flimsy swaths of satin, their performance would have been no more impressive than mine. It is the very devil, which Kesgrave knows, for I have pleaded with him several times to commission his boot maker to make me a pair of Hessians and he adamantly refuses. It is because he knows I would beat him in a race if properly attired, and he hopes to preserve his dignity."

At this rallying speech, the duke's expression lightened, and he assured her that he had surrendered his last shred of dignity at the altar when the minister asked him for the fourth time if he was *absolutely certain* he wanted to take her for a wife. "But you are not entirely wrong, for I do hope to preserve something and that is my relationship with Hoby. If I dared to ask him to make boots for a woman, he would cut me off without a second thought and I would be forced to buy my shoes from Poole in Cheapside."

But Bea shook her head, for she had heard this argument before and had no patience for it. "Hoby does not require chapter and verse of every pair you purchase. And if he does ask about the wearer, you can invent a young cousin lately arrived to the capital hoping to acquire a little town bronze. If telling even that small lie offends your sense of honor, then surely there is a young man of that general description knocking around your family tree whom we could dragoon into service."

Now the duke grinned as he contemplated her with

amusement. "Yes, because Mr. Twaddle-Thum would not immediately root out that deception. If left to your devices, I would be banned from every shoemaker, bookmaker, cobbler and cordwainer in London."

Bea, shaking her head with exaggerated sadness, heaved a hefty sigh and said to the dowager, "It is always like this, for your grandson harbors a crippling fear of the servants. It is always, 'No, Bea, we cannot search my housekeeper's quarters for a suspected clue at midnight,' or 'No, Bea, you cannot hide under the butler's bed.' It is bewildering to me that a man who was raised with so much privilege could be so wary of his own staff. If he felt an inkling of concern for the neighbors' servants, I would understand it better, but he was happy to trudge through the Mayhews' kitchens."

"Happy, no," Kesgrave replied mildly. "Resigned, yes."

The dowager smiled at these antics, as Bea had intended, while her aunt gawked like a fish suddenly exposed to air, her lips flapping wildly as her eyelids fluttered.

Pressing her hand against her bosom, as if trying to still her suddenly racing heart, Vera fervently assured the duke that Bea had not learned such appalling behavior in Portman Square. "Neither Mr. Hyde-Clare nor I would ever countenance such a want of conduct!" she said, then gasped as the implication struck her and she rushed to clarify that her niece could not have learned it at Kesgrave House either. "Books! Yes, yes, of course, obviously, that is the source, for she often had her head buried in one Gothic or another, and you know how those people comport themselves, always sneaking through hidden passages in the middle of the night and pretending to be ghosts."

"Your reading material sounds charming," the dowager said to Bea, her hands unclasped now that the matter had been settled. "I do hope you can lend me some of the more salacious titles for my journey. It is generally too bumpy for me to read in the coach, but one of the horses will throw its shoes and we will be forced to dither by the side of the lane or in a posting house for hours."

Aunt Vera flinched at the inevitable discomforts of the journey but smiled gamely and asked Bea to recommend some books for her as well. "I would hate to pester the dowager with conversation when her attention is engrossed elsewhere."

Bea, who knew her relative's reading preferences leaned toward flipping absentmindedly through *La Belle Assemblée* while criticizing her children, promised to have several weighty tomes delivered to Portman Square posthaste.

"You are too kind," Vera said, smiling stiffly.

The dowager, determined to get an early start for their trip, instructed Mrs. Hyde-Clare to return to her home and commence packing. She would send a footman to pick up her luggage in four hours. "Unless your maid can accomplish it sooner? I would like the coach with the bags to leave at first light to ensure that it arrives before we do. We do not have to depart until seven in the morning," she announced, her mood vastly improved by the requirements of the journey.

As her grace catalogued the many tasks to which she had to attend before she could leave for Cambridgeshire, Aunt Vera's complexion grew increasingly pale until she was practically ashen.

In making her generous offer, Mrs. Hyde-Clare had failed to consider the rigors of travel, and reminded now of how little she enjoyed the road, she appeared to sink into herself. Despite her efforts to once again hide in its depths, the wingback chair remained as impervious to her needs as ever. Kesgrave, noting her distress, owned himself grateful for her willingness to stand in his stead at the funeral and proffered his arm. Momentarily taken aback by the kindness in his voice, she flushed prettily, then simpered with delight.

Accepting the duke's escort, she promised to be ready to depart at six forty-five in the unlikely event her grace wanted to leave a little earlier, then rattled off a list of the many things she herself had to see to, the majority of which consisted of sending notes to various friends and acquaintances to alert them to the fact that she would be traveling with the dowager duchess as a personal favor to the duke.

Kesgrave indulged this turn, nodding at regular intervals and suggesting other people she might inform, such as Mrs. Ralston, who was among the most accomplished gossips in London.

Short of sending a missive directly to Mr. Twaddle-Thum, it was, Bea thought, the most effective way of notifying the *ton* of her increased significance to the Matlock family.

Delivering Aunt Vera to her carriage, the duke thanked her again for unhesitatingly offering her assistance and asked if there was anything he could do to help while she was away.

Ardently, she demurred, noting at length that he had far more important business to oversee than the minor details of her life. He persisted, and although she remained stridently opposed to his performing any service for her, regardless how small, she admitted that she could bear to accept a tiny favor from Bea.

"If you could find time in your busy schedule to have a peek in on your uncle, that would be remarkably calming to my mind," she said. "You know how he gets when I am not around."

Indeed, Bea did—and it bore little difference from when his wife *was* around. Accustomed to her prattle after decades of marriage, he was particularly adept at ignoring her entirely and every morning enjoyed his eggs and newspaper as if she were not sitting directly across from him at the breakfast table. She had yet to notice his lack of attention because she typically passed the meal in a flurry of anxiety, reviewing the prior day's events and making mountains out of the molehills with which her children continually supplied her.

"I am happy to visit with my uncle," Bea said.

"Thank you, my dear," Aunt Vera said. "You relieved my mind greatly."

Alas, it was only temporary, for she had no sooner said the words than her brow furrowed with apprehension and she voiced her concern about Flora, who had been acting strangely ever since suffering a terrible bout of food poisoning.

"Do look in on her as well and make sure she does not eat any more rotten eggs," she said. "I cannot believe Mrs. Emerson is at fault and can only assume the poor girl has a special sensitivity. 'Tis highly vexing! Nonetheless, perhaps you could look over the menus for the week and confirm there is nothing that will cause a bother."

Although she knew her cousin's recent spate of gastric issues was the product of subterfuge, not spoiled food, Bea readily agreed.

"And Russell," her aunt added. "He has a tendency to get into mischief if I am not there to guide his actions. If you could perhaps play a few hands of piquet with him for ha'penny a point to satisfy his desire to gamble. It is vital that you win, so that he can feel dreadful about owing you money, and although I would never condone cheating per se, you should feel free to tweak the cards while he is not looking to ensure you prevail. I find pointing out an imperfection in his tailoring, whether real or imagined, is sufficient to distract him."

As her aunt was far from subtle, Bea had to assume her cousin's vanity was so overweening as to allow this deception to succeed. "Piquet with Russell. Check."

Relieved, Aunt Vera permitted Kesgrave to hand her into

her carriage. As she perched on the bench, her lips pursed and she said, "Oh, and then there is Aileen."

"Aileen?" Bea asked, puzzled.

"The new upstairs maid. She is from Edinburgh and having a terrible time settling in," her relative explained. "It is her family. She misses them dreadfully. The only thing for it is to keep her too busy to brood. So, if you would not mind making sure she has enough to do? Mrs. Emerson, bless her heart, is a dear, but she lacks the ingenuity necessary to fill every minute of the poor girl's day. The linens, for example. Just because they were reorganized on Monday does not mean they cannot be reorganized on Thursday. We all know how insidious dust is. Honestly, I see no reason why the closet should not be reorganized daily, other than the fact that the maids cannot be incessantly folding linens. There is already so much to do around the house!"

Stifling a smile, Bea assented to this request and to the entreaty, issued sotto voce so that Kesgrave could not hear it as well, that she examine the western wall in the dining room for cracks because she feared a leak in the window casement was causing irreparable damage.

Graciously, Bea pledged to inspect the plaster and to even make sure that Flora did not read the new issue of Ackerman's before her mother did because the wretched girl always turned down the corners of the pages she liked.

She drew the line, however, at paying a call on Aunt Susan, who had been slow in recovering from the cold that had laid her low the week before.

Aunt Vera sighed dramatically, as if her niece were being unreasonable, and resolved to content herself with sending her sister a note.

About the Author

Lynn Messina is the author of almost two dozen novels, including the Beatrice Hyde-Clare mysteries, a cozy series set in Regency-era England. Her first novel, *Fashionistas,* has been translated into sixteen languages and was briefly slated to be a movie starring Lindsay Lohan. Her essays have appeared in *Self, American Baby* and the *New York Times* Modern Love column, and she has been a regular contributor to the *Times* parenting blog. She lives in New York City with her sons.

Also by Lynn Messina

The Fellingham Minx

The Bolingbroke Chit

The Impertinent Miss Templeton

Stand Alones

Prejudice and Pride

The Girls' Guide to Dating Zombies

Savvy Girl

Winner Takes All

Little Vampire Women

Never on a Sundae

Troublemaker

Fashionista (Spanish Edition)

Violet Venom's Rules for Life

Henry and the Incredibly Incorrigible, Inconveniently Smart Human

Welcome to the Bea Hive

FUN STUFF FOR BEATRICE HYDE-CLARE FANS

The Bea Tee

Beatrice's favorite three warships not only in the wrong order but also from the wrong time period. (Take that, maritime tradition *and* historical accuracy!)

The Kesgrave Shirt

A tee bearing the Duke of Kesgrave's favorite warships in the order in which they appeared in the Battle of the Nile

Available in mugs too!

See all the options in Lynn's Store.